To Andy + Ang

Promise

By M. Sue Alexander

M. Sue Alexander

SUZANDER PUBLISHING, LLC
VANLEER, TENNESSEE 37181

Other Books by M. Sue Alexander . . .

Resurrection Dawn 2014
Christian-Fiction Series
(Available as Print-on-Demand or E-book)

Resurrection Dawn 2014
The Christian Fugitive
Rebels in Paradise
Veil of Lies
The Anointing
Countdown to Justice
All Rise
Unlikely Suspect
Lethal Snapshot
Purgatory

Fictions E-books by Author

Adams' Bones
The Forum
Out of Time: The Vanderbilt Incident

Non-Fiction Books

Encounters of the God-Kind (2015)

Comments from Readers . . .

"Those who know cancer victims will identify with the main character as she suffers through surgery and recovery. Good novel, fast read; one of author's best stories."—Patricia Wilkins

"Author skillfully blends fiction and reality to show how God works in our lives to help overcome heartache, illness, and disappointment; a wonderful work of fiction."—Joyce Keller

Remarks from Author to Reader . . .

This creative work of fiction imparts my experience with double-ovarian cancer in 2001. The storyline in many aspects depicts my personal feelings regarding close friendships and faith in God.

Tomorrow's Promise

First edition 2011 by **CrossBooks**
Second edition 2015 by **Suzander Publishing, LLC**

Especially for Women Cancer Survivors

"God is our refuge and strength, an ever-present help in trouble"—Psalm 46:1, The NIV Bible.

♣1

GUNMETAL-GRAY CLOUDS hovered over Baton Rouge, Louisiana. For most people who worked a job, it was an ordinary Thursday. Not so for Jolene Salisbury who had just exited the doctor's office. Stunned over the diagnosis, she'd forgotten to leave off the pink slip required by the front desk.

Oh well . . . she stuck the paper inside her purse, deciding to mail it back later. *Ovarian cancer . . .?* What would that do to her? *Kill me, if a surgeon doesn't cut it out.* She grimaced at the thought.

Dr. Beatrice Kennedy was the best OBGYN around town. No soft-peddling the facts. Cancer was not a disease to be ignored—not like a painful abscessed tooth that could be pulled. Or a nasty cold she could medicate. Cancer *is* an aggressive killer that steals thousands of women's lives every year.

And now I have it. Or, it has me.

Rain dribbled down Jolene's face and soaked the collar of her crisp white blouse. Standing like a zombie under the portico, she was barely aware she'd exited the clinic. The storm raging inside her mind was far more threatening than the inclement weather.

Death . . . How would that feel?

Jolene shivered from the cold rain.

Her mother Kate had died at fifty-two from a *Mastocarcinoma.* In lay terms, it was a malignant and invasive epithelial tumor that spread by metastasis through her breast. Kate was sick and dying before she realized the disease ravaged her body.

Jolene was twenty-six at the time—should have sat beside her mother's hospital bed, held her hand, and talked about the good times in their past. But young and ignorant of suffering, it seemed far safer to keep her distance. Cancer would never attack her. She would eat healthy foods, exercise regularly, and maintain a positive approach to life. And hopefully live to a ripe old age.

Basically, Kate Lancaster had died alone. Jolene's father had been little comfort, working long hours and overtime at the post office as an avoidance tactic. A haughty laugh escaped Jolene's lips as she recalled the painful past. Why remember all that now?

She could only imagine what Kirk said to his sick wife when he squeezed in time at the hospital. "I paid the month's bills so you don't have to worry." Like that was important to Kate.

He probably pecked her on the cheek and promised to return soon. A lie, of course! Kate would nod and squeeze Kirk's hand—a gesture that said she understood his reason for staying away. *Go! Do whatever you think is best.* So her days passed.

Then Kirk would head on home without guilt, warm up a plate of food for supper, do the dirty laundry, or fill the void of Kate's absence with some insignificant activity in the scheme of life. So his days passed. That was then and this *is* now.

Jolene flipped open her umbrella and dashed down steps as slippery as greased glass. Water pooled at her feet, trickled around her boots and ran off the sides, flooding the pampered beds of the once lush shrubs. Filled with dread, she should tell David.

Would he treat her like Kirk had Kate? Pretend the cancer would go away if he didn't think about it?

Popping the door locks to her gray Buick, Jolene slid inside and let down the dripping umbrella. The car was brand-new last year, purchased as a write-off for her lucrative real estate business.

A reminder that she should call the office and check her messages, but somehow work wasn't so important anymore.

Cancer has changed everything.

Peter Cromwell was due in town to look for property later that day. *2:00 p.m.* The referral would earn her a handsome commission. Sales were what made a million-dollar producer.

Jolene stared at the face of her cell phone and shut it off.

No, she needed to tell David what was going on. *Now!*

His office was located a few blocks from Louisiana State University. David sold insurance for a private firm, Johnson & Bailey Associates, an affiliate of a larger national conglomerate.

Not Allstate, but just as lucrative when it came to pulling dollars out of citizen's pockets. He loved the work.

Bundled up with nervous energy, Jolene switched on the radio and punched in a Christian station. Max, her favorite disc jockey, was introducing a pastor whose wife was miraculously healed of lung disease. She listened a few minutes then decided God wasn't going to heal her. Like her mother, Jolene Lancaster Salisbury would suffer for a long time before dying alone.

What's wrong with me? Where is my faith?

Before Jolene realized it she had reached her destination.

David's ebony Cadillac was parked out front like a sleek wet monster. She counted five other cars in the side lot. One of them belonged to Ben Johnson, the CFO. She could do this.

Feeling immobile, with rain relentlessly peppering the windshield, and the engine running, Jolene crouched behind the wheel as the blowing heater staved off the cold December day, doing nothing to quench her icy mood.

Two weeks until Christmas—not one present purchased.

Finally, shutting off the motor, Jolene grabbed the umbrella at her feet, kicked open the door and dashed toward the covered front porch. After deflating the umbrella, she turned the golden knob and was inside, looking like a soaked muskrat.

"Is David busy?" she asked the secretary.

"Yeah, he's got someone in his office."

"I'll wait." Jolene took a seat.

"It's almost lunchtime," Sally commented. "Never knew David to miss a meal." She tossed a sideward glance.

"You're right." Jolene smiled. "He's predictable."

Some things didn't change.

To pass the time, Jolene plucked a real estate magazine from the rack and perused the new listings. Latter & Blum had twenty displayed in full color with agents' names underneath. CALL TODAY, WE HAVE THE RIGHT HOUSE FOR YOU.

She scoffed, *As if that matters anymore.*

David sauntered out of his office at 12:15, a joyful expression flooding his handsome face. No doubt, he'd landed a new client.

After showing the young executive to the door, he turned to Jolene with a puzzled expression. "Why are you here?"

"Can't I come see my husband for no reason?"

"What about your out-of-state client?"

"What about lunch?" Jolene hastily returned.

David stood loosely, scrutinizing Jolene, obviously evaluating his schedule to determine if he could fit his wife in. Handsome, tall and athletically lean, his wavy blond hair took years off his age.

Jolene only glared, her mind cluttered with what to say.

"I'll be back around 1:30," David informed Sally. "My cell will be on if anyone's looking for me." He turned to Jolene.

"So, I guess we're on for lunch."

"What's going on?" He grabbed Jolene's elbow and headed her to the door. *"Don't call,"* she mouthed back to Sally.

David would soon find out why she'd kidnapped him from his work. Like her, he'd need some time to adjust to the news.

He followed Jolene in his Cadillac over a few streets to a popular Cajun restaurant that featured fantastic luncheon specials. They ventured inside and approached the maitre d'. Despite the wicked weather, the restaurant was packed with joyful customers.

They waited twenty minutes to be seated, neither making small talk. She wanted to bawl, but resisted. Finally, they were shown to a corner table. Good, it lent a bit more privacy.

After perusing the menu choices, Jolene ordered the soup of the day, a spicy shrimp gumbo advertised only for the taste buds of natives born with asbestos mouths. David chose the creamy crawfish *etouffee*. They both had the sweet tea with lemon.

As if to cheer up Jolene, David chattered about the new client he'd signed. Not only had Hoyt Claymore purchased a policy on his own personal home, he had insured an apartment complex under construction. The commission would be gratifying.

"What?" David noted Jolene's disinterest. "I'm sorry if I'm boring you." He wasn't smiling. "I suppose you asked me out for a reason." He adjusted his bulk in the chair.

"Could you curb the attitude, David?"

"Sorry. So, tell me what's on your mind."

"I came straight from my doctor's appointment over to your office," she revealed. "I don't know how to tell you, David, other than to say it." Tears stung her eyes like acid.

"Okay . . ." Jolene had his full attention. "What's wrong?"

"I have cancer." She cringed at her disclosure.

David put down his fork and stared into his wife's flag-blue eyes for a few seconds. "What kind of cancer?"

"Ovarian."

"Honey—"

She put up a hand. "Don't, or I'll really lose it. I hate crybabies." Sympathy was not welcome at the moment.

He swallowed hard. "How serious is your condition?"

"I have two large tumors, one on each ovary," she replied, eyes wandering. "The cancer may have already spread."

He squeezed his eyes, said nothing.

"I won't know for sure until a surgeon opens me up."

His right hand slid warmly over Jolene's. With the other hand, he swiped red sauce from his lips and said, "Then you should schedule surgery immediately and hit this thing head on."

She nodded, tears bubbling.

"How can I help?"

Sincerity flooded David's expression.

How can anyone help? She heard hard rain becoming more aggressive outdoors. Her body belonged to someone else.

"Gosh. . ." she suppressed mounting fear, "I can't believe we haven't seen the blue sky in three days." A nervous chuckle erupted. "Do you realize that's how long Jesus was in the grave?"

David crookedly smiled. "I guess we're done eating."

A chill invaded Jolene's spirit as she glanced down at her delicious entree, barely touched. "Yeah, let's go home."

She grabbed her big purse off the floor while David asked the waiter for the tab and paid with a credit card.

What promise would tomorrow hold? Jolene wondered as they left the restaurant together. In the distance she heard a clock chime.

Tick-tock, tick-tock, time is running out.

♣2

JOLENE TRAILED DAVID'S Cadillac in her Buick. He took the ramp leading onto the interstate and headed east. Like a lamb following her shepherd, she kept her eyes on his pulsing rear lights, the musings of her mind floating in several directions.

She was forty-five years old, David two years older. They were hard-working Americans with above average dreams. Why didn't they have children like other couples? Or adopted a baby? David always said he wanted a family. She wanted to wait.

Didn't they need a nicer home before they brought a child into the world? What about their jobs? There never seemed enough money to buy all the expensive things they desired.

What was she thinking? That she had all the time in the world to start a family? Moments yielded to the past.

Jolene had stood over her mother's grave twenty years before and dismissed the idea that so horrible a disease as cancer could ever touch her. After a period of grieving, far too short in Jolene's estimation, her father had remarried a coworker and lived happily ever-after. Until heart disease took him out at fifty-six.

Jolene's cell phone chimed a tune. "Yeah . . .?"

"Are you okay?"

It was David. "I guess, considering."

"When I speeded up, you didn't follow."

"Sorry, I guess my mind was elsewhere." Jolene stepped on the accelerator and closed the distance between them. "I'm going to miss my two o'clock appointment." Fact was she didn't care.

"Did you let the office know you had, uh, a problem?"

"Cancer, David! Say the word, please!" Anger surfaced from nowhere. How could God allow this to happen? Was she so bad? Was this punishment for some unrecognized sin? Didn't she faithfully attend church every Sunday? David even taught a boys' class during the first service. She paid her tithe regularly.

No, this was totally unfair.

"Jolene?"

"Sorry, David," she apologized.

"I know this has gotta be hard on you, doll."

"Duh, you think?" She half smiled. David only called her "doll" when he felt tender towards her.

"I've never known you to ignore a customer."

That hurt. "Okay, I'm hanging up and calling Becky right now. Hopefully, she's free to show Peter Cromwell property."

If he's stupid enough to wade through mud puddles this afternoon, Jolene thought to herself. *Let Becky worry about that.*

"Okay, I'll see you at home."

Jolene dropped back as David sped up to negotiate the heavy traffic on I-10. She pulled over to the side of the road and pushed END on her cell phone. Seconds later, she had her real estate firm on the line. "Phyllis? Jolene. Is my appointment there?"

"He's here, all right. Doesn't look too happy that nobody has told him why you're late," the secretary rasped, always ready to hold down the fort for the agents. "What's going on, baby?"

Good question, Jolene considered how to answer. Everybody in south Louisiana calls their friends *baby*, probably because it was tradition to nestle a tiny plastic infant inside every King Cake as a sign of good luck as Marti Gras approached.

"Did you have an accident?" Phyllis asked.

"Just a glitch in my schedule," Jolene explained. "Is Becky Simms in the office by chance?"

"Yes, I'll put you through."

Jolene received the high producer's voicemail. Likely, Becky was on another line with a customer. While the national economy was collapsing, south Louisiana's oil drilling business had cranked up under a new presidential regime. Jolene left a message.

A mile down the road, Jolene's phone danced with a lively melody. "Becky?" She leaped to take the call.

"All day long," her real estate buddy replied. "Problem . . .?"

"Big time—my customer from Kansas City is waiting upfront as we speak. I was supposed to show him property this afternoon but I can't. His name is Peter Cromwell and he works for the CIA. Keep that under your hat. Could you show him around?"

"Sure. Is your folder on Cromwell at the office?" Becky asked.

"Yeah, it's on my desk. Apologize for me, please."

"Are you going to tell me what's wrong?"

"I will later. David and I are headed home to discuss the problem." She wasn't ready to announce cancer to the public.

"Well, now, I'm really worried if Mr. Success took time off work to solve *your* problem." Becky huffed. "Okay, tend to personal business, I'll hold down the fort."

"Thanks, Becky. I owe you."

"Yes, you do." She chuckled.

Jolene ended the call, her thoughts bogged down in the past. Refocusing, she spied David up ahead pulling into their concrete driveway. *Already home?* She had been cruising on automatic.

Jolene pulled inside the garage next to David and killed the motor. They simultaneously exited their cars.

"Messy day," she commented.

"Awful." Keys jingled in David's hand as he headed for the side door, taking big strides with purpose.

"I'll put on a pot of coffee." She shivered. "Something hot sounds good." She parked her umbrella by the door.

"Something dry sounds better." He unlocked the door to their enclosed porch that served as a breezeway to the kitchen. "It's getting much colder outside." Tit for tat, oh hum.

"You think we'll get snow?" Warm air touched her face.

"Channel 5 reports we might get ice tonight," he offered.

"Wonderful."

Jolene shrugged off her full-length waterproof parka and slung it on the back of a kitchen chair, going straight for the Community Coffee in the cabinet. David disappeared into his office off the den next to the kitchen and parked his belongings. He stared at the blinking light on the phone then ignored his messages.

Menial tasks like making coffee felt useful. Jolene knew how to do it with her eyes closed. *Cancer?* That was a new task.

It wasn't long before David returned to the kitchen. "Coffee smells great!" His huge hazel eyes targeted his wife.

"It's the real thing—no beverage for the fainthearted."

She removed a carton of fortified cream from the fridge. Cajuns liked their coffee loaded with caffeine.

"Did you pick up the mail?" he asked.

"You know I didn't," she replied.

"I'll get it later." He peered out the bay window, hands folded over his chest. "I guess winter is definitely here." They made eye contact until he looked away. "I'll go get the mail."

A few minutes later, when Jolene had filled two mugs with the dark chicory, they sat down at the round oak table for a powwow.

Jolene took a sip of coffee and sighed. "Perfect." Her gaze latched onto David. "Anything important in the mail . . .?"

"No, just the usual bills," he replied while stirring a spoon of sugar into his coffee and adding cream.

She took a sip of her coffee and sighed.

"You'll need to take a sabbatical from work, you know."

Time for the real conversation, she blinked.

"You'll need time to heal," he added.

Her eyes cut over on him. "Won't be a problem—Becky will love inheriting my business." Her lips tightened with a scowl.

"For a referral fee, I hope." He lifted the mug to his lips.

"Of course, I'm not stupid." Jolene shook her head and frowned. Dark glossy hair parted in the crown and fell loosely in a straight style, framing her pretty face. Her blue eyes must have darkened, reflecting her increasing intolerance to criticism.

"What? Did I say something wrong?"

"It's always about earning more money, isn't it?" She felt like taking a few swings at the furniture with a sledgehammer. "When have we taken a vacation, David?"

Why am I picking a fight?

"Where did that come from?" He shot back.

"Answer the question."

"Whoa, baby! You're the workaholic! I wanted to take a break last fall, you said no. *You* had to work."

"So, you think *I'm* the problem in this family."

"Ha, you said it, not me! I was the one who wanted to have a family and you said later. I suggested we adopt and you refused."

Silence ruled the kitchen as his statement impacted. How did this conversation about cancer switch to fatherhood?

"Now it's too late," he mumbled. "And it's your fault."

Wow. Tears bubbled up in Jolene's eyes.

"You're right, I'm the Ogre. Blame me for failed parenthood."

The drenching rain poured loudly through the gutters as David blinked with realization. "Tell me, Jolene, how did we get from *your* cancer diagnosis to discussing *our* failed marriage?"

Jolene released a sigh. "I was thinking the same thing."

"Great minds run in the same channel?"

This is not the time to fight. Jolene made a snap decision. "I'm not going to have my surgery here," she announced with resolve.

"Huh? What—why not?" David's forehead furrowed.

"I'm going home, to Tennessee."

"Did I miss something, Jolene? *That* doesn't make a shred of sense!" His hazel eyes flashed. "Your friends live here. Are you giving up a ten-year real estate career, for Christ's sake?"

"Leave Jesus out of this!" she screamed.

"Okay, okay, calm down. I know you're upset." He grasped Jolene's hand. "Please think this through, okay?"

Jolene withdrew her hand. "Okay, I'll pray about it."

♣3

WHEN MONDAY ROLLED around, Jolene spoke to her office manager at Latter & Blum about putting her license on hold and referring her business to Becky Simms.

"What's the problem?" Paula inquired. "Quitting is not like you." She scrutinized Jolene. "Have you thought this through?"

"Enough. On the contrary, I'm stepping up to the plate and taking responsibility." Jolene viewed her decision to return to Tennessee as a way of addressing grievous past mistakes.

After learning that Jolene needed cancer surgery, Paula said she understood why taking time off work was necessary. But moving to Tennessee? Giving up a ten-year career didn't seem wise, she'd pointed out. Why did it matter where she had surgery? Weren't the doctors and hospitals in Louisiana good enough?

"You should reconsider," Paula concluded.

But her advice fell deaf on Jolene's ears.

Jolene needed to speak with Becky before leaving the office. She soon learned that Peter Cromwell purchased a $300,000 home on Saturday, and according to Becky, his credit was impeccable. As promised, Becky would split the sale with Jolene.

Although Becky disagreed with Jolene's decision to leave, going to Tennessee felt like the right thing to do. So, Jolene stuck to her guns. Then later, feeling unrest over her decision to leave home and revisit her past, Jolene made an appointment with her pastor. Maybe Dr. Burt James could shed insight on her dilemma. She could sure use a little parental-like wisdom about now.

At 4 p.m. Jolene was seated in the anteroom to Burt's study, nervously chewing on a fingernail. His nosy secretary Frieda inquired why Jolene was there. A clam didn't have a tighter mouth. Frieda was nice, but she had a quick tongue. So, making light conversation, Jolene waited for her pastor to emerge.

After a few minutes, Burt's door opened and he motioned for Jolene to enter his private sanctuary. "Thank you for seeing me on such short notice," she uttered, her brain stumbling for the right words to explain the rampaging confusion.

"No problem, you were due a visit." Burt scrutinized Jolene.

"Has it been that long?" Jolene managed to smile as she took a seat in front of his cluttered desk. "I hope I haven't interrupted your work." Burt usually counseled people by appointment.

"No problem." He cleared his throat. "I'm like a doctor on call, or a fireman putting out brushfires." He chuckled.

Dr. James was an educated man in his mid-fifties, married with two children, and a proud grandfather of eight balls-of-fire, as he fondly called them. A strict adherent to the teachings of the Bible, his daily walk with Christ appeared impeccable.

Still, Burt managed to stay connected to reality, making those in his presence feel completely welcome and comfortable. To Jolene, he was like the father she'd always wanted; but then everyone in his small Episcopal congregation felt the same way.

Burt sat quietly in his swivel rocker, head tilted to one side, hands forming a tent, marble-sized gray eyes set firmly on Jolene's face. "Did something bad happen?" he queried.

She nodded as tears bubbled in her eyes. "I have cancer."

He stamped feet on the floor and leaned forward. "I see."

"No, you don't!" Jolene shook her head, eyes glued to the multicolored carpet. "My mother died of cancer."

He said nothing.

Jolene quivered with emotion. "After attending her funeral, I left Tennessee and never looked back. I've hardly thought about my parents since." She made firm eye contact. "I'm an only child, Burt. And I ran away. Do you know anyone more selfish?"

"Is this about guilt?" The big man eased out of his chair and shuffled around his desk. "Come here." He motioned with arms wide open. "Let ol' Burt give you a hug."

Jolene nearly fell against the soft folds of his paunch and boohooed. Shame on her, said a part of her psyche. Let it all hang out, said another. Like two bulls fighting it out.

"Now, doesn't that feel better?" he rasped.

She nodded, sniffled, and accepted a tissue.

"Let's talk about it, shall we?" He hitched up his polyester pants. "Nothing offers more relief than the heart's confession."

In the next thirty minutes, Jolene poured out her regrets, reminiscing about how she'd grown up in middle Tennessee, in Dickson County where she graduated high school, and later received a degree in marketing from the University of Memphis.

She'd met David while working as a pharmaceutical rep in Jackson, Mississippi. After a whirlwind romance, they had married. With his business located in Baton Rouge, Louisiana, she'd moved there with him and never looked back.

In a sense, she'd abandoned her family for her future. Her remarried father certainly hadn't needed her. Life marches on.

Burt adjusted himself in his padded chair.

"What has all this got to do with your cancer, dear?" he inquired; a puzzled expression nagging his aging face.

"I might die, Burt. Before I make peace with my past," she confessed. *God expects no less*, she thought to herself.

"So you need to return to Tennessee." His bushy white eyebrows arched. "And do what, my dear? Punish yourself for past mistakes?" He paused to give Jolene time to reflect.

"It's hard to put into words, but I have to do this."

"Say you go," Burt uttered with sincerity, "do you have relatives there who will help you during this crisis?"

"Dad's dead, I can't change that." Jolene plunged her nose into a wad of Kleenex and blew hard. "Somehow, I must find a way to confront my failures as his daughter. Make amends."

Burt placed arthritic hands on his desk. "How does David feel about your decision to leave?"

The question lingered like frost in the air. David? Will he even care? Jolene blinked, realizing she hadn't answered Burt.

"Who's going to treat your cancer when you get there?"

"I haven't thought that far," she admitted. "David can come with me to Tennessee, if he's willing." What about his work?

"What about your friends? Not to mention your job?"

"David asked the same questions." Jolene sighed. "I know I'll need people around I can count on. I'll work it out."

"I see. Well, if you've already made up your mind, what's the problem?" he asked. "Why have you come to see me?"

That was a good question.

"Do you want me to talk you out of going?"

Now, that was a better question.

"I want you to talk to my husband," Jolene declared with renewed resolve. "David refuses to see my reasoning and won't budge an inch. He thinks I've lost my mind."

Burt winced and tugged at his double chin. "Maybe David feels like you're abandoning him. Love can be selfish."

"What?" That was an angle she hadn't considered.

Sure, they had their share of marital problems, but she wasn't leaving him for good. *Am I?* Now she was more confused.

Burt heaved a sigh. "So, I guess, following your heart is more important than pleasing your husband at this juncture. Because you have cancer and might die." He nailed the lid on the coffin.

Jolene nodded, tears pulsing to be released. "I was too busy with my own life to comfort my mother while she was dying in the hospital. And didn't see my father lowered in the grave, still furious at him because he remarried so soon after Mama died."

"So this trip *is* about resolving guilt." Burt diagnosed Jolene's problem. "Have you sought God's forgiveness?"

"Of course, I did."

"No one walks in another's shoes, Jolene. In a sense, every soul is an island." He leaned back in the swiveling-rocker.

Jolene nodded, rolled her shoulders and slumped in her chair. Through the window she spied remnants of the weekend snow clinging to greenery. Soon it would be spring down south.

"Who will take care of you after your surgery?" Burt brought the subject of Jolene's dilemma into focus.

"I have one cousin in Murfreesboro—that's a bedroom community located in south Nashville," Jolene explained. "We exchange cards at Christmas. I'll call her."

"Well, at least there's someone there."

Burt's smile was rewarding.

"Mitzi is six years older than me, my first cousin. Aunt Lila—that's my daddy's baby sister—she died four years ago from lung cancer." *Another cancer victim*, Jolene cringed, feeling a measure of relief from sharing her chaotic family heritage.

"Home is where the heart is, or so they say." Burt's smile was comforting. "My only suggestion: do what God tells you."

"Unfortunately, I haven't heard His voice in awhile," Jolene admitted. "You're the next thing to God I know that has vocal chords." She nervously chuckled, hands clutching her abdomen.

Surprise put a light in Burt's eyes.

"You know what I mean," she said, half giggling.

"That's truly a sweet compliment, my dear. Let's pray, shall we?" He pronounced the most beautiful prayer Jolene had heard in years. A fierce peace invaded her soul as she confirmed in her heart that the path she'd chosen was the correct one.

Perhaps going to Tennessee was more than just about herself. Maybe God was setting her feet to a mission that would fulfill some higher purpose than alleviating her emotional pain.

When the prayer ended, Jolene opened her glazed eyes.

"Would you look at the time?" Burt glanced at the wall clock. "Past time to close up shop," he uttered. "Promised the wife I'd take her out for dinner tonight; it's our anniversary."

"How many years . . .?" Jolene asked.

"Thirty-six," he smiled. "Best decision I ever made was marrying Cora. She's been the crown jewel to my career. "

"Congratulations!" Jolene exclaimed, considering if her marriage would last another month. Would choosing to leave town be the last straw that broke their marriage? David might decide she wasn't worth waiting for and start divorce proceedings.

"I'll see you to the front door." Burt eased from his chair and exited the office. She followed as he shuffled down the narrow hallway. "Be carefully driving home, dear."

The front door yawned open, an invitation to go.

"I will. And thanks."

Jolene stepped out into the cold crisp day. The sky was a flawless Robin blue. That would change again as a warm Gulf breeze fast warmed the atmosphere. It could even be seventy-two in New Orleans by Christmas. Every so often, a winter snow fell, surprising everyone. Children loved making snowmen and sliding down concrete driveways in cardboard boxes.

Oh, to turn time back and change my past.

Tomorrow, Jolene decided, she would call Dr. Kennedy and ask for a referral to an oncologist in Nashville. By the end of the week, her real estate license would be on hold, her office cleaned out, and all her clients turned over to Becky Simms. Then, God willing, she was off to Tennessee with or without David's approval. It wasn't a textbook life, but it was hers.

Jolene climbed in her Buick and headed home.

♣4

JOLENE HADN'T EXPECTED a knockdown drag-out fight the night before she caught a flight to Nashville on Saturday.

Early Friday, Burt James had spoken to David about Jolene's decision to return to Tennessee for surgery. Rather than help, the conversation had sparked a war. Apparently, David viewed her decision as abandonment. Nothing she said helped. Like the words to an old country song, *that's his story and he's sticking to it.*

David had tried every way in the world to convince Jolene that her decision to *run*—as he put it—was stupid. Who would take care of her after surgery? Mitzi had her own family. How could she think of imposing on a relative she hardly knew?

What about the months of pain she'd endure as a result of chemotherapy? Did she think her cousin would welcome the challenge? She had no one but him. Face it!

Nevertheless, Jolene's heart was set on a mission.

She'd asked Becky to take her to the airport. David hadn't spoken to her since their fight. Operating on autopilot, she checked in and boarded the Delta flight to Nashville. The jet lifted off the runway with ease, five days before Christmas.

Yet, not one gift purchased for anyone.

God's gift to man was free. *Jesus.*

All Jolene took with her for the adventure were two suitcases filled with the warmest clothes she could purchase at the mall. According to the national weather forecast, it was snowing in Nashville at a miserable twenty-eight degrees Fahrenheit. She closed her eyes and slept for the direct one-hour-and-half flight.

Time was meaningless. Dreams vanquished.

As the plane descended, a bell dinged. Flight attendants moved about the cabin to collect trash and empty plastic water bottles. Awake now, Jolene glanced out the small slice of window.

Below, she spied the beautiful glistening rolling landscape covered in snow as the jet broke through the cloud coverage and the airport terminal appeared in the distance. Right or wrong, foolish or wise, she had arrived at her destination.

Jolene followed a horde of travelers through the Jetway and hurried down the terminal toward BAGGAGE. A sense of adventure spurred her on, almost like the thrill of a first ride on a roller coaster. She had no long-term plans. This was playing it by ear, as the old adage went. While waiting for the carrier to float her luggage around, she dialed Mitzi's cell phone number.

"I'm on the ground," she said. "Where are you?"

"Parked outside the terminal, can't wait to see you, honey."

"Give me five, I see my bags coming." Jolene folded her phone in one hand, a glimpse of her future materializing.

It was eleven o'clock and the Titans were playing a home game that afternoon. Winning was everything to most people.

In a way, I'm waging a war, too.

Traffic was heavy, and sluggish, due to the slick roads. But the interstate had been soaked in a chemical the night before to melt the falling snow. Mitzi drove at an even, safe speed.

She was full of talk about her new daughter-in-law, a second marriage for her son Chris. Jolene listened with interest as her mind replayed David's accusation that she'd never had time for children. He was right, of course. She'd put off having babies until it was too late. Place the blame where it was due, baby!

As Mitzi exited the interstate at Murfreesboro forty-five minutes later, she turned to Jolene, a question mark etching her face. "You've hardly said a word during the trip."

"Sorry." Jolene shrugged.

"Have I talked your ears off?"

Jolene smiled. "Yes, but I've loved hearing how happy you are. It's helped my day, trust me."

All is not well at my house.

"I sense you're not. Entirely happy, that is."

"Happiness is a state of mind, I'll get there."

Will I if David never speaks to me again?

"I'm sorry David couldn't get away," Mitzi piped. "Is there a problem?" she queried. "He's not mad at you, is he?"

Jolene haughtily laughed. "Worse."

"He'll come around—hey, who knows? You might decide you don't like your doctor here and go home." She turned right at the next stoplight and picked up speed. "We're almost there."

Jolene spied the two-story Colonial home featuring a wraparound porch. A humongous snowman, with a carrot for a nose and two black rocks for eyes, smiled at them as Mitzi drove her Ford Explorer into the triple-garage and lowered the doors.

"How long have you lived here?" Jolene asked.

"Six years. Jack works in management for a local book company. My daughter lives in Franklin—she has two girls, ten and seven. Chris and his new bride live one subdivision over. I get to see my grandkids on a regular basis, which is a blessing."

"More than you realize."

"I don't know what I'd do without them." Mitzi stepped out of the SUV and unlatched the rear door. "Leave your luggage. I'll send Jack to fetch it when he returns from the gym."

They hustled out of the cold garage into a warm, inviting house. Over lunch, Jolene caught up on years of family heritage. Mitzi knew more about the last few years of Kate's life than Jolene did. Shame cornered her feelings, but that was about to change.

"I hear you're having surgery," Jack said when he came home.

"Yes. It isn't an option." Jolene's blue eyes flickered.

Was this the time to ask for a roof over her head?

"Is your condition serious?"

"I'll soon know," she replied. "I have an appointment with an oncologist on January fifth. After my surgery, we'll see."

Jack caught Mitzi's eye as she uttered, "Of course, you're welcome to stay with us, dear. We'll not accept a refusal."

"It's not that I don't appreciate the invitation, but I don't want to be a burden." Options were limited. "You have your lives, and taking care of a grouchy patient won't be pleasant."

"Don't be silly, we have plenty of room," Jack insisted.

"I'll think about it, but first I'd like to rent a car and drive out to Dickson County. I kind'a have my heart set on renting a place close to Charlotte." It was part of the healing plan.

"Do you still have friends who live there?" Jack inquired.

"I'm not sure; I'm kind of on a safari," Jolene explained. "The wild animal I want to slay is Fear." The imagery was all too real. "I'm exploring my failures as an only child in the face of my parents' untimely deaths." There was no plainer way to say it.

Jack shot Mitzi a look. "And now you're facing cancer."

"Yeah, I am. Stinks, doesn't it?"

"You're a survivor!" Mitzi said. "And you shoot straight."

They all had a good laugh followed by a rich, chocolate dessert. After a long tiring day, Jolene retired at nine thirty.

Sleep came with vivid dreams, disconnected and troubling. She woke often to check the time. Finally, around four a.m., she fell into a deep sleep and didn't wake up until late morning.

Mitzi had left a note on the breakfast bar: *Gone to church. Be home around noon.* Sunday: David would probably be at church.

With time on her hands, Jolene removed her Bible from the suitcase and read a passage from Psalm. King David had hurt over his mistakes, too. Yet, God had forgiven and even blessed him. She was counting on the same God of Abraham, Isaac, and Jacob to show up for her, too. If the Lord of Life couldn't sustain her through cancer surgery, she was lost to despair.

God, help me. Give me courage to face what comes next.

♣5

MIDDLE TENNESSEE'S SNOWFALL melted away on Tuesday as the temperature rose into the mid-fifties. It was two days before Christmas. Jolene needed to shop for gifts so Mitzi took her to the mall for lunch and a buying excursion.

Excitement permeated the atmosphere as folks, young and old, rushed around purchasing last minute gifts. Jolene bought gift certificates and found herself accepting Mitzi's invitation to stay with them until she met with the oncologist in January. Surgery would follow, then a time of recuperation.

Life is tentative, at best. What about David?

Though it was Jolene's choice to leave Baton Rouge, she'd hoped David would change his mind and follow her to Tennessee. But he had not called. And stubbornness wouldn't let her.

That afternoon, Jolene rented an Audi from a Murfreesboro dealer and drove toward Dickson County. The manager claimed the rental was only two years old, but from the way it drove, she suspected it had been wrecked. If the car gave her trouble, he'd told her, trade it for another one in Dickson at no extra cost.

Jolene needed to rent a house or apartment before having surgery so she could recuperate in Charlotte while exploring her jaded past. On her way there, at every turn, the car threatened to stall. "Oh, brother," Jolene grimaced, praying for travel mercy.

Dickson was thirty-five miles west of Nashville via Interstate 40. Jolene exited on Highway 46 and spied a Cracker Barrel on her right. In a hurry to get ahead of her day, she followed the familiar signs north then turned left toward the downtown district.

Main Street was a narrow two-way street flanked by mom-and-pop stores and a coffee shop called HOUSEBLEND that drew people like bees to honey. Feeling the need for a blast of caffeine, Jolene pulled into a parking space and entered the bistro.

Approaching three, and feeling in need of nourishment, she ordered a large hazelnut latte with an almond scone. She chose a seat at the vacant table next to the window. With Christmas on the doorstep, the ambiance of frivolity permeated the bistro as high school students gathered to fraternize and enjoy specialty coffees. One elderly man sat in a corner reading a book.

A feeling bordering nostalgia invaded Jolene's spirit as she sipped on her latte and munched on the scone. Observing how friendly the locals were stimulated a surge of loneliness as she thought of David. He'd not bothered to phone once. That he was still mad at her was a given. Should she break the silly standoff and be the first to apologize?

And admit she was wrong? Jolene tucked the cell phone in her purse. *No, he's the stubborn one. Let him call first.*

The Dickson Herald, a bi-weekly local newspaper, lay within reach on the next table. Snagging it, Jolene perused the short list of rental houses. Apparently, Dickson County was growing while other counties nationwide tanked because of a sagging economy. If one believed the bad news, America was not faring well.

After polishing off her latte, Jolene left the bistro and drove north on Highway 48. Charlotte lay eight miles in front of her.

Almost there, she thought. *Home, has it changed much?*

With excitement mounting, Jolene drove past a few rural homes with cow pastures and barns lining the highway. A funeral home perched on a hill to her left, and farther down the road, a couple of churches. With humidity still low and the sun blazing above, frozen patches of vegetation were slowly melting.

Jolene automatically let down the window of the Audi to feel the cold breeze against her face. Although a bit tired, it felt exhilarating to be in familiar territory. Nearing the heart of Charlotte, she rolled past a grocery store and came to a stop sign.

On her left was a graveyard next to a rustic hardware store with an Ever-ready Battery Sign attached to one side.

Making a right turn, Jolene proceeded slowly until she took a left at the next through street. Down a ways, and cattycorner to the federal Post Office, stood Charlotte's historic courthouse.

Jolene turned right to circle the square.

Hefty trucks, the color of sweet pickles and cherries, were slant-parked facing the courthouse around the perimeter. Serving as the county seat for Dickson County, many a murderer had been tried there. Jolene shivered at their dire futures.

To Jolene's right, a newer two-story municipal building had been erected to accommodate taxpayers. For a small town, Charlotte bustled with activity. She circled the square once, pulled into a vacant parking spot then exited the Audi.

The late afternoon air was pleasant as the sun peeked through a thin haze of cirrus clouds. Sunset would come early, so there was no time to waste. She wasn't sure why she'd stopped.

Icicles perilously clung to naked bushes shaded by the tall buildings. A sign that winter wasn't going away anytime soon. This wasn't south Louisiana's weather, she considered while traipsing across the street. Seconds later, she entered a three-story, turn-of-the-century house, utilized as a bed-and-breakfast.

Pleasantly surprised, Jolene discovered a small bookstore with a delicatessen near the front where one could order drinks. The odor of coffee brewing and lingering lunch odors provided just the right atmosphere. Glancing through the archway into the next room, she spied square tables set for future customers.

Keeping one eye on people entering and leaving, Jolene perused the book titles lining the wooden shelves. Mothers with children were seated at low tables. This was family time.

Had any of these people known her parents?

Most of Jolene's high school classmates had left for parts unknown after graduation. Wanting to escape the country culture like her, they were after better paying jobs. "The other side of the fence always looks greener," her grandmother often said.

But is that always true? Isn't there something grand about home?

"Excuse me, but I haven't seen you in town before," the pretty young woman perched behind the sales counter noted.

"Who me . . .?" Jolene glanced around.

"Do you see another stranger?"

"No." Jolene laughed.

"Call me curious, but what brings you to Charlotte?"

"I grew up here," Jolene replied. "My mother was a Gilmore. Are any still around?" She paused for input on the subject.

"Sure. That's a name that's been around Dickson County for ages." The tall, thin employee curiously stared at Jolene.

"My mother's first name was Kate. She's deceased," Jolene offered. "She was married to Kirk Lancaster. He's dead, too."

Humph. "Guess that was before my time."

Jolene offered no comment.

"Beverly's my name." A bony hand shot out. "My aunt owns this place and pays me to help run it."

"Jolene." She reciprocated. "It's a beautiful vintage home. Didn't someone used to run a kindergarten in here?"

"Yeah, they did." Skinny leaned elbows on the front counter. "Until 1950, it's recorded in a book my aunt wrote."

"Really . . .?" Jolene wondered if her mother's name was in that book. "I graduated from Dickson High School," she offered. "My mother died a few years after I graduated from college."

"Shoot, maybe you've still got relatives living here. Might check the courthouse records for births and deaths," Beverly suggested. "Or take out an ad in the local newspaper."

"That's an idea." Jolene recalled that Mitzi said there were no living relatives in the county—plenty of dead ones, if Jolene decided to visit the cemeteries. "Thanks for talking to me."

"No, problem, make yourself welcome."

If Jolene could only talk to someone who had known her mother before she died, to get a feel for her state of mind.

Was Mama terrified? Or brave like Jolene wanted to be?

"Staying in town long?" Beverly struck up the conversation again, offering Jolene a cup of java. "It's on the house."

"You sure . . .?"

She waved a hand. "My aunt can afford it."

"How nice of you," Jolene smiled, "To answer your question, Beverly, I'm just visiting."

Am I? Or will I end up staying longer?

"What are my chances of renting one of your rooms?" Jolene inquired, glancing up at the bead-board ceilings.

"None available, I'm afraid."

Jolene's flag-blue eyes widened.

"My aunt, Claire Wilkes—she usually doesn't rent rooms during the winter season. Ceilings too blame high to heat," Beverly explained. "Sorry, but that's her rule."

"Is there a motel nearby where I can get a room for the night?" Jolene wasn't going to be so easily run out of town.

"'Nope," Beverly huffed, "you gotta go back to Dickson. Best choices are on Highway 46 South near the Interstate."

Clearly, Jolene was disappointed.

"'Spect you'd have no trouble getting a room, seeing Christmas is almost here. Most folks are either out of town or spending time with their family."

Family was something Jolene didn't want to think about.

"Oh, and Cracker Barrel's close by the interstate, too," Beverly exclaimed. "The restaurant has great food, and gas across the street is a whole lot cheaper at the truck stop than here."

"Thanks for the info and coffee."

Jolene exited the B & B, praying for wisdom as to how to proceed. It was as if her hometown had cast her out.

Once back in the Audi, she opened the *Dickson Herald* and spied the ads of two rental houses she'd previously marked in red. Both properties were located on Highway 49, a stretch of curvy, hilly paved road that ran between Charlotte and Vanleer.

With daylight still burning, Jolene decided to drive past them before setting an appointment. However, she had to find a room before sunset. She wasn't Mother Mary about to deliver a baby, but a stable dwelling had no special appeal for her at Christmas.

A couple miles out of Charlotte, on Highway 49, the Audi sputtered and stalled. Dead as a doornail!

No, no, no! She pounded the steering wheel and took her foot off the brake. The dud rolled down the steep hill and Jolene guided it off on the side pavement. This was not in her plan.

Shoving the door open, she climbed out and looked at the stretch of empty highway in both directions. There was no one local she knew to call for help. Suddenly, she felt very old and weary. Were the cancers stealing her vitality? She felt the chilly wind as it scurried across the meadows, dragging a plastic grocery bag with it. At least she had on warm clothing.

No other choice, she'd have to walk back to town. Or hitch a ride. Looking both ways again, not a car was in sight.

Oh, dear. Standing next to the stalled car in a quandary, Jolene spied a dilapidated-looking farmhouse with an overgrown yard in need of mowing. *No help there.* And no cell phone service.

She'd be forced to walk back to Charlotte and seek help.

Thankfully, Jolene wore leather boots over heavy socks, and her long woolen coat was hooded to break the cold brisk wind. Hands tucked inside warm furry gloves, she locked the Audi and started backtracking on foot, thinking around every curve she'd spot an occupied residence where she could borrow a phone.

No such luck, baby. This might not be your best day.

Jolene hadn't gotten half a mile toward town when an old Cadillac whizzed past with its canvas top lowered. The driver's curly hair blew like threads of fire in the wind as four tiny heads bobbed up and down in the back seat. A boy around ten was perched on his knees in the passenger seat, braced for an impact.

Who is this crazy mom driving like a maniac in freezing weather?

♣6

WHEELS SCREECHED AS tires burned rubber on the asphalt road and Road-Rage behind the wheel slammed on the brakes. Speeding in reverse, the clunker backed up and stopped beside Jolene. "Need a ride, lady?" the wild driver asked.

"I don't think so." Jolene had more sense than to trust the crazy mother. "It can't be far back to town."

"Are you nuts, lady?" The woman huffed. "It's mor 'n two miles back to Charlotte. Sun's almost down, can't stay out here."

"I guess not." Jolene sighed.

"Know I'm not the best driver in the world, but I'd be happy to squeeze you in—Cloy! Get in the back seat and holt tight to Carla!" The redhead told the girls in the back to move over.

Jolene blinked, her mouth hanging open. She had *not* yet given her consent. Who was this sassy young woman?

"Get in, lady. I've used up all my patience for one day." She kicked the passenger door open with her right foot.

Jolene walked around the front of the Cadillac, staring at the children in the back seat. "Do you know anybody in Charlotte who will tow my car at this late hour?" she asked the testy mom.

"That it stalled on the side of the road back a' ways?"

"Yeah, I knew it was a lemon," Jolene replied. "It needs serious help." *Like some people I know.*

"Apparently, you do, too."

Touché. Jolene actually smiled.

"On your way through town, you passed a business that handles the repair of wrecked cars," Mom-with-the-heavy-foot uttered. "If you'll get in, I'll take you there in a jiffy."

"Thank you." Jolene filled the passenger seat. "I'm Jolene Salisbury," she introduced herself, looking for seatbelts.

"Nancy Blake. Live in that ol' farmhouse a' ways back."

Mama Bear revved the engine and the noisy car shot forward, taking the next curve with plenty of attitude.

"Where are the seatbelts?" Jolene felt for the leather straps.

"Cut 'em out when the baby started chewing on 'em," Nancy said. "Is that a problem?" Stony jade eyes glared at Jolene.

"I guess not." *Don't look a gift horse in the mouth.*

The ride was fast and bumpy. Nancy came to an abrupt stop in front of Jamie's Solution for Troubled Vehicles.

"Clever name," Jolene noted. "What do I owe you?"

Nancy drew in her chin with indignation. "People who live around here don't take handouts for being nice, Jolene," she protested. "Evidently, you ain't from here!"

"Sorry, Nancy, I didn't mean to insult you—is there any other way I could help?" Jolene was truly grateful for the lift.

"I said no, didn't I? What part don't you understand?"

Jolene took in a breath. "Actually, I grew up around here. I'm back for a visit." She evaluated the girl's interest. "I was scouting for a house to rent when my rental car stalled."

Does she really want to hear all this?

"Oh." The steam went out of Nancy. "That stinks."

"Yes, it does. I tried to rent a room at the B & B in Charlotte, but the young woman at the front desk told me there wasn't a bed to be had," Jolene explained.

"That would be my cousin, Beverly," Nancy said. "My mother owns the place." A frown settled in her face.

"Really . . .?" Jolene tried to open the car door but it resisted. "I can't get the door open." She shoved it harder.

"Lean back." Nancy kicked the door hard with a foot. "Gets stuck sometimes, but it's still a good car, and it gets me places."

"Why don't you let Jamie fix it?"

"No extra money," Nancy said. "Besides, I'm leaving town."

"Why?" Jolene found herself prying.

"I'm leaving my no-good husband!" Nancy cursed then turned around in her seat and said, "You didn't hear that, kids. Mama's just upset. Cloy, wipe that grin off yo'r face!"

Jolene was embarrassed for the children. Cloy, the older boy with shaggy red hair and freckles frowned.

"Mama ain't leavin', lady. Don'chu believe her!"

Little ears know things.

"Shut your mouth, Cloy!" Nancy exploded. "You haven't lived long enough for an opinion!"

By this time the two younger children were bawling.

"Sorry." Nancy appeared genuinely embarrassed. "I didn't mean for you to get in the middle of a family squabble."

"It's okay." Jolene eased the warped door open and stepped outside. "I insist on paying for the door to be fixed."

Nancy haughtily laughed. "Oh, well, if you've got money to burn, who am I to refuse?" The wind fizzled out of her sails.

In the next five minutes, Nancy and her five children, along with Jolene, piled into the manager's office and waited for assistance. A muscular man with oily black hands named Jake came through a side door. "What'cha need, ladies?"

"Uh, I need my stalled vehicle hauled to a car rental agency in Dickson," Jolene spoke up. "The motor won't turn over."

"Hi, Nancy," Jake popped his gum, "how's Buck?"

Wrong question, from the look on the mom's face. "Nancy was nice enough to give me a lift into town," Jolene intervened.

Jake plopped down at his cluttered desk and started filling out an order. "Name . . .?" He glanced up at his customer.

"Jolene Salisbury. I rented the Audi in Murfreesboro. I was told to turn it in at the rental place in Dickson if it gave trouble."

Jake put down his pen and studied Jolene. "It'll cost you seventy-five for a wrecker. Rental insurance oughta cover it."

"No problem, I'll pay in cash or credit card, your choice."

Jake's grape eyes slid toward Nancy and hung there a long moment. "Buck still truckin' every week?"

"He's fine, Jake. We're all fine." Nancy stared into space.

There's more here than meets the surface.

"Do I pay you now?" Jolene asked Jake to fill the void.

Evidently, Nancy wasn't sharing the fact she was leaving Buck for Tim-buck-too. Or maybe she was simply going home to mama. *Claire Wilkes:* the woman was a person of interest.

Jake scribbled on his form then said, "Okay, that wraps up the paperwork." He swiped his nose with the back of a hand.

"How soon can a wrecker get here?" Jolene asked.

"Got one parked out back," Jake replied. "You can hitch a ride into town with Ken. He's going that way, anyhow."

"One more thing, Jake . . ." Jolene smiled at Nancy. "I want to pay for the Nancy's passenger door to be fixed."

"Come again?" Jake's face scrunched as he dug a finger in one ear. "That beat-up ol' Cadillac ain't worth fixin'."

"Shut up, Jake. Don't be a jerk!" Nancy snapped.

"She ain't got car insurance," Jake informed Jolene.

"That doesn't matter," Jolene countered. "It's not safe for the children to ride in a car where the door might jar open."

Jolene insisted that Jake do the job then added, "And put in used seatbelts on front and back seats while you're at it."

Jerk! Jolene sided with Nancy.

Nancy's face opened like a blooming flower. Poor girl must really feel like an orphan. Jolene wanted to help her even more.

"Okay, I'll need your credit card 'fore I start the work," Jake said to Jolene. "Nancy, can you leave the Cadillac with us?"

"I guess—if the kids and I can get a ride to the house."

Jolene guessed her generosity had defused Nancy's anger at her husband. That was the easiest marriage she ever saved.

After signing more of Jake's paperwork, Jolene walked outside with Nancy and the children. Her girls were antsy from sitting still so long and had begun poking jabs at each another.

"That's enough, kids!" Nancy cautioned. "You don't want to make mama mad." The fighting immediately ceased. "Sorry, it's way past their suppertime," she apologized to Jolene.

"I can't imagine how you do it."

"Do what?" Nancy appeared puzzled.

"Raise five children," Jolene said. Baby Carla had cried herself to sleep in her big brother's arms. "Considering the circumstances, I think your children behaved wonderfully."

"That's so sweet." Nancy relaxed; a warm smile surfacing. "I stopped to help you and you turned around and helped me."

"It was my pleasure. Do you need to grocery shop?"

"Actually, I could use a jug of milk to tide us over."

Jolene handed Nancy a ten-dollar bill and asked Jamie to take her to the grocery store before driving them home.

Ken was anxiously waiting in the wrecker for Jolene to show him where she'd abandoned the Audi. "I'd better get going."

Nancy nodded. "Guess this is goodbye."

"Will you be okay?" Jolene asked.

Nancy's nose wrinkled. "I'll manage."

"Will I see you again?"

Jolene felt as if she'd made a new friend.

"You know whur I live."

Before parting ways, Nancy hugged Jolene like she was Santa Claus and asked her to stop by the house tomorrow.

Jolene agreed, worried that Nancy might decide to take off again with the children and divorce Buck if she didn't make her presence known. Not that it was any of her business.

Where is Claire Wilkes? Why isn't she counseling her daughter?

~

Tuesday folded in on Jolene like a gloved hand as the sun's last rays blinked out behind the rolling hills of Dickson County. A melon glow suffused the atmosphere as dusk fell.

It had been a challenging day.

Actually, meeting Nancy and her five children was the highlight of Jolene's coming-home experience. A blessing to boot, the Dickson Rental Agency had arranged for the damaged Audi to be towed back to Murfreesboro at no added expense.

And now she was driving a reliable six-month-old Buick.

Jolene had no problem renting a room at the Holiday Inn next to the interstate. After taking her bag up to the room, she drove over to the Cracker Barrel and gorged on a vegetable plate.

By seven forty-five, she was back in her room, collapsed on the bed in her nightie, and about to turn on the TV when the phone beside the bed rang. She pounced on it. "Hello!"

"It's Mitzi, Jolene."

"I meant to call you earlier."

"No problem, I was getting my nails done. Got your message that you were staying in Dickson another day," Mitzi sputtered.

"It's been an interesting day."

"What's going on with the rental car?"

"Bummed out on me," Jolene replied, "but I caught a ride into Charlotte and arranged for it to be towed."

"Anyone I would know?"

"Nancy Blake. She has five adorable children, ten and under." Jolene went on to explain how Nancy was in the process of leaving her husband until she defused the situation.

"I see—well, don't get too attached to Nancy and her kids, you have enough on your plate," Mitzi warned.

Jolene knew that to be true.

"Did you arrange for a better ride?"

"Yes, a Buick. It purrs like a charm."

"How did it feel to go home?" Mitzi asked.

"Good. For a little while, I actually forgot I had cancer."

"Tomorrow's Christmas Eve, did you forget that, too?"

"It hasn't been foremost in my mind." Jolene thought of David, alone for the holidays. *Will he miss me?*

"You should really be with family on Christmas."

"I will, I'll be at your house by five o'clock tomorrow."

"Perfect. Don't break my heart," Mitzi said.

"Promise not to go to any extra trouble on my account."

"Around my house, we celebrate Christmas in a huge way. If your plans do change, call me on my cell," Mitzi said.

"See you tomorrow afternoon."

Jolene ended the call and called home. The line rang four times before the machine clicked on. "Where are you, David?"

After reading a few Bible Scriptures, she prayed for Nancy's marriage to Buck. Locked into a novel drama, ten o'clock rolled around quickly. Closing the book and setting it aside, she yawned and switched on the TV to catch the news.

Another cold front was forecast for Christmas Eve, expected to dump four inches of the frozen white stuff over Middle Tennessee and plummet temperatures into the teens.

Jolene smiled. A host of children would be excited about Santa's sled gliding through the moonlit snowy night to reach their houses and deliver presents. *Joy to the world! The Lord has come!*

She felt her swollen stomach, a telltale sign of the growing cancers. Snuffing out the lamplight, she realized how very scary cancer was. Would the New Year signal her final months on earth? Without faith, there would be no hope of survival.

All things are possible through Christ Jesus Who strengthens me.

♣7

LIGHT SLIPPED THROUGH the crack in the curtains and filled the motel room, signaling morning. It took Jolene a couple minutes to realize where she was before bolting from bed.

"I'm really in Tennessee!" she announced.

Christmas Eve came with the promise of snow, Jolene recalled last night's weather report as she dressed, packed her bag, and checked out of the Holiday Inn. Hopefully, the Charlotte Courthouse would be open. She wanted to examine the tax rolls to see if anybody she knew still owned property and lived here.

Jolene parked in the back of the courthouse and exited the Buick. Across the street, Claire's B & B was lit up like a Christmas tree. Blue shutters on the elongated windows gave the home a gingerbread look. A huge glittering banner sagged across the front porch announcing BREAKFAST WITH SANTA.

Jolene found a notice on the courthouse door, CLOSED FOR CHRISTMAS. She turned around and started walking toward her rental. Growing curious about Nancy's mother, she ventured inside the B & B, ordered a hazelnut latte, and waited for Santa to arrive. The odors of baked cinnamon cookies permeated the bookstore, drawing inside a dozen or more children trailed by smiling parents. The children's laughter clearly defined their anticipation of viewing the jolly ol' elf up close and personal.

Of course, their parents would make sure Saint Nick filled their toy orders. As Jolene observed the festivities in progress, the noise level escalated, though diligent mamas and daddies did their best to control their excited offspring. Jolene wondered why Nancy hadn't brought her five children to the event.

Maybe they didn't have transportation, seeing the Cadillac was at Jamie's Solution for Troubled Cars being fixed.

She approached the counter. "Excuse me."

"Oh, hi. You were here yesterday. Jolene, wasn't it?"

"You have a good memory, Beverly."

"Not like we get outsiders every day," Nancy's cousin spoke above the loud chatter. "But visitors are always welcome."

"Do you have a phone book I can borrow?" Jolene couldn't hear herself think. Kids were screaming and running all over the place like excited rats. "I hope Santa comes soon."

"Who're you lookin' for?" Beverly inquired. "I might know the number by heart." Charlotte was still a small town.

"Your cousin, Nancy," Jolene replied.

"Oh, that's easy." Beverly dialed the number. "What you want her for?" She handed over the land phone.

"I thought I'd see if Nancy needs me to pick up the kids and bring them over here for the party." Jolene heard the phone ringing. "It's the least I could do for her."

"Wait!" Beverly grabbed the phone. "No use askin'. She doesn't let the children do *anything* that involves her mother."

"Do you mind if I ask why?"

"Well, it ain't like it's no big secret."

"Then you can certainly tell me," Jolene declared.

Beverly placed her sharp elbows on the counter and leaned inches into Jolene's face. "You didn't hear this from me." She glanced around for eavesdroppers. "Claire's still mad at Nancy 'cause she got pregnant before finishing high school."

Stunned, Jolene erected her body. "But that's been at least ten years ago!" She recalled the age of Nancy's eldest boy, Cloy.

"That's right. But for Claire, forgiveness doesn't come easy."

"That's a real shame." Jolene clamped her lips.

Who am I to pass judgment?

When Jolene's father had married Olivia Kemp, she cut off all communication with him. Forgiveness requires humility.

"Yeah, it truly is." Beverly sighed. "Still, I don't see them two ever changin'. Nancy's got her life with Buck—such as it is. And Claire is the belle of every ball held in Charlotte."

"Why is that?"

"Didn't Nancy tell you? Her mother is married to the mayor." Two more people came through the door.

"Well, thanks for the info." Jolene shrugged on her coat. "It looks like you have a busy morning, and I need to get going."

"Leavin' before Santa arrives?" Beverly raised an eyebrow.

"Yeah, I think I'll go out and see Nancy and the children. Maybe I can be of some help with Christmas preparations."

"Good luck with that!" Beverly mouthed. "My cousin has a bee up her butt. She doesn't make friends so easily."

Jolene smiled as she slipped on her leather gloves.

"We're already friends, Beverly."

Exiting the B & B, Jolene climbed into her rental and drove straight over to Nancy Blake's dilapidated farmhouse.

The front yard wouldn't win any awards. It was grown up with tall grass, making it a deplorable haven for snakes and other varmints. The guts of four cars peeked over the dead weeds out back, next to a peeling red barn with a collapsing roof. The cab of a semi was parked in the driveway in front of a red truck that had seen some years. Not having called ahead, Jolene hoped Nancy's invitation to visit still stood. Well, she would soon find out.

The houselights were on downstairs, though the second and third stories had no life in them. Jolene took the path leading up to the house, a series of uneven flat stones. The front porch roof, supported by six rotting wooden pillars, hung slightly askew. And the white paint on the home's clapboard exterior was peeling.

Buck and Nancy's house had barely survived the war zone going on inside. Jolene politely knocked at the door and waited.

A cold wind kicked up and snow flurries peppered down. A few minutes later, Nancy opened the screen door.

"It's you." The mama smiled.

"Yes, am I interrupting anything?"

The door yawned wade open. "House is a mess. Kids are crazy with Santa on his way. And my husband is home."

"I'll only stay a moment," Jolene said.

A blast of heat siphoning from a wood-burning stove inserted into the brick fireplace against an outer wall hit Jolene in the face as she stepped in the Blake's compact living room. The floor was scuffed oak planks, what was not covered in threadbare rugs.

"This is cozy, real nice," Jolene announced with a smile.

"You don't have to lie, it's awful!" Nancy scowled.

"Who're you?" A bulky frame plugged the doorway leading deeper into the farmhouse. "Who is she, Nancy?"

"Excuse me?" Jolene peered at a towering male, handsome in a woodsy way with dark locks of curly dark tumbling over his forehead. Shaggily bearded, his eyes were an intense topaz.

Intimidating came to Jolene's mind.

"Who is this woman?" Buck asked again.

Jolene observed the look that passed between the couple.

"This is my friend, Jolene." Nancy parked a sassy hand on one hip. "She paid for *our* Cadillac to be fixed."

"You must be Buck." Jolene took the bull by the horns and offered her right hand in friendship. "I just wanted to make sure Nancy and the children were all right."

"Why wouldn't they be?" Buck spouted.

"I caused her to have a late and challenging day."

"Well, I'm home now." His long, taut legs spread eagle.

"You weren't home yesterday," Jolene shot back. "Pardon me if I was concerned." *I'm not your punching bag, buddy!*

"Well, now that you've seen that *everybody* is just fine, I guess you can leave!" He moved a step closer to Jolene.

She blinked with disbelief. Never had she encountered so rude a human being, not a clue as how to respond to Nancy's husband. She wanted to light into him like a mama hen brooding over her chicks. "Do you want me to leave, Nancy?"

"Absolutely not!!!" Nancy sauntered over to Buck and slapped him hard on the chest. "Go somewhere else and smoke. Get a beer. Cool off. Jolene and I are gonna have us a visit."

Buck softened like putty. "I'll see you later." He turned to Jolene. "Don't go putting silly ideas in this woman's head."

Then he stormed out the door like a wounded animal.

"I'm glad you came," Nancy said.

"I hope I haven't caused you more trouble."

"Buck's bark is worse than his bite."

Secretly smiling, Jolene took a great deal of comfort in the fact Buck couldn't bully Nancy. She guessed they slugged it out now and then when nobody was around to report them.

"I was about to have some coffee. Want some?"

"I'd love a cup." Jolene parted the living room's ragged curtains and observed Buck as he got in his red pickup, revved the engine, and tore out of the driveway. "Will Buck be okay?"

"Buck is Buck." Nancy made a face. "He keeps a burr up his saddle to prove he's still boss. I swear if I didn't love the man, I'd kill him with my own two bare hands!"

Jolene hoped that was a hyperbole.

"Where are the children?" She trailed Nancy into a country kitchen with tired vinyl floors and took a seat at the scarred oak table that looked like something from an 18th-century log cabin.

"They're in the back bedroom watching a Disney video."

Nancy filled an old-fashioned percolator with tap water and added four scoops of Folgers' vanilla-flavored coffee.

"Your house is charming, Nancy. I admit it needs some upkeep, but I think you are a very lucky lady," Jolene said.

"It's a roof over our heads."

"It's a private plantation, away from the rest of the world."

Nancy turned around, her mouth hanging open. "Sometimes I think it's so far from the rest of the world that I'll never get out."

Jolene understood, she was running from something, too.

"People in town call us 'poor white trash.'"

"I don't think that's true." Jolene watched Nancy plug the percolator cord into an electrical outlet. "My mother used to have a coffeemaker like that," she said. "She dearly loved her coffee."

"I thought you were headin' back to your cousin's today," Nancy said, slim hips parked against the kitchen counter as the water heated and burped through the percolator's metal funnel.

"I am, later." Brewing coffee teased Jolene's taste buds.

Nancy sloughed off her floral apron and joined Jolene at the distressed table. "Did your mother grow up in Charlotte?"

Jolene nodded, tears pressing against her eyelids.

"Is that why you came back?"

"It's complicated, Nancy." Jolene bit her lower lip. Should she tell Nancy about her cancer problem? They had only known each other for twenty-four hours. Still . . .

"What?" Nancy peered at Jolene. "'Fess up!"

Jolene lifted sad eyes. "I have cancer."

"No!" Horror flooded Nancy's face then softened with concern, no words that mattered to offer Jolene comfort.

"I'm afraid it's true." She placed a hand over Nancy's. "It's all right, really. I have an appointment to see a surgeon in early January. The cancerous growths will come out and I'll likely have chemotherapy. I'll be fine." *Would she?*

Nancy drew in a deep breath. "Where's home, Jolene?"

"Baton Rouge."

"So why come here for surgery?"

"Like I said, it's complicated." Jolene glanced away.

If David were only here I'd feel better.

"You can tell me, I grew up with complicated."

♣8

NOT BLAMING DAVID entirely for their distressed marriage, Jolene explained her situation to Nancy. Together for eighteen years, and true workaholics, she and David had never taken time to identify and meet each other's psychological needs.

Haven't we both chosen work over growing a family?

Now, too late to become pregnant and afraid that cancer might cut her life short, Jolene had returned to Charlotte in an attempt to resolve guilt in failing to be present in her parent's lives when they needed her most. As an only child, she'd been selfish.

"In what ways were you selfish?" Nancy asked as she filled two mugs with coffee and placed a carton of cream on the table.

Jolene hesitated answering while adding cream and sugar to her mug. "Well, that's what I'm facing. After finishing college, I chose to avoid going home. Back then, I thought Charlotte was a hick town with people I didn't care to know anymore."

"Wow! Is that supposed to make me feel better?"

Jolene chuckled. "That was then, Nancy, not now. I was so stupid to think I could abandon my family roots and never look back. Eventually, the past comes home to roost."

"So now you are a philosopher?"

For the next ten minutes, Jolene elaborated on her life choices. Somehow, confessing to a stranger was easier than confronting people she knew well. "So, you see . . ."

Rising from her chair, Nancy noticed that Jolene's coffee had grown cold. "Could I heat up that cup for you?"

Jolene put up a hand. "Let me get the rest of this out first."

Nancy nodded and eased back down.

"Admitting my faults doesn't come easy."

"You're not alone in that."

"So, after some serious deliberation with myself, and talking at length with my pastor, I knew what I needed to do. So I packed up and left Baton Rouge last Saturday," Jolene explained.

"Hush your mouth. That is . . . amazing."

"My husband David didn't think so. He was furious with me. He might never forgive me." Jolene knew it was so. "I called to apologize last night but he didn't answer his cell phone."

"What do you think that means?" Nancy asked.

"I'm not sure."

Is he interested in someone else?

"Why not find out?" Nancy walked over to the counter and grabbed the land phone. "Here, call David. It's Christmas Eve and it'll make you feel a whole lot better if you two talk."

"You're right." Jolene's jaw muscles tightened. "I should apologize to him for leaving so abruptly."

Jolene dialed his office number.

"May I speak to David?"

"Jolene? Is that you?" Sally returned.

"Yes, is David there?" Her gaze drifted toward the two elongated windows at the back. Snow was falling at a pretty good clip. She should head back to Murfreesboro before long.

"No, he's not. Would you like to leave a message?"

"Sally, do you know where he is?"

"Yeah, he's in the Bahamas. With Ben and Lyle, celebrating closing out a great insurance sales year," Sally replied. "You should be proud of David. This past week, he landed the biggest commercial account in the history of this company."

"I see." A catch was in Jolene's voice. "I am proud of him."

Inwardly, she was disappointed David hadn't bothered to tell her his company's plans. What if she needed him?

"Shall I tell David you called?" Sally asked.

"No. When do you expect the guys back?"

"Not until January 1. The office will be closed until then. In fact, I'm winding up everything now so I can leave."

"Merry Christmas, Sally, enjoy your time off."

Jolene hung up and stared at Nancy.

"Well, that certainly went well."

Jolene stood motionless in thought. "He's out of the country, sunning with his bachelor bosses in the Bahamas."

Am I bitter or not?

"I'm back!" Buck hollered as he pushed open the front door, interrupting Nancy's response.

"Hey, babe, I could use a little help about now!"

"Crazy guy, as if we thought he'd left for good!" Nancy laughed. "No such luck." She set her empty cup on the counter and headed for the living room. Jolene followed.

"Got us a Christmas tree as tall as our ceilings!" he announced. "Where you wanna put it?"

"Who would've thought?" Nancy mouthed at Jolene.

"Git the kids and let's start decorating it!"

"Are you outta your mind, Buck Blake? This tree's as big as Goliath! We don't have enough decorations to go on it."

"Get the kids and let's show 'em." Buck hitched up his jeans, a proud daddy, Nancy's comment not deterring his enthusiasm one iota. "Go on. Tell the kids to git in here now."

"Hold on, partner!" Nancy held up a restraining hand. "How much did this monstrosity put us out? We still got December bills to pay. What were you thinking?"

Buck grabbed Nancy and swung her around. "It's Christmas, Babe. Where's your spirit? It don't happen but once a year."

"Have you been drinking, Buck?" Nancy smelled his breath.

"Tree was marked down half price. Kids 'll love it."

"No doubt, Buck." Nancy caved.

Jolene had to admit it was an awesome spruce, its limbs full and fresh with green needles. "Let me help decorate," she said. "If you need more trim or lights, I'll make a run to Wal-Mart."

Do I have the time? Mitzi is expecting me later today.

Last year Jolene hadn't put up a tree. In fact, she'd shown property on Christmas Day to a couple from Houston, Texas. Afterwards, she and David had eaten out and called it Christmas when they exchanged gift cards—$200 each from a popular clothing store. *Tit for tat!* So the season passed uneventfully.

"We'd love to have you help us. Wouldn't we, Buck?"

His lips twisted to the side, not totally convinced.

"The kids miss having a grandmother around on holidays—not that you're old enough to be one," Nancy said to Jolene.

"It's okay, I ain't exactly no spring chicken."

They both laughed as Buck walked into the hall and hollered, "Kids, Christmas tree's here! Come help Mama and Jolene put on the trimmings." A measure of joy flooded his expression.

Jolene heard the scrambling of tiny feet, a testimony to the children's excitement. Buck turned around and peered at her.

"Guess this means you're staying fer a spell," he said.

"You're darn tootin!" Jolene laughed as her spirits lifted. "I wouldn't miss a tree-trimming for a million bucks!"

Wild horses couldn't drag me away.

In the next twenty minutes, Buck carried six boxes filled with decorations from the outside shed and placed them on the living room floor. Nancy dug into the packaging and removed strings of old-fashioned bubble lights, colors ranging from a bright red to extreme purple. Helping the Blake family trim the tree brought back fond memories of Jolene's childhood. Back then, Kirk and Kate were good parents who made sure their daughter had plenty of presents for Christmas. Her past hadn't been all bad.

So why have I dwelled on the negatives for so long?

The living tree stood tall, symbolizing Christ's birth and His death. Jesus was fully alive, fully God's Son, before being nailed to a lifeless tree, the cross, for sins He didn't commit. He was pierced for our transgressions, crushed for our iniquities. Three days later, Jesus vacated the grave and offered new life to all who would call on His name in faith. As a reminder, Burt James often read Isaiah 53 to his congregation at the Christmas Eve service.

To Jolene, the glittering star at the top of the tree represented her glorious Savior, the light of the world. Those shiny, colored balls depicted a range of human feelings. Life was not always bright like red, sometimes dark and somber like purple. Presents under the tree were a reminder that Christ gave gifts to the world: love, joy, and peace. Best of all was the free gift of salvation.

Jolene observed Burt and Nancy's children seated in a circle, giggling and chattering like monkeys as they threaded white popcorn through a long red string. Nancy leaned over and placed a large bowl of salted popcorn in the middle of the circle for them to nibble on. In the background, the radio droned softly with one Christmas carol after another playing as Buck strung the lights.

Spellbound, Jolene soaked in the moments. When Buck had climbed the ladder and placed the angel at the top of the tree, she glanced at her wristwatch. It was time to go. Nancy noticed Jolene retrieving her coat and purse from the wooden rack.

She asked, "You don't have to go yet, do you?"

"The snow's accumulating fast. I should go while I still can."

"Actually," Buck caught Jolene's eye, "you could spend the night with us." He wrapped an arm around his wife.

Buck's generous offer caught Jolene totally off guard. Nancy's eyes grew large and soft. "Why, honey, that's so sweet of you." She nestled even closer, squeezing his muscular arm.

Buck leaned over and kissed Nancy. "I love you, Babe."

"I love you, too." Nancy nearly cooed.

Jolene thought of David. When had they said those words to each other: *I love you?* They hadn't been sleeping in the same bed for months. He claimed her snoring kept him awake. Until now, she hadn't wanted to think of what that forecast.

"Buck's right," Nancy uttered to Jolene. "We'll put up a cot in here so you'll be nice and warm near the woodstove."

"Maybe another night," Jolene declined. "As you can see, I've grown quite fond of your family." If she hadn't already promised Mitzi . . . "You've actually made my Christmas."

"Well, all right then," Buck remarked, "give me your car keys and I'll start up the motor and scrape your icy windshield."

He grabbed his jacket off the rocker.

After handing over her keys to Buck, Jolene hugged the children goodbye and gave each one of them a dollar bill. To the eldest boy first: Cloy, then nine-year-old Craig, the spitting image of his father. Claire, seven, her grandma's namesake, clung to Jolene's leg with fervor, huge emerald eyes staring adoringly up at Jolene. Catherine, four and a half, raced around Jolene giggling until she was dizzy and fell out on the floor. Last of all, Nancy placed two-year-old Carla in Jolene's arms for a sloppy kiss.

The children squealed and held to their money like it was pure gold, making Jolene feel like she'd cleaned out her bank account. "Merry Christmas to all!!" she bid the family adieu.

And to all a very goodnight!

♣9

THE WAY NANCY had forgiven Buck in less than twenty-four hours from leaving seemed no less than miraculous. Jolene recalled how she and David had spats during their early years of marriage and the joy she experienced in making up a few hours later. Maybe she'd forgotten how love was supposed to work.

The Bible defined love as compassionate and understanding, not stubborn and unyielding. Her cell phone suddenly rang.

Jolene pounced on the call. "David . . ?"

"No, it's Mitzi."

Disappointed, she couldn't eek a response.

"Are you in the car on your way here?"

"Yes, the snow is falling so hard I can hardly see out."

"Please take it slow and easy," Mitzi warned. "The melted snow from yesterday has become black ice. Channel 5 is reporting multiple accidents on the roadways. Do you have plenty of gas?"

"I'm fine, Mitzi. Don't worry about me. I'm almost to the Bellevue exit and, so far, so good. Smart folks are at home."

"Great! I was worried. After you get on I-24, you will outrun the snow front. We have only one inch on our yard while Nashville is reporting three," Mitzi informed Jolene.

"Just pray I get there safely, I have enough on my plate without being involved in an accident." Jolene's swollen stomach growled at the remark. Maybe that was because she hadn't eaten anything but a bowl of cereal and popcorn since early morning.

"I should arrive in another hour," Jolene added.

"Okay, call us if you get into trouble."

"I will. See you soon." Jolene ended the call.

She was already in big trouble. David was in the sunny Bahamas, sipping on *pinacolatas* with two known womanizers.

Both Ben and Lyle had divorced their wives and chosen a dating lifestyle defying Christian values. They had plenty of money to burn, and David had contributed to their stockpile.

Is he also cheating on me with another woman?

Jolene looked at her cell phone. She could call him. "No." She realized how hurt she was. Maybe David was glad she left. That would give him a reason to take the first step toward divorce.

Jolene turned up the radio and joined the singer in *Away in a Manger.* Mother Mary must have felt out of place in Bethlehem. She had travelled with her husband Joseph a long distance to register on the Roman tax roles. No one had offered to take the couple in when night grew cold and Mary felt her first cramps of childbirth. Finally, they found a newly carved-out cave, offered to them by a man who owned a B & B. Jolene smiled.

"Like Claire's," she uttered and dialed Nancy's number.

"Hi, it's me. I've made it safely almost to Interstate 24. Did you finish cleaning up the decoration mess we made?"

"Yeah, and Buck helped," Nancy reported. "We just had hotdogs and the girls are napping. Cloy and Craig 're watching a Christmas video in the playroom. All is peaceful."

"I can't thank you enough for your hospitality. It brought back so many wonderful childhood memories," Jolene said.

"Hey, you helped us, too—might've saved our marriage."

"My pleasure," Jolene said, filled with joy.

"Buck's a big ol' lug. Stubborn as a mule, still surprises me sometimes. He loves me, though I'm a hothead when things don't git done around here like I think they oughta."

"I understand. We're like that in Louisiana, too." Guilt mounted as Jolene grieved over the rift between her and David. "Well, enjoy your day." She would try to do the same.

"Call me when you git to Mitzi's. I'll worry until then."

"Thank you. By the way, when will your Cadillac be fixed?"

"First week in January," Nancy replied. "But that's okay. Buck's taking time off trucking, so I'll have a ride when I need it."

"Well, remember how *not* to get pregnant," Jolene said before thinking. "Sorry. That came from, I don't know." She giggled.

"Now you sound just like my mama."

"I'm just a bag of advice that nobody wants to open."

"It's okay, I know you mean well, and for your information, we take precautions." The airways fell silent. "Fact is, we don't have the money to raise the five kids we got," Nancy admitted.

"Love goes a long way," Jolene uttered.

"I hope so," Nancy said.

It was well after four p.m. when Jolene rolled into Mitzi's driveway. The snowfall had followed her southward, but luckily the state had taken the precaution of layering the interstate with chemicals that would melt the ice. It was almost sundown.

After grabbing her overnight bag from the backseat and locking up the Buick, Jolene covered her head with a hand and raced to the porch, nearly sliding on the first icy porch step.

Mitzi flung open the door, pulled Jolene inside. "Brrr . . ." she shivered. "It's miserable weather out there!"

"Tell me about it." Jolene shook the snow from her bobbed brown hair. "But it's sure nice and toasty in here." She spied a roaring fire in the hearth. Two young girls sat on pillows in front of the fireplace playing cards. "Are these Dorothy's girls?"

"Yes," Mitzi replied. "Meet Amy and Priscilla, Jolene."

She bent over eyelevel with the girls and said, "Hi, girls. I'm Jolene, your Granny's first cousin. Her mother was my father's only sister. That makes you girls my third cousins."

Clueless, Amy ten, Priscilla seven, peered up at Jolene.

"They get confused over family relationships." Mitzi placed a hand on their shoulders. "Girls, give Cousin Jolene a big hug."

"Yes ma'am." They each wrapped an arm around Jolene's neck and squeezed hard. Then they ran and hid behind Mitzi.

"Is Santa bringing you something special?" Jolene asked.

Priscilla's violet eyes lit up. "A baby doll that wets."

Amy rolled java-bean eyes. "She doesn't know yet."

"Oh." Jolene caught Mitzi's eye. "About Santa Claus . . ."

Mitzi flashed a grin. "Wash up, girls. We're having an early supper, your favorite, spaghetti and meatballs. Dessert is a surprise." She motioned for Jolene to follow her.

With yelps and squeals, the children rushed down the hall to the bathroom. "They are beautiful children," Jolene told Mitzi, following her into the kitchen. "Can I do something?"

"No, the table is set, and Jack is upstairs making some calls."

"I can't thank you enough for inviting me to stay with you over the holidays," Jolene said. "I just learned from David's secretary that he's in the Bahamas with his two associates."

"Well, you might want to catch a flight and join him, honey." Mitzi filled five tumblers with crushed ice and poured the sweet tea. "What's that look for?" she curiously inquired.

"He didn't tell me he was going," Jolene revealed.

"Well, call the man and find out what's going on."

"No," Jolene stubbornly said. "He has my cell number."

To that remark, Mitzi had no comeback.

After everyone was seated at the dining room table, Jack bowed his head and said a blessing: "Our Heavenly Father, we thank you for sending us the Light. Bless the food we are about to partake, and keep us safely in your hands throughout the night. Amen." He glanced at Mitzi. "Meal smells great, honey."

Amy used her fork and dove into her spaghetti. "It tastes real good, Granny." She licked little pink lips.

"Are the girls staying the night?" Jolene asked Jack.

"No, Dorothy and Harold are at a company Christmas party, so we're just keeping them for a few more hours," Jack explained, forking a crisp Caesar salad while he reached for the pepper.

"The streets are pretty treacherous," Jolene noted.

"If they can't make it back to pick up the girls, we'll keep them overnight. There are plenty of presents under the tree to open tomorrow morning. Dot will bring the rest."

"It's nice that you live so close to family." Jolene nibbled on her salad. Despite the good company, she felt lonely, misplaced.

David should be here with me.

"Jolene?" Mitzi paused between bites. "Did you find out anything new about Uncle Kirk and Aunt Kate?"

"No, the courthouse was closed today," Jolene replied, "but I did get to spend some time with the Blake family and their five adorable children." She tried to suppress her depression.

"That was where you were earlier today?" Jack interjected.

"Yes, I helped them decorate their Christmas tree. I'd forgotten how much fun it was." Jolene's lips trembled with a smile. "David and I didn't bother to put up a tree last year."

"Why not . . .?" young Amy innocently asked. "Everybody I know has a pretty tree at Christmastime."

Jolene set blue eyes on the girl. "My husband and I don't have children, Amy, and we work a lot of hours. Pulling out the decorations didn't seem worth the effort for just two people."

"What's *effort* mean?" Priscilla asked her grandfather.

"Not worth the trouble," Jack answered.

"You don't think a Christmas tree is worth the trouble?" Amy blurted out, getting Priscilla's attention. "Why not . . .?"

"I do now." Jolene chuckled. "I just needed a reminder."

"That's enough questions, Amy," Mitzi scolded. "Finish your supper, girls, and we'll find something fun for you to do."

"Yes, ma'am," they politely chimed.

♣10

WITH ROADS IMPASSSABLE, Amy and Priscilla ended up spending the night with Jack and Mitzi.

As Wednesday evening waned on, everyone settled down for a long winter's nap. The house grew silent. Santa was on his way.

~

By the time Jolene heard noises Christmas morning and tiptoed down the stairs to investigate, she discovered Mitzi's granddaughters in the den, ripping open their presents. Spying the joy on their young faces made Jolene regret even more that she hadn't seized the opportunity to bear children of her own.

Now, her baby factories were damaged, so creating a new little human being in God's normal fashion was impossible.

The coffeemaker had been set on automatic the night before so the coffee was brewed and ready for consumption when Jolene entered the kitchen. Pancakes sizzled on the grill as Jack whistled a tune while cooking. Jolene spied Mitzi seated at the breakfast table perusing the morning paper. It was a perfect family picture.

"It's after nine, Mitzi, why didn't you guys wake me?" Jolene asked as she took a seat at the table opposite her cousin.

Glancing up, Mitzi smiled. "I peeked in your bedroom earlier and you were sleeping so soundly I thought some extra rest was the best gift we could give you today."

"I did sleep well." Though Jolene's deep sleep had spawned nightmares about David. "Can I set the table or pour the juice?"

Jolene locked eyes with Jack. "Really, I'm not helpless."

"Just relax and enjoy, I'm about done cooking."

"He's been up since sunup," Mitzi said. "Already shoveled snow from the driveway so Harold and Dorothy can safely pull in their suburban. We told them not to try it, but what do parents know?" Mitzi shrugged her shoulders. "It's Christmas, after all."

"Did I say Merry Christmas yet?" Jolene's eye widened as she yawned. "Excuse me. I just can't seem to wake up." She was still wearing her pajamas with a chenille bathrobe over them.

"A cup of Joe will fix that." Jack pointed with a spatula at the coffeemaker standing on the counter. "It's our custom to snap pictures at the breakfast table. If you want in them, you might want to get dressed. Otherwise, I'll let you take the pictures."

"It would be my honor to photograph your moments." Jolene helped herself to a cup of the specialty coffee then added cream. "But first I'll make myself presentable."

Jolene carried her java upstairs.

Twenty minutes later, Jolene was back. She snapped a dozen or more pictures of the family gathered around the breakfast table when the front doorbell sounded. The girls squealed.

"I'll get it!" Mitzi hustled into the den.

"Come on in and join us for breakfast," Jack hollered when he spied Harold and Dorothy in the archway. "If we need more food, I know the cook personally." He chuckled.

Everyone laughed as the parents sloughed off their coats and hung them in the hall closet. "Brrr . . . I forgot how cold twenty degrees feels!" Dot shivered as her children hugged her legs.

"No way can my heater compete with the cold." Harold rubbed his two large hands together to stimulate warmth. "Sure we're not interrupting your breakfast?" He spied the food.

Jack pulled two more chairs up to the table. "Heaven's no, we were about to put down a whole box of pancakes, a bottle of Maple syrup, and a pound of bacon. OJ, if you want it."

"Coffee smells inviting." Harold settled into a chair. "Is this your pretty cousin, Mitzi?" He peered at Jolene with cinnamon eyes endowed with interest. "From Baton Rouge, right . . .?"

"Harold, this is Jolene Salisbury," Mitzi said. "She grew up in Charlotte many moons ago—not that she's old."

"That's debatable," Jolene uttered, making a face.

"Pleased to meet you . . ." Harold reached across the table and shook Jolene's hand, "and welcome home."

"Can we eat now?" Amy impatiently asked; fork poised over a huge pancake weeping with sweet Maple syrup.

"Let Grandpa say a blessing first," Mitzi insisted. "Bow your heads, girls. Jesus can hear everything we say."

"Dear Lord. We are grateful it's Christmas again and we can celebrate Your Son's birth. Bless this food to our health and give us a joyous day. Amen." Jack unfolded his paper napkin.

Harold had a ton of questions for Jolene, particularly why her husband David wasn't with her. Without being too critical, she explained that coming alone was her choice. Her trip was about investigating family roots. Everyone laughed when little Priscilla said: "Is that like finding out what makes a family tree grow?"

"You're a pretty smart little girl," Jolene told Priscilla.

"That's what Granny says." Priscilla eyed Mitzi. "She's smart, too." Her grin reflected immense happiness.

Everyone laughed at the remark.

"Don't forget about me!" Amy gushed. "I'm smart, too."

That comment earned smiles around the table.

After the family finished eating, and the dishwasher was loaded, Harold brought in the rest of the presents from the car.

The girls whooped at each new trinket they unwrapped, running around the den to show each spectator their prize.

"Forgive me for purchasing gift cards for all of you," Jolene apologized, "but I wasn't sure what you wanted."

"You know how I love to shop." Mitzi presented Jolene with a gold tinsel-wrapped box tied with a frilly red ribbon. "Christmas is about giving and our family sure likes doing it. Enjoy."

"Thank you so much. All of you." Tears peppered Jolene's eyes. Hands nervously shaking, she opened the box and spied two beautiful nightgowns. Surprise grazed in her face. "Oh . . ."

"It's for your stay at the hospital after surgery," Mitzi announced. "I noticed that you already had a warm, snuggly robe—the one you were wearing earlier this morning."

"It was a Christmas gift from David." *Three years ago.* Jolene felt tears trickling down both cheeks. "He went to the Bahamas on a vacation without telling me." The truth surfaced like scum on pond water. "He doesn't love me anymore."

Jolene realized her announcement must put a damper on the family's celebration. "I'm sorry, I should not have said that," she apologized. "It's just that having cancer makes a person more, uh, susceptible to hurt." She dried her bleary eyes with her hands.

"Jesus loves you," little Priscilla announced.

"I know He does," Jolene said to the little girl. "Thank God, I can always count on Jesus." She tried to think positive.

It took a few minutes for the conversation to recover after Jolene's outburst. But when the awkward moment did pass, and the family had opened most of their presents, she slipped upstairs to the guest bedroom. It was time to call David and wish him well, even if he hadn't shown concern for her welfare.

Nervous fingers dialed his cell number.

Please answer this time.

Ring . . . ring . . .g! David had international coverage, so why wasn't he picking up? *He knows I'm calling.*

Jolene imagined the worst. He might be involved in activities contrary to their marriage vows.

Is there a new love in his life?

His voice mail intervened: "This is David. Busy at the moment, leave a message at the beep and I'll get back at'cha."

Distraught with emotion bordering anger, Jolene was not leaving a message. It was clear that David didn't want to talk to anybody today. But there was one other call she should make.

Buck answered the phone. "Yeah . . .?"

"Merry Christmas!" Jolene sputtered.

"Hi, Jolene. Merry Christmas."

"Did the kids open their presents?"

"Yeah, it wasn't much, but they loved whut they got," Buck replied, sounding like a proud daddy. "How're you doing?"

"Good. I'm with my cousin and her family. Mitzi's son and new wife will be over this afternoon to share the evening meal."

"Here's Nancy—she wants to talk to you."

A man of few words, Jolene heard Buck whisper to Nancy as he handed over the phone. "He says to invite you to stay with us after you have surgery," Nancy reported. "I know . . ."

Jolene could imagine Nancy rolling her big eyes.

"Really . . .?" Jolene was uplifted at the invitation. "Won't I be a bother—with all you have to do on a daily basis?"

"Not that I've seen. Besides, the kids love you."

"I love them, too." Emotion welled up and caught in Jolene's throat. "Don't forget I'll be grouchy as an ol' hen and sick as a dog after surgery. Can you put up with that?"

"Absolutely! You've already helped us so much, Jolene," Nancy sputtered. "Please, let us help you back."

"Oh that. Getting your car fixed was nothing!"

"I don't call three thousand dollars *nothing*!" Nancy exclaimed. "Consider it rent for a room at our B & B. That way we both get a blessing." She waited for Jolene's response.

"Are you sure?" Jolene's mind raced in several directions.

"Positive. You can watch the kids if I have to run an errand."

"Okay, let me give it some serious thought," Jolene said. "I need to run it by Mitzi first. I don't want to hurt her feelings."

"Okay, but while you're thinkin' about it, Buck's gonna put a fresh coat of paint on the walls in the extra bedroom and lay down some new carpet. We want everything fresh and clean by the time you move in." Nancy said it like it was a done deal.

"That is so kind of you." Jolene was overwhelmed at the Blake's generosity. God was truly blessing her.

"Buck thought living close to Charlotte would give you the chance to find out more about your family," Nancy offered.

"We'll start askin' around, too. Who knows? We might find somebody who knew your parents well, can feed you some info."

"I sure hope so." Jolene rejoiced in her spirit. "I guess I already know my answer." She decided. "Yes, I'll come and stay with you and Buck after I get out of the hospital."

"Great! Have a Merry Christmas!" Nancy exclaimed.

"I already have." Jolene hung up the phone and bounded down the stairs like a giddy teenager with a first date.

"You look like you just saw Santa in person." Mitzi noted. "Did you talk to David? Is he coming to Tennessee?"

Her cousin assumed far too much.

"No, but I talked to my friend Nancy. Her husband Buck invited me to stay with them while I recoup from cancer surgery. It will put me close to Charlotte where I need to be." Jolene's eyes moved across the room to Jack. "I hope you understand."

"Honestly, we do," Mitzi answered for them both. "You have a mission to accomplish and who are we to stop you?"

"Thank you for understanding." Jolene smiled. "It really means a lot." She paused. "Is that the coffeemaker bubbling?"

"Just made, have some," Jack said.

Jolene ventured into the kitchen for another cup of java, grinning and thinking *Santa is a sneaky ol' elf.*

♣11

CHRISTMAS WEEK FLEW by, as did the following. Jolene did not hear from David. He'd be back in his office by January second. The New Year would define how the rest of their married lives turned out—whether they were together, or separate.

Likely, Sally would inform David she had called the office on Christmas Eve looking for him. That was fine by Jolene. If he felt guilty for not wishing her Merry Christmas, so be it.

Hurt surfaced, though she denied another outburst.

January 5th was ushered in with overcast skies. Jolene found herself seated in Dr. Helen Blazer's office, waiting to be examined.

"Jolene Salisbury," the receptionist called out.

"That's me." Jolene weakly raised one hand then scrambled for her purse. The walk through the open door down the hallway felt like she was facing a death sentence.

As she passed a large room on the left, she spied a nurse seated at her desk. Five female cancer patients filled various colored padded recliners, three of them wearing head wraps.

So that's chemo. Jolene continued down the long hallway.

The attentive young nurse with curly blond hair motioned with a hand for Jolene to enter the room on her left.

Obedient, like an innocent lamb submitting to slaughter, she limped inside and waited for instructions.

"Strip to the skin and put on the thingy," Goldie Locks ordered. "Dr. Blazer will be with you momentarily."

Jolene nodded, a lump lodged in her parched throat.

The wait for the oncologist was excruciating. If only David were here. But then, maybe he didn't care what came next.

To investigate ovarian cancer Jolene had gone on the Internet and explored stories about women who survived the disease.

Popularly described as the "silent killer" of thousands of women in America every year, many had identified their own cancers.

Physicians admitted most victims didn't realize something was wrong with them until it was too late. Symptoms were often minimal, except for a swelling abdomen as the growths imbedded in the ovaries slowly enlarged. Since mature women tend to gain weight around the middle, and menstrual periods caused swelling, the signs signaling cancer were often ignored. That had not been the case with Jolene. Two years without getting a checkup had proven to be an unwise decision. Now, here she was.

A woman who didn't appear much older than Jolene, wearing a crisp white frock over her black slacks, entered the room.

"Hello, Jolene. I'm Dr. Helen Blazer."

"I'm pleased to meet you." Jolene shook the woman's hand like she was another potential real estate customer about to purchase property in Baton Rouge and put money in her pocket.

"Beatrice Kennedy and I were in medical school together," Helen explained as she hugged her chart and hitched a slender hip on the edge of the desk where a sink was installed.

"She told me you were nice."

Nice?

"We spoke of your condition at length."

Helen's soft golden gaze and unpretentious mannerisms immediately put Jolene at ease as she relaxed a bit.

"I'll take good care of you, I promise."

"Did Dr. Kennedy also tell you I sold real estate?"

"Yes, and she said you were pretty and smart. If anybody could beat cancer, you could." Helen pumped up Jolene. "I'd like to think that with proper care you've already won this battle."

"What makes you say that?" Jolene inquired.

"Part of a medical solution is recognizing the problem. Those of us who receive cancer treatment are better off than the thousands of women who are walking around unaware."

"You had cancer, too?"

"Yes, at forty-nine. I know what it's like to fear the disease."

Jolene's confidence in Dr. Blazer took a huge leap, her spirits uplifted for the first time that day. Life is about overcoming trials.

"Well, sweetheart, if you'll lie back, I'll take a look inside your belly and see what we're up against." Helen motioned for Jolene to mount the table as she slipped on clear surgical gloves.

The examination didn't take long.

"Get dressed and we'll steal some blood to see if you need help getting your red count up before surgery," Helen ordered.

Jolene sat up and shivered. "You're going to operate."

"Definitely," Helen replied.

"Good. I feel like a walking time bomb."

Helen placed a warm hand on Jolene's shoulder and looked deeply into her eyes. "Like Dr. Kennedy said, you have cancers on both ovaries; one the size of a grapefruit, the other smaller."

Jolene nodded, clutching the sheet around her body.

"I'll cut out the tumors, remove a layer of lining in your abdomen, and order six chemotherapy treatments to wash your blood just in case any loose cancer cells are present."

Questions flooded Jolene's mind, but she remained silent.

"During the chemo process, I'll monitor your progress. After that, you'll see me twice a year for the next three years, plus have yearly pap smears and mammograms for up to ten years."

"Are you saying the cancer could come back another place in my body?" Jolene had believed surgery would cure her.

"Let's not assume the worst. If the tumors are contained in the ovaries, and haven't spread throughout the abdomen, your chances of a complete recovery are excellent."

Helen picked up her chart. "Do you have other questions?"

"I guess not," Jolene replied. "When will I have surgery?"

"You'll get a call in a few days with details," Helen replied.

Jolene nodded, signaling she understood.

"You can get dressed now and Bonita will show you to the lab now. After your blood is drawn, we're finished for today."

"Thank you, Dr. Blazer." Jolene hopped off the examination table and grabbed her clothes off the straight chair.

~

Back at Mitzi's, Jolene took a shower and bawled. Her emotions were all over the place with a mix of fear and hope. She desperately needed to speak to David. It was utterly foolish to believe her silence punished him. He was still her husband.

At David's office, Sally answered Jolene's call.

"Hi, it's me. Did the guys get back from the Bahamas?"

"Yes, but David is with a client. Shall I tell him to call you?"

"Yes," Jolene replied. "He has my cell number."

She was propped up on a huge pillow in the middle of the bed, snuggled inside the warm chenille robe David had given her while staring out the window at the cold bleak, overcast day.

Tennessee residents seldom see the sun in January and February, unless a cold front passes through to push back the humid Gulf air masses. Then the sky turns a brilliant cold blue.

Jolene was reading a Bible passage when David called.

"Yes?" She tentatively responded.

"It's me."

"I know. Did you have fun in the Bahamas?"

"Sure. But I missed you."

"Of course, that's why you didn't take my call."

"My cell phone didn't work on the island," he said.

"That must have been inconvenient." She imagined Hula girls swaying with the palms while the guys gawked at them. "I bet the ocean was warm and the scenery breathtaking."

Here I go, picking a fight again.

"What do you want, Jolene?"

"I know you're busy so I'll make this short. I saw the oncologist this morning. In a few days, I'll have a surgery date."

"Is this a competent doctor?"

"Dr. Kennedy attended medical school with Helen Blazer. She seems competent, and she's been very encouraging."

"Encouraging how?" David wanted details.

"She had ovarian cancer a few years back, so she understands how the disease affects the body." Jolene thought of Christ, how much He had suffered on the cross on behalf of humanity.

Both involved in speculation, David was the first to end the uncomfortable silence. "Do you want me there for your surgery?"

"Would you mind? Having you root for me will be helpful."

"Let me know the date and I'll be there," he said.

"Is that a promise?"

"Tomorrow's promise," he replied.

"Thank you, David. I'll let you know the date."

"Sorry, I need to go. My appointment is waiting."

Jolene ended the call and cried again. Their conversation had been so formal, so perfunctory. David didn't sound like the man she married eighteen years ago. A tall wall existed between them.

What has happened to us? Did we forget how to love?

♣12

AS PROMISED, DAVID arrived in Nashville the day before Jolene's scheduled surgery. She packed her belongings, placed the suitcase in the back of her reliable rented Buick and hugged Mitzi. "This isn't goodbye, you know," Jolene said.

"I know." Mitzi stood shivering at the end of the sidewalk as Jolene climbed in the car. "Hey," she called out, "if you change your mind, you can stay with us after you get out of the hospital."

Jolene rolled down the window. "I'll keep that in mind. You're not only family, Mitzi, you're a wonderful friend."

"Tell David hello for me and that I'd like to meet him one day," she said, the freezing wind whipping her hair. "You'd better raise your window now, before you lose all the heat inside."

"Pray for me?" Jolene's breath vaporized in the January air.

"You know we will. Everyone in our Sunday School class at Murfreesboro Baptist Church will be lifting you up, too. Have faith, Jolene. God will take care of you."

"He's always faithful," Jolene uttered, thinking of her pastor. "Well, I should go. David has already checked into the Ramada Inn near Baptist Hospital, and we have a great deal to discuss."

Mitzi offered no marital advice.

"Well, I guess this is bye for now."

"Yes." Tears threatened to pour. "Bye."

Jolene rolled up her window and put the car in reverse. *This is it*, she considered. *Who knows what tomorrow will bring?*

The sun peeped from behind a cloudbank moving in from the west as Jolene drove out of Mitzi's subdivision. Winds were gusting in the thirties at temperatures hovering near freezing. Jolene hoped David brought along enough warm clothes to be comfortable. He wasn't used to a winter in Tennessee.

While she drove toward the city, Jolene recalled the conversation she'd had with David the last night before boarding a Delta flight to Nashville. "Don't go, Jolene! This is a crazy."

"This is my body, David!" she'd screamed back. "It's selfish of you to want me to stay when my heart yearns for home."

"I may be selfish, but you are unreasonable!"

At his words, Jolene's tears had poured.

"Why can't you understand my point of view? I could die during surgery. What if I never resolve my anger against Dad? Will God forgive me for not visiting Mama while she was dying?"

"Don't be so dramatic, Jolene! If I'm not there, who will care for you after surgery? You need to think this through."

"I'll figure all that out after I get there." She had haphazardly tossed her clothes into the suitcase and slammed it.

"Don't go." He'd pleaded with her.

"I have to. Come with me."

One last request . . . she'd hoped David would change his mind. "You know I can't. I have clients, I have a job here."

"What about us?" Jolene had asked.

"What's left of *us*?" he'd returned. "You never touch me."

"Whose fault is that? You chose to sleep alone."

"Does this mean you want a divorce?"

"Did I ask for one?" Jolene hadn't meant for the argument to go that far. Were they down to their last words spoken?

His chin was set hard, anger seething underneath a steel façade. Then he'd turned and walked toward the guest bedroom.

"Wait! Is this it?" she'd called out loudly. "I just leave?" She'd had a moment of second-guessing her decision.

He'd spun around, a despicable glance. "I guess so."

Then she'd heard the bedroom door slam hard.

And that was how they'd left it, an unresolved matter as to whether they would stay married. Now, she would face him again.

What will I say to David?

Forty-five minutes later, Jolene was standing in the motel lobby, shaking like a leaf about to be disconnected from its branch. She knew his room number; they'd talked not ten minutes before. The elevator doors scrunched open.

Jolene stared into the empty cavity.

Lord, I don't know if I can face him.

On autopilot, she stepped aboard the elevator and punched a button. Ascending two floors, the doors reopened. She walked down the long hallway, her overnight case in one hand. Her larger bag, packed for her hospital stay, she'd left in the car trunk.

"Oh, David . . ." She tapped on the door to Room 302, deciding not to use the key he'd left for her at the front desk.

This feels like his room, not mine.

The door came open and their eyes met. David's hazel gaze sent chills straight through Jolene. She still loved him.

How could that be?

With no hesitation, she wrapped her arms around his neck and vacationed a moment. "Thank you so much for coming."

"No problem." He took a step back, holding her at arm's length, somewhat startled at her greeting. "You've lost weight, woman, and you didn't have any to lose."

"I know." She sighed and set her bag on the round table near the TV. "It's cold outdoors, did you bring a warm jacket?"

"Always the one taking care of me . . ." David's stare lingered. "Actually, I purchased one at the mall," he admitted.

"I didn't order snow," she uttered.

"Does the winter sky always look this dingy in Tennessee?"

Jolene shrugged then smiled. "God loves variety, David. But springs, summers, and autumns are beautiful in these rolling hills."

"I guess that makes up for awful winters."

Jolene nodded, a few good thoughts playing in her mind.

"I'd be out on the golf course if I were in Baton Rouge," David said. "Can't beat Louisiana weather, sixty-five degrees and partly sunny. King cakes in stores, and parties in the wing."

"It's not that I don't miss all that . . ." Jolene collapsed in a plush wingback as David took a seat on the edge of the bed.

"Were your flight arrangements satisfactory?" she asked.

"Couldn't get a one-way, took a detour through Atlanta."

"Sorry."

From there, the conversation became chitchat, but that was perfectly fine with Jolene. Nothing too serious was a good thing, she thought. He'd heard from her office and shared some details.

Then he talked about his work, always his best topic.

"We've closed our biggest year yet." He got up and switched on the coffeemaker. "I could use some caffeine to wake up my senses? How about you . . .?" Mr. Success-of-the-Year inquired.

"You know how I love my coffee," Jolene muttered, staring at the queen-size bed. Where would she sleep tonight?

"Do you want me to get you a separate room?"

So now he's a mind-reader?

"It's your call, David."

"What does that mean?"

"I'm comfortable sleeping in the bed beside you."

He laughed. "No problem. We can snuggle to keep warm."

Would they? Then what?

The coffee finished dripping and David filled two Styrofoam cups, adding cream and sugar like they both preferred.

"Did Dr. Blazer tell you what to expect tomorrow?"

"Pretty much," she replied. "I'm prepping now."

"What does that process entail?" He sipped his coffee.

"Well, except for liquids, I can't eat any solid foods. I've already taken my first laxatives," Jolene revealed. "You might want to go out for a while to avoid the odor."

"We'll see how bad it gets," he replied. "What else?"

"At the hospital, they'll do some more prepping for surgery and sedate me," Jolene explained. "The procedure is expected to take several hours, depending on what Dr. Blazer finds."

"Have you seen the tumors on a screen?"

"Yes." A lump lodged in Jolene's throat. "Both ovaries are enlarged with growths." Her eyes drifted to the frosted window as she considered the terrific pain that would follow. Outdoors, sunlight filtered through the gray mound of clouds.

"I can see talking about it bothers you."

"A little," she admitted. *A lot*, she told God.

David got up and turned up the sound on the television.

"Why don't we watch a movie and try to forget it's the day before," he suggested. "Can I get you anything?"

"A glass of water, please. I have to drink all I can."

He made a trek to the bathroom and returned with a filled hotel glass. "What's showing on the movie channel?" she asked.

And so the day went.

♣13

TIME FOR JOLENE'S surgery arrived. She lay in a bed of white sheets in a sanitized room tiled in green. A man with a gauze mask, wearing a green surgical suit and cap, stood to her left. "How're you doing?" the anesthesiologist inquired.

"Okay, considering—" she giddily remarked —"the doctor is about to slice me open and find God-only-knows-what inside."

"You'll do just fine, Jolene. Tell you what, when you see this needle . . ." he thumped it to assure no air was left between the liquid and the exit point, "inserted in your IV . . ."

She nodded. "Uh huh . . . then what . . .?"

"Bye-bye, sweet dreams . . ."

Unsure of what that meant, she frowned.

"Don't be scared. Okay? Dr. Blazer has done this surgery many times and she's never lost a patient." The technician peered down at Jolene. "Ready?" He checked the tubing to the IV bag.

"I guess—if I wake up in Heaven, I'll save you a place."

"That's a deal." He inserted the needle in the tube.

Lights out! Time had no meaning.

~

Jolene opened her eyes and looked at the technician. "I thought you said I was going to have surgery."

He crookedly grinned. "How do you feel?"

"Not sure. What happened?" Medicinal odors stung Jolene's nostrils as she realized she was strapped to a gurney.

"You're just waking up from surgery that occurred . . ." the anesthesiologist glanced at the wall clock, "exactly four and a half hours ago." He continued monitoring his patient.

Jolene still felt woozy. "The cancers are out?"

"Yep," he said. "All done, you'll remain here in recovery for a while so I can track your vital signs. In an hour or so a nurse will gurney you to a private room on the fifth floor."

"Why there?" Jolene wondered.

"Cancer ward. You'll get special care there," he reported. "You'll love the nurses. They'll be at your beck-and-call. Bring you chipped ice galore. Their pain meds are wonderful."

"I can handle that." Jolene's mouth was powder dry. But she guessed that would soon pass. The meds would help.

David? She suddenly thought of him then slipped away.

~

Hours later, Jolene woke up and glanced around the hospital room for David. He was seated in a chair not three feet from her bed. "Hi," she peeped, feeling her first tinge of discomfort.

"Hi," he said. "How do you feel?"

"Like a train hit me."

"How was surgery?" He laid *The Tennessean* on the window ledge and directed his full attention to Jolene.

"I don't know." Attempting to turn over was a mistake. *Ouch.* "Has Dr. Blazer been by? What's my prognosis?"

There was that big word again.

"I guess we'll find out soon enough."

"Okay." She tried to accept the waiting. "What time is it?"

"After six p.m. Your surgery was at ten this morning."

"Talk about being out of it." Jolene started to roll over on her side then thought better of it. "Could you raise the head of my bed slightly? And I really need a drink of water."

"Sure." David pressed a button and the hospital bed automatically adjusted to the right height. Then offered her some crushed ice. "Not too much at first, it'll make you sick."

The ice was wet and cold, and most welcome.

"Thank you for being here, I know you made a sacrifice."

"Work can wait. You needed me here worse."

"Please, one more spoonful of crushed ice." Jolene's throat felt like she'd swallowed a cupful of Gulf sand.

David held the spoon at a tilt for Jolene.

"Thanks, that feels better." She tried to get comfortable in the bed, an impossible feat considering the pain in her belly.

"Try to get some rest, Jolene." David stretched long arms and yawned while leaning back in the padded green recliner.

"You look tired, David. When did you last sleep or eat?"

"Me? I'm okay." He half grinned. "I had cafeteria food while you were in surgery. Don't worry about me."

"If you need to go back to the hotel and rest, I understand," Jolene said. "The nurses will take care of me." She suddenly felt chilled. "Throw an extra blanket over my feet and fluff my pillow?" She shivered between the crisp white sheets.

"Sure." David snagged a blanket from an empty chair and spread it over Jolene. "You should know my flight leaves on Sunday at four, but I'll stay longer if you'll come home with me."

For a moment, she considered his offer then said, "I want to, but you know why I can't. We've already plowed this territory."

He shrugged. "Why does that not surprise me?"

She'd run out of words to express how she felt.

"It's not like your parents are living, Jolene," he uttered. "Your home is in Baton Rouge with me. And you have a good job, I might add. What's wrong with your priorities?"

"I—" the words were trapped in her throat.

Just in time, a nurse bolted through the door and saved Jolene from giving David an answer he wouldn't like.

"Time for your meds . . ." the nurse fed Jolene four small white tablets with a sip of tap water. "You need to sleep so the pain won't get too bad." ANNE was the name on her badge.

"Okay, but can I talk to Dr. Blazer first?"

"She'll be in to see you tomorrow morning." Anne faced David. "Dr. Blazer had an emergency surgery," the nurse explained. "Are you staying with your wife overnight?"

His hazel eyes wearily drifted on Jolene. "Yes, for a bit."

"Good idea. Night staffing is limited," Anne said. "If you decide to stay, the recliner doubles for a single bed." She raised the bars on Jolene's bed. "I'll get some bedding and pillows."

"Thanks, I'll hang around until I'm sure Jolene is sleeping peacefully before I leave," he said to Anne. "What time in the morning does Dr. Blazer do her rounds?"

"Before seven; she has a surgery scheduled for nine."

Jolene yawned. "I guess food is out of the question."

"Why risk getting an upset stomach?" David peered at Anne.

"No solid food tonight, Jolene," Nurse Ann reported. "I'll make sure you have a nourishing breakfast tomorrow morning."

"Thanks." She felt the sedative taking charge of her body.

"Go on to the motel, David, I'll be fine. Leave your business card on the bedside stand. If I need you during the night, I'll ask a nurse to phone you." Jolene's eyelids demanded closure.

"Are you sure you won't need me?"

"If I'm asleep, I won't know the difference."

"Push the red button on the cord if you need assistance," Nurse Anne instructed. "We'll take good care of you, Jolene."

"I know the routine." She managed a weak smile.

David squeezed Jolene's hand and sat down in the recliner. Sometime later, near eleven, he slipped quietly from the room.

Jolene's discomfort woke her up, but she fell back asleep as the pain meds did their job. Finally, no dreams interrupted her dreamless sleep. The sedatives were so effective she might have been lying in her own grave, sleeping peacefully for all eternity.

♣14

WHEN JOLENE OPENED her eyes Friday morning, Dr. Blazer was standing there talking to David.

"Hi." She summoned their attention, feeling left out of some urgent information. "Am I okay?"

Helen walked over to the bed and grasped Jolene's hand. "I gotta tell you, sweetheart, somebody is watching over you. Yours was the most perfect surgery I have ever performed. Everything went right in that operating room."

"Really . . .? What does that mean?" Jolene glanced at David.

"It means she got all the cancer and it hasn't spread."

"Thank God!" Tears poured. "Will I need chemo?"

"My advice is, take the medicine as a precaution."

"How many treatments did you say I'll need, Doctor?"

"Six. Each dosage increases in strength. Your body will adapt to the medication and it's sure to work effectively."

"Explain the process of how that works," David said.

"Sure," Helen replied. "The surgeon will install a portacath in Jolene's vein above the heart when she arrives for her first appointment. The chemo will be fed through the device."

"What kind of adverse reaction should Jolene expect during the process?" David was concerned about infection.

"She'll lose all the hair on her body within the first month and experience flu-like symptoms for the duration of treatment," Helen explained. "Some people get nausea, but we'll give Jolene medication to help with the problem before each treatment."

"I haven't said I'd take chemo, yet," Jolene chimed in.

"You need to take it," David declared. "Don't chance the cancer coming back." He grasped Jolene's hand. "Do it for me."

Does that mean he still loves me?

"Your husband's right," Helen promoted the treatment. "The Taxol we administer acts as a blood wash to prevent cancer cells from spreading. It's protocol for ovarian cancer patients."

"I see." Jolene evaluated her choices. "I guess I'd better."

"Good girl!" David smiled.

She felt like it was a pep rally. *Hooray for Jolene! She just scored.*

David spent the day and left Jolene after she'd eaten a light supper. If she developed no fever, an indication of an infection, she'd check out of the hospital on Monday. Buck had agreed to pick her up in his truck since David was flying home on Sunday.

~

Monday rolled around and Jolene felt some better, but she was sore and still required strong pain medication. As promised, Buck Blake came to the hospital to give her a ride to his house.

The trip to Charlotte proved challenging, but Jolene didn't complain since the Blake's were boarding her for the next month. After that, she intended to rent a suitable house near Charlotte.

The success of her marriage was still in question. David had continually refused to reveal what went on in the Bahamas. His silence conjured up the worst scenarios: prostitutes parading in and out of the guys' rooms, offering drugs and sex.

No, David wouldn't do that.

She was merely projecting what Hollywood portrayed on the big screen—debauchery with no limitations. If David wasn't telling her what happened, he had a good reason.

Bottom line: she would have to trust him.

He'll tell me when he feels the time is right.

But the Bahamas trip was a mystery that wouldn't leave Jolene's thoughts for one second during the drive to the Blake's humble abode. However, when they finally arrived, the children's screams of excitement, and the delicious odors of a home-cooked meal, restored Jolene's faith in mankind. This was a new start for her, a better one. God would right all wrongs in His timing.

The guest bedroom makeover turned out beautifully. Buck had painted the walls a teal blue, and Nancy had sown new floral-patterned curtains for the two elongated windows. The furniture had been purchased at a Salvation Army in Dickson.

The mattress on the four-poster bed was brand new, firm at the base, with a pillow-top covering. Jolene was appreciative.

"Guys, you went to a lot of trouble!" She tested the mattress.

"Our pleasure." The couple smiled as their children pressed close behind them. "We wanted you to feel at home."

"I do. Thank you so much. It's such a kind gift."

"No problem," Buck said, a grin spreading. "We got our Cadillac out of hock on Saturday. Kevin even fixed the top so it would come up. We hope our hospitality expresses our thanks."

"You look tired, Jolene." Nancy observed. "Get in bed and I'll bring your lunch." She pulled back the bedcovers and helped Jolene crawl in—not an easy feat, considering the level of pain.

"Get the prescription pills from my purse," Jolene called out to Buck, the weariness of the trip impacting her sore body.

"I'll get you a bottle of water," Nancy offered.

Popping two pain pills into her mouth, Jolene gulped them down with quick sips and tried to get in a comfortable position that would allow her to sleep. "Thanks, guys, I'm fine now."

"Rest is the best medicine," Nancy said, closing the door.

With every subtle movement, Jolene's stomach muscles pulled like needles as a result of major surgery. The stitches itched. But that would get better soon, Dr. Blazer promised.

An hour later, Nancy brought in a tray of food.

"Are you awake, Jolene?" she whispered.

Jolene opened her eyes and spied Nancy through bleary eyes.

"Here, let me help you sit up." She supported Jolene's back with a hand then adjusted the two king-size pillows for her.

"The food smells wonderful."

"It's just plain country food." Nancy minimized her talent.

Jolene tucked a napkin under her chin and picked up a spoon. "Enjoy." Nancy escaped the room as she heard Carla crying.

After eating a slice of pork roast lathered in gravy, and half a buttered sweet potato, Jolene felt full and exhausted. She pushed aside the tray and lay back against the fluffy pillows. Sometime later, she woke up at sounds of the frolicking children.

Jolene's revived senses jolted to attention as the pain in her stomach returned. She needed help going to the bathroom. With the bedroom door shut, she didn't want to scream to be heard.

Then she noticed a baby monitor on the bedside table.

Duh. "Nancy, can you come in here a minute?"

"What is it, dear?" Nancy peeked into the room, hands swiping her cotton apron. "Need help getting to the bathroom?"

"Are you a mind reader, too?" Jolene nervously chuckled.

"You name it, sister, and I'm it!"

"I had no idea it would be this hard—maneuvering around."

"You've never had a baby, that's why."

"Frankly, at this moment, I'd welcome that kind of pain."

"Sorry, I guess I hit a sore spot," Nancy apologized.

After the bathroom trip, and another nap, Jolene pulled on her snuggly chenille robe and shuffled into the kitchen to enjoy a bowl of soup with the family. It was already dark outdoors.

"Are you sure you're up to sitting?" Nancy inquired as Buck helped Jolene settle into a chair padded with a small pillow.

Jolene nodded. "Doctor said to be up some."

"I don't mind serving you in bed," Nancy said.

"I need to work out my soreness." Jolene's gaze slid to the children. "Hi, kids. How are you doing?"

"Fine," said Cloy, the usual spokesperson for the others.

"Does it hurt?" Four-year-old Catherine dared to ask.

"Some, but I'm doing better. How was your day?"

"Good." Catherine peered at her mother as the two younger children giggled. Jolene guessed houseguests were a rarity.

Buck cleared his throat, a signal to "cool it."

"I've ask the children to be on their best behavior for the next week," Nancy explained to Jolene. "That means they can't ask you a lot of questions." Her emerald eyes widened.

"What do you want to know, kids?" Jolene asked.

In obedience to Mom, not one mouth opened.

"Your children are so well behaved," Jolene remarked. "Congratulations! You and Buck are good parents."

Why hadn't she taken the time to be a parent?

"Did you have a nice visit with your husband?" Buck asked.

"Yes, but he's a busy man. He sells insurance policies."

"He must be real smart," Nancy said between sips of soup.

"David is a good man, smart and honest."

"Then why didn't he stay here with you?" Buck mouthed.

"He couldn't, but I understand his commitment to the job. I sell residential real estate, or I used to. But now, I don't know, it feels like my life is changing." Would it be for the better?

"Sometimes change is good." Buck grinned. Dressed in jeans, and smelling woodsy, his dark hair had grown longer.

"That's what I'm counting on," Jolene said.

"What about chemo?" Nancy asked. "Is it a go?"

"I don't have much of a choice," Jolene replied. "Dr. Blazer says it will help guarantee that the cancer won't' reoccur."

"That must be scary—thinking about it, you know," Buck uttered, exuding sympathy to Jolene's medical situation.

"A little," she admitted. "I need to trust Jesus and believe He holds my future." She testified of her faith in God.

"We don't go to church," Cloy said, wagging his head.

"My mother, uh, Claire—" Nancy had trouble even saying her name, "she's taken the kids on special occasions and they loved it. Buck and I just don't fit in with *that* crowd."

"Sunday School is good for kids," Jolene said. "It helps them learn about Jesus and teaches many important social values—like respect for your parents, and loving your neighbor as yourself."

"Mama says Grandma is mean," Craig uttered.

"I didn't say that, Craig!" Nancy countered. "I said she was difficult. There's a difference." Her cheeks reddened, clearly embarrassed over her son's disparaging remark.

"I don't see no difference." Buck sided with Craig.

"Can we talk about something else?" Nancy barked.

Jolene ascertained the rift between Nancy and her mother was serious. Mothers and daughters should be close. Though Jolene cherished playing the role of grandmother to Nancy's children, she was no substitute for the person with blood ties.

Surely, there was a way to help Nancy and Claire find forgiveness in their hearts. Jolene decided to work on it.

"How is your soup?" Buck moved the conversation forward.

"The best I've ever had. Nancy's a great cook." Jolene smiled. "I understand you're a trucker, Buck. What's that like?"

He shrugged. "It's a pretty good living. Pay depends on the kind of loads I carry. Some weeks I make better than others."

"He's gone from home a lot," Nancy interjected.

"I know you miss Buck when he's on the road," Jolene said.

"Do you?" He stared at his wife. "Miss me even a little?"

"Of course, I do, you big goon!" She smacked his arm.

The kids guffawed and chatted about school, listing some of the supplies and books they'd need for the spring semester.

Buck told Nancy to see if she could buy used books.

"If it's okay with you," Jolene addressed the parents, "I'd like to help with that expense." Her gaze skittered between them.

"That's mighty kind of you, but not necessary," Buck said.

"Consider it a Christmas gift," she said to the couple.

Nancy locked eyes with Buck. "In that case, we accept."

♣15

ON WEDNESDAY, THREE days after leaving the hospital, Jolene spoke with David by phone. Their conversation had felt stilted. Avoiding talking about their separation, they spoke mostly about Jolene's health. In early February, a surgeon would install her portacath at Baptist Hospital and she would receive her first dose of poison in Dr. Blazer's office. Poison was how Jolene perceived the prescribed Taxol. *Why?* Because the drug destroyed both red and white blood cells alongside any roaming cancer cells.

Since Jolene had inherited *Thalacemia Minor*, a blood disorder that caused stippling in some of her red blood cells, she would also receive regular Procrit shots to boost her immunity.

Jolene had dressed casually for her first appointment. Nancy had insisted on driving her to Nashville and waiting why Jolene had the portacath installed and the chemo treatment.

"What about the children?" she'd asked.

"A friend is keeping them," Nancy had replied.

They were in the car, Nancy driving and Jolene musing over what to expect as they entered Nashville city limits.

"I'm grateful for the ride," Jolene told Nancy.

"My pleasure, just sit back and relax."

During the trip to Baptist, Nancy sited complaints about her mother's critical nature, how Claire labeled her and Buck as "poor white trash" to her rich friends because they struggled financially.

Jolene half listened, her heart not into Nancy's plight today. "I'm so sorry," she occasionally added. "Is there anything I can do to help?" There wasn't, unless God delivered a miracle.

Time to spare, they drove into the belly of the three-story medical complex and Nancy found a parking spot. After entering the complex through automatic glass doors, they took the elevator down to the surgery floor where Jolene would receive a portacath.

An hour later, woozy from the medication, she was wheeled up to Dr. Blazer's office for her first chemo treatment. The wound from the device stung like bees. Nancy took a seat in the waiting room, concerned over Jolene's weakened condition.

"I'll be fine," Jolene reassured her friend.

Dr. Helen Blazer came from the back and greeted Jolene, inquiring how the procedure went. "Fine," Jolene said.

A nurse pushed Jolene in her wheelchair down the narrow hallway toward a room that was set up for chemotherapy.

"Are you hurting much?" Dr. Blazer inquired

"Some." Jolene's heart skittered. "Nothing I can't bear."

"That's not unusual. You'll have some discomfort until the wound around the portacath heals. It's important to keep the pinpoint opening clean. You don't want to deal with an infection while taking chemo, trust me." They stopped at the door.

"What kind of infection?" Jolene asked.

"It's rare but, occasionally, staphylococcus infects the area."

"Are we talking about *staph,* the kind that might kill me?"

"Yes," Dr. Blazer replied. "I don't advise taking hot baths following a treatment, though a good soak feels mighty good to an achy body." She eyed her patient. "Wait a couple of days."

"Okay," said Jolene, "and thanks for the tip."

"Wynn, see that Jolene gets a comfortable chair," Dr. Blazer ordered. "Try to relax, it'll make the time go faster," she advised Jolene. "The treatment will last approximately four hours."

"I don't know if Nancy can stay that long."

"I'll speak to your ride and send her home," Dr. Blazer said. "We'll arrange for an ambulance to transport you to your destination after your treatment. Insurance will cover it."

"Well, okay, I guess."

A ride home in an ambulance seemed rather luxurious. However, how could a little pampering hurt under the extreme circumstances? *Go with the flow* entered Jolene's mind.

Inside the rectangular room, a nurse Jolene hadn't met was seated at her desk recording patient data.

"This is Jolene Salisbury," Wynn introduced the newest patient to the technician. "Sonya will take it from here."

"Hi, Jolene," Sonya said. "I'll be here every time you come in for a treatment," she explained. "See that padded green chair at the end of the room. That's yours for today."

Jolene blinked as she walked toward the chair, eyes darting at the mute faces of four other women involved in treatment. Each patient was seated in a different colored leather recliner.

Color coordinated, Jolene smiled at the unique situation.

The IV contraption that held the Taxol cocktail hung on a metal stand beside each chair. Many wore head wraps since they were bald and the room was cold. Their eyes were closed.

"Are they sleeping?" Jolene asked Sonya.

"Probably not, just relaxing," the technician answered. "As soon as you're connected to the IV, you'll get fifty milligrams of Benadryl. It helps with sitting still for four hours."

"Okay." Jolene eased from the wheelchair into the recliner.

As promised, Sonya attached the IV to Jolene's port and inserted a needle into the tubing. Seconds later, Jolene felt the cold liquid Benadryl flow through her veins and jolt her brain like a strong sedative. "Wow! That was pretty interesting."

"Yes, wow!" Sonya smiled. "Like a magazine to read?"

"No, I'll pass."

Jolene leaned back in the recliner and shut her eyes. Trapped in memories she envisioned the first day she and David spent together. They were so into one another, so emotionally charged.

Falling in love is a beautiful experience.

Four hours slipped by and the IV came off. By this time, the sun was receding on the bloody horizon. Jolene was wheeled downstairs and taken outside to board an ambulance.

The ride to Charlotte seemed longer today than before, the dying day more dismal at the thought of poison running rampant through her veins. So this was what it felt like—surviving cancer.

If Jolene had her druthers, this experience would all be an insane nightmare. But it wasn't. It was all too real. And the outcome of her treatment could determine if she lived or died.

The idea of God being in control was a great comfort in these dark days. In a perfect world, David would be there with her.

Oh, David, when did we fall out of love?

♣16

EVERY THIRD MONDAY, Jolene was scheduled for treatment. Like Dr. Blazer predicted, her body ached most of the time from what felt like an influenza virus that never quite went away.

And there was the potential for weight gain and nausea.

While some patients grew sick at their stomachs and threw up after a treatment, Jolene thrived on Procrit and actually increased in energy. Feeling hungry most of the time, she yearned for salty snacks to counteract the continual gnawing in her stomach.

The third day after receiving the Taxol cocktail was the worst. Like clockwork, her body ached unmercifully and nothing seemed to cure the nagging pain. Those few troubling days she spent in bed, nursing her body with sleep and continual prayer.

Weeks twittered past and Nancy proved a gracious hostess.

As expected, Buck was gone most weekdays. Nancy wouldn't hear of Jolene moving into a rental. Going with the flow, routine rigorously set in at the Blake's. Daily house chores, paying bills, and parenting skills remained a challenge for Nancy.

The children became precious treasures to Jolene and she got to know them better and appreciated their idiosyncrasies.

Before her third chemo treatment, her hair began falling out. Standing motionless in the shower, Jolene held a clump of the precious commodity in one hand. Time to get her head shaved.

She should have listened to the other patients who'd gone before her. They warned that going bald was devastating. Luckily, she'd already purchased three wigs of different colors: red, frosted-blond, and dark brown, deciding in advance she'd have some fun by changing her physical appearance to accommodate her outfits. The do-rag was strictly for home use.

"You want me to do what?" the beautician at the salon asked Jolene. "Shave my head," she replied then snap my picture.

The visual concept was almost comical, but no one in the salon was laughing except Jolene. How else could she cope?

So the deed was accomplished.

~

David came to visit Jolene in early March. He rented a car at the airport and drove over to Dickson Country. Nancy let him in the front door. "Hi, I'm David." He shook her hand.

"I guessed that." Nancy pointed. "She's in the kitchen."

"Thanks." David walked through the archway and spied his wife seated in a rocker in front of a big picture window. Rolling hills lay beyond the cluttered backyard.

"Hi." Jolene glanced up from her spy novel.

"Hi back." He pulled a straight chair away from the table and mounted it backwards, arms resting on the top slat.

"I'm surprised to see you're here," she said.

He smiled. "You look well, too."

"Liar, liar, pants on fire!"

Jolene held his gaze for a moment.

"You hurt much—from the chemo, I mean?"

"Does fire burn?" Jolene quipped at her absentee husband. She had only herself to blame. Separation had been her choice.

"You don't have to be so sarcastic, Jolene," he scowled. "I was only trying to be sensitive to your, uh, condition."

"Cancer, David. Say it, please!" Jolene rose from the rocker and walked over to the sink. Nancy had perked a pot of Folgers in anticipation of his coming. A plate of oatmeal cookies covered with wax paper lay on the counter. "Care for some coffee?"

"Sure." He got up, flipped the chair around, and walked over to the cabinet. "Don't I get a hug from my wife?" He wrapped his arms around her plump waist, nestling his face in her neck.

Jolene froze. "Sure." She gave his hand a slight squeeze.

"You're mad at me," he said, taking a step back.

"I just don't like you tiptoeing around the facts, David. Cancer is a killer, and we both need to face that." She took in a big breath. *Be nice, Jolene. David's here like you wanted.*

"I know that." He grabbed two mugs from the oak cabinet, set them on the counter and reached for the peculator.

"Careful or you'll get burned." Jolene removed a carton of real cream from the fridge and added some to her cup.

"I'm sorry, Jolene, if I hurt your feelings when I left last time." He made firm eye contact. "I was upset, too."

"I don't want to spend our day discussing the past." Jolene sipped from her mug. "Sorry is enough for me."

"So you're through tormenting me."

David's gaze sent ripples down Jolene's spine.

"I didn't realize that was what I was doing."

"I guess we've both made mistakes."

"Well, I'm fine now, doing quite well battling this illness." She enhanced her position of independence. "I only have four more treatments. And I expect to fully recover."

"Then you'll be coming home?"

"I actually don't know what the future holds."

"You mean *our* future." He grasped Jolene's hand, tenderness resting in his hazel eyes, a blond curl tumbling onto his forehead.

"I've missed you a lot," he said.

She looked away, her thoughts rushing back to his trip to the Bahamas over Christmas. *Is he hiding something?*

"My grandmother always said home is where the heart is. I need to be here long enough to accomplish my mission in coming, which is to learn as much about my parents' last days as I can."

"Is that really necessary?" He snagged a cookie from the platter. "Let bygones be bygones, is a great policy."

"It's important for me to know what I've missed. When you face death, suddenly unfinished business takes the forefront. I don't expect you to understand, if that makes you feel any better."

"I see." His expression reflected displeasure.

"It's not that our marriage isn't important," Jolene qualified.

"It's about choice, isn't it? Don't forget about love."

"Do you still love me, David?" She searched his face.

"Yeah, I do." He heaved a sigh. "It's not the exciting kind of feelings I used to have when we first were a couple."

The raw truth was difficult to absorb.

"I know what you mean," Jolene agreed. "It's more like we're a two-family unit now. Know what I mean?"

"That doesn't mean we should exclude sex," he said.

"You were the one who moved out of *our* bedroom!"

Here I go, picking a fight again.

The critical moment passed as they each collected their wits.

"I already told you," David spoke slowly, "I can't sleep when you constantly flip over in the bed. And you snore."

"Okay, I guess we settled that matter." She took her coffee outdoors to the porch rocker, plopped down, and set it in motion.

He followed her outside. "Are you mad at me?"

"No." She glanced up. "I appreciate your visit."

"But you're still aggravated, I can tell."

"We should call a truce." Tears bubbled in Jolene's eyes. "You do what you have to do at home, and I'll take care of things here. Let's just try to enjoy the day; it's really all we have."

"What do you mean?" Wrinkles furrowed his forehead.

"A day at a time, somebody said in a song. Remember?"

He nodded, heaved a breath. "How long do you plan on staying with the Blake's?" He collapsed in the swing.

"Until they kick me out, I guess."

"Don't you pay them rent?" He halted the swing.

Jolene told David about the money she'd spent up front in getting Nancy's Cadillac repaired. "I also stay with the children when she runs errands, do a few chores when I'm up to it." She paused to summarize. "Actually, I help her and she helps me."

"Sounds like a win-win situation. Symbiotic."

"Actually, my duties feel almost motherly."

"That's a good thing, huh?" He gazed at the junk buried in deep grass in the side yard. "Where's Nancy's husband?"

"Buck's a trucker, he's gone a lot," Jolene replied.

"That's tough on a wife with five children."

"Tell me about it." Jolene nursed her coffee slowly.

"The grass hasn't been mowed in weeks."

"Yeah, and that's a sore spot with Nancy."

"So how much time does Buck spend away from home?"

"He's home on weekends. Since I moved in, they seem to be getting along better. When I met Nancy, she was leaving Buck with the kids. I think saving her car door saved the day."

David grinned. "What do you want to do with our day?"

"I don't know. What do you have in mind?"

He handed her a brochure of a historic home in Clarksville and Jolene reviewed the information. "Looks pretty interesting," she commented. "We'll go, if that's what you want to do."

"It will give us both a break from our normal routines."

She kept her eyes on David, offering no opinion.

"Then it's settled. We'll need to be back by mid-afternoon since my plane departs from Nashville at 6:30 p.m.," he said.

"Then we'd better get going. I'll tell Nancy."

♣17

DAVID HAD JOLENE back at Nancy's by 2:30 p.m. He promised to visit again soon. After a light kiss, he drove away. She watched him leave through the kitchen window until his car disappeared over the hill, feeling abandoned once again. How many more goodbyes could their marriage survive?

"I heard ya'll arguing out on the front porch this morning." Nancy interrupted Jolene's thoughts. "Is that wise?"

"What? Suddenly, you're a psychiatrist?" Jolene uttered. "It wasn't exactly an argument." She gave her landlord a look.

"Sounded like fussing to me." The younger woman stood at the kitchen sink peeling new potatoes. "Grab the buttermilk from the fridge and stir us up some cornbread."

"I can do that." Jolene set her mind to the task.

"Okay, maybe not an argument, but your conversation sounded less than friendly—not that I purposely eavesdropped."

Nancy swung her knife toward Jolene like a weapon.

"Look," Jolene returned Nancy's stare, "David wants me to come home but I can't do that right now. You know why I'm here. Now that I feel better, I wish I knew what came next."

"Maybe I have an idea." Nancy dumped the potatoes in a pot.

"I'm open to suggestions." Jolene cracked two eggs, added them to the mixing bowl with the cornmeal, buttermilk and oil.

The two women locked eyes.

"My grandmother's been 'round for a while, and she knows a ton of people, some living; some dead." Nancy wiped her wet hands on an apron. "You should talk to her."

"You think she knew my parents?" Jolene hitched a breath.

"Granted, Granny Mercer is sometimes off her rocker." Nancy switched on the gas burner and put on the potatoes to boil.

"A touch of dementia doesn't always make for clear thinking. Gets things mixed up sometimes, but sweet as a person can be."

"Still, I'd love to talk to her about Kirk and Kate Lancaster."

"Okay, we should do that now," Nancy decided. "The potatoes can wait." She turned off the gas burner.

"Are you sure?" Jolene queried.

"Yeah, I'll drive you over to Granny's house and you can ask your questions." Nancy shoved the milk in the fridge. "I'll bundle up Catherine and Carla and strap them in their car seats while you get your coat and meet us out front."

Jolene glanced at the kitchen clock. The county school bus let the older children off at 3:15. "What about the kids?"

"Not a problem today," Nancy said. "Claire's picking them up after school and spending a couple hours with them."

Considering Nancy's begrudging tone of voice, Jolene couldn't resist remarking, "You sound like that's a bad thing."

"Don't judge me when you don't know Claire."

"I wasn't, just trying to understand why you keep your mother at bay. If my mother were alive . . ."

"I don't want my children getting any fancy ideas that money buys happiness," Nancy barked. "Claire showers them with gifts every opportunity she gets—like it can buy their affection. She's still punishing me for getting pregnant in high school."

Jolene wasn't going there today. "Okay, I'll grab my coat and purse and meet you at the car." She hustled to the bedroom.

The drive over to Granny Mercer's only took fifteen minutes. Blanche lived in the small cottage behind the B & B Claire owned.

"I'd better go inside first and see what condition Granny's in," Nancy warned. "Mind waiting in the car with the girls?"

"No problem." Jolene glanced in the backseat at four-year-old Catherine and two-year old Carla, fast asleep in her car seat.

Nancy came back. "Granny's fine, up for a visit."

Not sure what *fine* meant, Jolene helped Catherine out of the car seat while Nancy carried her sleeping child to the front porch.

Blanche Mercer held the door open for them.

"Lordy mercy, girls, come in and get'cha se'f warmed up!" She motioned them inside with a bony hand. "What'cha think yo're doin' takin' them kids out on sech a cold day?"

"Car's warm and kids have on coats, Granny," Nancy said.

"Folks don't think the same as they used to."

The frail woman wearing flip-flops shuffled across the width of her tiny living room, and poked the hot coals in her woodstove.

"Better heat up this ol' house for the babies," Granny said.

The frame house was a step-back into the 1940s, a typical block-styled, all-wood construction; plenty of space for Granny. The floor layout featured two bedrooms, one bath, and a compact living room opening into the kitchen. Wood floors throughout were scarred from decades of use, but the walls had a fresh coat of beige paint. Somebody was taking good care of Granny.

Was it her daughter Claire? Jolene wondered. *If so, why didn't she feel the same way about Nancy?*

Nancy helped Catherine shed her coat before taking off her own polyester-lined parka. "This is my friend, Jolene."

"Not often I gits a pretty, young visitor," Granny said.

"Jolene wants to ask you a few questions."

Blanche patted the couch, signaling for Jolene to sit close. "Sure. But don't hear so well these days, so speak up, honey."

"I hope our visit isn't an imposition," Jolene said.

"Smart, too, as well as pretty."

Nancy removed a coloring book and crayons from her purse then sat Catherine on the rug at the task. Carla slept.

"Thanks for seeing us on short notice," Jolene added.

"At my age, guests are a godsend. Ya'll want som'in to eat?"

"I want some'in," Catherine chimed in.

"No, baby, not now," Nancy told her daughter. "Won't be long 'fore suppertime, you can wait." She eyed Jolene.

"No thanks, none for me." Jolene stared at Blanche, thinking it was the first time she'd been around a person who had lived so long. The woman had witnessed many changes in her hometown over the decades. Blanche had likely outlived all her immediate family and many of her friends. Her tight smile produced a dozen wrinkles at the corners of her thin lips. Wispy hair, white as fresh-fallen snow, formed a kinky nest of cobwebs on her round head. With ears too large for her body and a face resembling parchment paper, her best feature was her eyes, burning black like live coals.

"Do you have Indian blood running in you?" Jolene asked.

"Grandpa was part Cher'kee. I got his looks."

"Some say I look like my mother," Jolene revealed.

"When I wuz young . . ." Blanche began to reminisce. "The young fellas shore kept their eyes on me, I can tell you. Ever'time I walked 'cross a room they took notice. Them were the days."

Jolene watched the old woman as she shuffled over to a whatnot cabinet and retrieved a photograph inside a tarnished gold frame. "See fer yo'r se'f, took in 1945."

"You were beautiful," Jolene noted. "Still are," she added.

Blanche threw an arthritic hand. "Don't go lying to an ol' woman, Jolene." She collapsed in a squeaky oak rocker. "Age done cast its spell o'er me. Whut's a poor woman to do?"

Nancy chuckled. "Granny will be ninety-one soon. She's in good health except for rheumatoid arthritis and some memory loss. And she knows this town like the back of her hand."

Jolene curiously eyed Blanche. "Did you know my father, Kirk Lancaster? He's a generation younger than you."

"Lancaster? Oh, yeah . . ." Blanche peered out the window. "Wasn't he that postal deliv'ry guy?" Her gaze drifted lazily on Nancy. "Guess you'd be too young to 'member."

"Daddy worked for the post office," Jolene told Blanche.

"Seems to me, I heer'd tell he married that prissy little coworker of his after his wife died—or was that somebody else?"

Blanche wagged her head in reflection.

"No, you're right." Phlegm clogged Jolene's throat.

"Folks said Kirk was cheatin' on poor Kate," Blanche recalled. "Gossip. Who pays attention to that?"

"Sounds like my daddy," Jolene quipped.

"But you turned out all right, didn't you?" Blanche said.

"Oh, I suppose. As an only child my parents spoiled me, though at the time I didn't recognize it. After I graduated from college, I didn't come home much. When Mama got sick—" Jolene sniffled and fought tears, "I wasn't here for her."

Fresh grief gripped Jolene as she covered her eyes with both hands, stunned at her display of emotion. "I'm sorry."

"Guess that troubles yo'r poor soul, child." Blanche patted Jolene's hand. "No use cryin' over spilt milk, my mama always said. Do som'in 'bout it. Make it better."

"That's what I'm trying to do." Jolene believed Granny understood her plight better than anyone. "Now that I look back, I wonder if my parents were ever a happy couple."

"Now, child, happiness is hard to come by."

"I wonder if they were ever in love."

"Tha's a question only they can answer," the old woman said. "Love is commitment, not always exciting like in the movies."

"Kirk and Kate married right out of high school." Jolene mused over the past. "Mother had trouble getting pregnant until I came along. I hate to think of myself as a mistake."

"No creature of God's is a mistake!" Blanche balked. "He knows our lives, beginnin' to end, don't you never forgit that!"

"I wasn't a faithful daughter," Jolene admitted. "From the time I was twelve, I never wanted to live in this town." She didn't preface town with 'hick'. "Now, I'm compelled to be here."

"Is that 'cause of the cancer?" Blanche questioned.

"I'm sure it triggered some repressed emotions," Jolene replied. "You go through life a day at a time, doing what's necessary, not thinking a particular day might be your last."

"Who wants to think about that?" Nancy interjected.

Jolene smiled. "No one, until they realize the end is closer."

"Well, ever'body makes peace in their own way," Blanche piped, a beguiling expression clawing in her mature face.

"I guess they did their best raising me," Jolene said.

Blanche snapped out of her reverie. "Charlotte's a fine town, Jolene. Jes ask Nancy." She glanced at her granddaughter. "But all folks ever'whur got their troubles. We ain't no different."

Jolene thought about the rift between Nancy and Claire and wished there was some way to repair their relationship. At least, in helping someone else she could pay penance for her mistakes.

"Thank you, Blanche, I feel better after talking to you."

"My pleasure," Granny said. "Cake and coffee . . .?"

"Sure." Nancy went into the kitchen to prepare the snack.

♣18

AFTER TALKING TO Blanche Mercer, Jolene realized what she should do next. It was time to visit the graves of her parents. So on the first warm sunny day of spring, she drove into Dickson on the pretense of picking up a few groceries. Turning right off Highway 48 onto 70, she made a left turn at the next traffic light.

Half a block down on North Charlotte Street, Jolene's heart lurched as she spied hundreds of white tombstones nesting on the rolling green hills of Union Cemetery. Wherever magical sunlight touched the wet soil, green grass had emerged like gangbusters.

Slowly driving up the paved road between gravesites, Jolene shut off the Cadillac's engine and stared at the orange fabric tent, wondering who lay in the coffin. She was surprised when the sight brought tears to her eyes. Hurt surfaced like a rising flood.

Did it matter if Kirk cheated on Kate now that they lay side by side in their graves? If Kate had heard the ugly rumors Granny Mercer mentioned, did she choose to ignore them? Did my mom love my dad enough to be generous even on her deathbed?

Jolene sucked in a quick breath of cool air infused with the odors of fragrant spring flowers and considered her past failures. She'd had plenty of practice ignoring marital issues. At least now, she wasn't avoiding facing family issues for one last time.

More worrisome, if David didn't file for divorce, could she muster the courage to make the break? That she even considered splitting up said something about the fragile bond of love.

Life's situations were complex, human feelings complicated.

Back in the nineteen eighties, cancer was still a mysterious fatal disease. Surgery was the victim's only option. In some instances, cancerous tumors were subjected to radiation to reduce the size, but once it had spread, hope for survival was over.

By the turn of the 21st century, medical technology had taken a giant leap with the mapping of human genomes and stem cell studies. Treatment for cancers became more specific. Medicine to eradicate ovarian cancer had been tried and tested for a decade before Jolene needed it. The use of Taxol had passed the test.

No longer was cancer an automatic death sentence. But Kate Lancaster had been born too soon in the 20th century for technology to save her. How did knowing Kate was going to die affect Kirk? Did he turn to another woman for comfort? Was his heart attack God's punishment for committing adultery?

Or did he die because he ate red meat and too many sweets?

Jolene smiled at her foolish meanderings.

Finally the grieving crowd gathered under the orange tent scattered. One by one, vehicles moved out of the cemetery.

By now, the sun was dropping low on the western horizon. Sunlight winked through the budding trees like waking fireflies.

It was time to view her parents' graves.

They were both buried near the top of the hill. Jolene slowly drove up the paved drive to the approximate location and parked.

Exiting the car, she walked between the scripted granite stones, examining the newer ones. Then she paused.

Kirk and Kate Lancaster: there they are.

No mention of a second wife on Kirk's tombstone. As if Olivia had never existed. If she and David divorced, would they be buried side by side? Unprepared for the gripping volatile emotions, Jolene stumbled to her knees at the base of the graves.

She'd attended her mother's funeral, but had refused to watch dirt shoveled over the gray steel casket. Self-preservation had driven her away from the cemetery too soon that day.

"Mama, I just didn't understand," Jolene uttered. "But I do now, and I am so sorry." She laid a fresh rose on the mound of the grassy grave. "Accept my apology."

Jolene's eyes drifted to where her father lay.

"How long should I stay mad at Daddy for marrying Olivia?" she said, as if Kate could hear her. "Doesn't he deserve a rose for helping raise me? Who am I to place blame? Am I so perfect?"

Jolene lingered on her knees awhile longer.

The western sky evolved into a dark maroon color as dusk pulled down its shade on daylight. A cold wind cut eddies across the cemetery before Jolene decided it was time to leave.

I've done what I came to do, apologize.

She rose to her feet. A lightheartedness suffusing her spirit, Jolene drove to the nearest grocery store to buy milk and bread. Then she drove back to Charlotte, admitting to herself that the act of forgiveness had made a difference. Shouldn't she extend the same graciousness to David, her husband of eighteen years?

Didn't they both deserve a second chance?

Foolishly, Jolene blamed him for her unhappiness. But hadn't she refused to get pregnant? She'd placed her career ahead of starting a family, thinking there would be a better time.

Now it was too late to birth a baby.

But maybe it wasn't too late to save their marriage.

How hard had Kate and Kirk tried to mend fences? When life gave them lemons, did they let the taste of bitterness linger, or make lemonade? She would probably never learn the answers to those questions. Speculation over the past would drive her crazy.

Sometimes, it took a leap of faith to move forward.

While driving through Charlotte she called David on his cell phone. "It's me, how was your day?" she asked in a quiet voice.

"Fine, it's been a busy one. What about you?"

"I visited my parents' graves today," she said.

"Was it therapeutic?"

"Thought provoking," she replied.

"In what ways, explain?"

"I came to realize I'm a terrible wife." Admitting her faults didn't come so easy. "I wanted to say I'm sorry."

He chuckled. "What if I think differently?"

"Let me get this out, okay?" She fought for control over her emotions, to say the right thing. "I've put off having a family because of many reasons. One, I love my work. Plus, I've wanted the finer things money could buy. For both of us," she added.

"Wow, you've been soul searching."

"Denying us children wasn't fair, I apologize."

"We can always adopt."

"It's not the same as having our own child and you know it."

"I realize that." He released a breath. "Are you saying you want to adopt?" A vaporous void ensued.

"I'm just saying, shouldn't we talk about our problems? Discuss what's gone wrong with us as a couple?"

Are you having an affair, David?

"Does your change of heart mean you're coming home?"

"I can't yet. I still have three chemo treatments left."

"Then you'll come home," he concluded.

"I don't know. That's the best I can do for now."

"I know you like Tennessee." He thrummed a pencil on his desk. "I just don't know if I can move to a small town you once described as hick." He chuckled. "That was insensitive. Sorry."

"Well, that was *then* and this is *now*. I'm meeting an awful lot of nice people," she revealed. "Maybe you can take some vacation time before long and come here for an extended visit."

"I'll think about it," he said. "Things are odd here."

"Odd, how . . .?" Jolene thought of his Bahamas' trip.

"Trust me, I can't say yet."

Trust . . .? "Okay, do I have a choice?"

Silence ruled a moment.

"Well, I'll go now." What else was there to say?

"Jolene . . .?" David uttered.

"Yeah?" She prayed for some insight into his secretive life.

"Nothing, I guess," he said. "We'll talk more, later."

"Keep safe, David."

What big secret is he guarding?

♣19

A WEEK AFTER Jolene's fourth chemo treatment in April she began feeling better. Realizing there was a small window of time between each treatment when she hurt less, wouldn't it make sense to use those days to plan something interesting to do?

"Where is your mother?" Jolene asked Catherine. The little girl was busy molding animal shapes with colored Silly Putty.

Catherine glanced up and batted her baby blues. "Wanna play with me, Aunt Jolene?" the four-year-old asked.

"Maybe later, honey." Jolene heard music coming from the front porch. "Where is your little sister?" she asked Catherine, worried Nancy had taken off without telling her.

"Sleeping," she answered, scrutinizing her artwork.

"What about your mother? Did she go somewhere?" Jolene failed to compete with Silly Putty's mystique.

"She said to leave her alone." Catherine looked up at Jolene.

"Oh." *Humph.* Had Buck gotten booted out of the house because he'd failed to mow the overgrown yard again?

Curious about the source of music, Jolene parted the living room window curtains and spied Nancy seated in the front porch swing, playing a guitar and singing to the top of her lungs.

The melodic contralto sound coming from Nancy's vocal chords was unbelievably beautiful. Jolene opened the door and poked out her head. "Hey," she uttered.

"Hey, you back!" Nancy stopped her performance.

"I had no idea you were such a talented singer." Jolene ventured onto the porch and sat down on the first step leading down to the yard. "Don't let me stop you." She waved a hand. "I'm just starting to enjoy the show. Please continue."

Nancy smiled, finished her song, and sat down on the steps next to Jolene. "I wrote the words and music."

"Wow!" Jolene felt a catch in her throat. "Buck told me you wanted to sign up for the talent contest last year. Does your mother know how well you write and sing?"

"Yeah, well," Nancy cleared her throat, "you can forget about signing me up for that contest! My mother would never allow me to participate." She placed the guitar in its battered case.

"Has she heard you perform lately?" Jolene asked.

"No, but she knows I have a gift. Claire gave me umpteen dozens of lessons and expected me to be on a Nashville stage by the time I was twenty-one. I let her down. It's called failure."

"Then she does care about your talent." Jolene smiled.

"That was before Baby Number One." Nancy stared at Jolene. "It's too late for me to have a singing career."

"I don't consider you a failure at all!" Jolene collapsed in the swing beside Nancy. "You have five beautiful, healthy children. That's an important accomplishment. And you have Buck."

"So what? You're a successful real estate agent."

"In Baton Rouge, I was." Jolene stared into space. "Top of the Latter Club, to prove I earned it." She engaged Nancy's eyes. "But I can tell you, sweetheart, I'd give it all up to be a mother. What do I have to show for my work now?"

"Imagine!" Nancy exclaimed. "Who would've thought?"

Jolene gazed at the robin-blue sky. "It took cancer to make me realize what's important in life. Success and money can't buy happiness. It can't guarantee love." She thought of David.

"Did you learn all this because you've lived longer?"

"Age helps." Jolene made eye contact and smiled. "I've made more mistakes than I have right decisions."

"Been there, done that." Nancy frowned.

"Don't beat up on yourself too badly."

"I knew better than to sleep with Buck 'fore we got married, but I did it anyway," Nancy admitted. "When Mama found out I was pregnant, she blabbed it to her pastor. Made me so mad, I hoped I'd have a dozen kids to spite her."

Jolene let out a chuckle. "Why didn't you?"

"Five is enough, plus Buck and I can't afford more."

"About finances . . ." Jolene said, "I'd like to pay for a lawn service to come every other week and clean up around the place."

"You'd do that?" Nancy perked up.

"Yes, the kids could play in the backyard and I wouldn't have to worry about so many insect bites and grass snakes."

Nancy smiled. "That's sweet, but I shouldn't let you."

"Give me one reason why I shouldn't? I'll even throw in a new swing set and a sandbox, if that's okay."

Nancy bowed her head then lifted her dazed eyes. "I don't want you to think you owe us, Jolene. You don't."

"That's not why I'm offering."

"Living here, well, you've been a big help already."

"I know, and I'm not trying to diminish your generosity, believe me. If I hadn't had your support in the beginning of my chemo treatment, I think I would've high-tailed it back to Louisiana," Jolene revealed. "I have a dream, what's yours?"

"To record songs, my own," Nancy said.

"Then somehow let's make that happen. I'll help."

"Help how?"

A quizzical expression frolicked in Nancy's expression.

"Well, for starters, let's make you look like a star."

"Now that's a tall order!" Nancy leaped to her feet and playfully spun around in circles. "Look at me! I'm twenty-eight years old. I haven't worn anything but jeans and tee shirts for a decade. The two dresses hanging in my closet are too big now."

"That's a good thing, Nancy. You have a great figure."

Collapsing in the swing, tears bubbled in her eyes.

"I'm sure there's a business in Nashville that does beauty makeovers," Jolene said. "You'll be twenty-nine soon, so let me treat you, as a birthday gift. It would give me great pleasure."

"Oh, I don't know, what does something like that cost?"

"Less than the check I just received from my broker at Latter & Blum." Jolene smiled. "My cohort Becky has been selling my listings like gangbusters and the dough's rolling in."

Nancy laughed. "You make changing my life sound simple."

"Look like a gospel-artist, sing like one, and become one!"

"I love the way you think." Nancy heard her two-year-old cry out. "But right now, motherhood calls."

"Let me get Carla. Finish practicing, and write some more tunes." *What is friendship for, if not to help?* Jolene considered.

"About the contest—how do you plan to get me signed up?"

"Don't worry, honey, I have my ways."

"You don't know Claire."

"And she hasn't met a Top-of-the-Ladder salesperson."

They both laughed hard.

♣20

ON FRIDAY, NANCY arranged for Catherine and Carla to stay home with a sitter while she rode with Jolene into Nashville to visit Kent, the owner of IMPRESSIVE MAKEOVER, a beauty salon with the positive subtitle: *Guaranteed to Please.*

"I should've told Buck I was going to do this." Nancy and Jolene exited the Cadillac and made their way to the front door.

"Let me handle Buck," Jolene said.

"What if he hates the way I look?"

"Trust me, he won't. Your improved image is bound to be a nice surprise for your husband," Jolene expounded. "It might even help your sex life." *Bite my tongue.*

Nancy chuckled. "He doesn't need help with that."

"Name and your time of appointment?" the receptionist at the front desk said, face flushed at hearing the personal comment.

"Nancy Blake, ten o'clock," Jolene said.

"Kent's running a little behind."

"No problem," Nancy said. "But I need a guarantee I'll be outta here by two. I have kids coming home from school around three thirty and it's more than an hour drive to my house."

"I'll tell Kent. He's doing you personally."

Nancy grimaced. "I never had a guy cut my hair."

"Oh, sweetheart . . ." a melodic male voice called out as a handsome man flowed to the front of the shop like he was skating, "you're going to get much more than a haircut."

"You must me Kent." Jolene shot out her right hand. "This is my friend, Nancy. I'm treating her to a makeover for her birthday, so do a fantastic job that will please us both."

"With me in charge, you need not worry! Fill out a card, Nancy, and we'll take $20 off your bill," Kent instructed. "Consider the discount a birthday present from the salon."

"Thank you." Nancy smiled at Jolene, suspecting Kent's kindness came with a healthy bill at the end of the session.

Jolene looked at Kent, mid-thirties, with a powerhouse frame for a petite guy. It was evident he hit the gym regularly. Dental-generated white teeth shown beneath his smile. Seeing how his thick brown hair glistened with gel, he'd had his own makeover.

Nancy filled out the information card and followed Susie to the back of the salon where she entered a closet and stripped down to her bra and panties. Clean pink jumpsuits were provided Kent's clientele, comfortably warm in the air-conditioned shop.

On the wall in the dressing room hung photographs of women of all ages, the *before* and *after* Kent's makeover. The contrast was amazing. Nancy was hopeful that maybe she could look like a star when he finished. Ready to begin her metamorphosis, she emerged from the dressing room.

"You don't have to hang around, Jolene."

"I don't mind waiting." She picked up a magazine.

"We'll be at least two hours," Kent said. "You should do something productive. Trust me, I know my craft."

"Go on," Nancy threw a hand, "I'll call you on your cell phone when I'm finished." She brushed back an unruly red curl. "Have some fun while Kent performs his magic on me."

"You're sure?" Jolene slipped the magazine in the rack.

"Positive. I'm in good hands."

"She is." Kent flashed a smile. "I'm good at magic."

"Okay, I'll drop by the doctor's office and get my blood taken since it's not far to the hospital," Jolene said. "Maybe I can get my Procrit shot a couple days early, save a trip on Monday."

"Get some lunch while you're out," Susie suggested. "Nancy will eat with us. We've already ordered a delicious tray of gourmet sandwiches for our morning customers."

"Sounds like a plan." Jolene slipped on her light jacket, grabbed her purse, and turned to Nancy. "I don't mind staying, if it will make you feel more comfortable with the process."

"No, you're my first firewall. If you don't recognize me, I'll know the makeover was a success." Nancy nervously laughed. "I might even need to splurge for some new duds."

"Okay. I'm going." Jolene considered if she'd forgotten anything. "I'll be back before two, even if you don't phone."

"Have a good rest of the morning," Nancy said.

"You, too, and enjoy."

Jolene pushed open the front door, stepped outside into the crisp April morning, and inhaled the bakery odors coming from the shop next door. She felt pretty well today, minimal aching in her bones. Not a cloud in sight, a round ball of fire glistened in the sky, nestled in a backdrop of blue arcing over Nashville.

Jingling Nancy's Cadillac keys, Jolene manually unlocked the aging vehicle and climbed behind the steering wheel. The hospital was ten minutes away and the morning traffic was negotiable. Come noon, gleaming steel would be lined up at traffic lights.

After pulling into the high-rise parking garage at the Doctors' Building, Jolene caught the elevator going up to the fourth floor.

A nurse stepped into the waiting room and called out the next patient's name. Spying Jolene, Sonya queried, "Hey, aren't you three days early?" She checked her mini-calendar.

"Yeah . . ." Jolene replied, "but since I was downtown, I was hoping to get my blood test and Procrit shot."

"Let me check with Dr. Blazer," she said. "Have a seat."

Jolene settled in the comfortable leather chair by the window and plucked a health magazine from the crafted wire bin. At the corner of her vision she spied an elderly man, seated across the room on the plaid sofa, looking distraught. Jolene's quick smile brought him out of his reverie as he acknowledged her.

"Someone you love taking chemo?" she inquired.

"My wife Angela," he said in a gravelly voice, scratching his chin. "She's seventy-two and chemo's hit her pretty hard," he explained. "I see you're wearing one of those headwraps, too."

"I have three wigs, but they all itch by scalp. Motorcyclists with baldheads made these do-rags popular." She smiled back.

"How long 'ave you been taking treatments?"

"Since January," Jolene replied. "Monday's usually my day to give blood and get my Procrit shot, but since I was already in Nashville I figured, um, maybe I could do it today."

"Oh." His black eyes peeked from under saggy eyelids. "Timothy Caruthers, good to mee'tcha." He waved a hand.

"Jolene Salisbury," she said. "Is your wife going to be okay?"

"Don't know. Got age and heart disease going against her," Timothy explained. "Doc Blazer couldn't operate on the tumors but thinks the chemo will reduce their sizes. We'll see."

"I'm so sorry to hear that." Jolene empathized.

"Our time's running out, anyhow." He listlessly stared out the window, a shadow of depression settling in his expression. "Don't suppose a body can live forever."

"Time waits for no person." Jolene realized her window of opportunity to repair her relationship with David was running out, too. They hadn't spoken in over a week. Did that mean he'd given up on love? Or cared what happened to her anymore?

Or has someone else already taken my place?

"Jolene?"

The window to the secretary's cage was open. "You can go on back now and get your blood drawn," Laura said.

"Nice meeting you, Mr. Caruthers. I'll pray for Angela."

"Thank you." He winked a grin, dimples bookending his droll mouth. "We'll pray for you, too. What else have we got to do that helps?" Wrinkles gathered around his sad eyes.

"God is good, Timothy. Don't forget that?"

"Sometimes a fella needs reminding."

"See you." Jolene approached the door as it opened.

"You know the routine." Wynn led the way down the hall to the lab. "The technician will be right with you."

"Anyone I know here today?" Jolene inquired.

"No, but one of your Monday seatmates had a reaction to medication and died earlier today," Wynn reported. "She took an over-the-counter drug without checking with us first."

Jolene hadn't expected the news to impact her so severely. Patients like her bonded at times like these. "I'm so sorry."

"We all are."

"Well, that's certainly something I need to remember."

"You're doing great, Jolene." Wynn optimistically chattered. "Two more treatments and you're done here for another six months. Then you'll see us twice a year, if all goes well."

Am I doing great? Not so much emotionally.

Jolene stepped into the compact lab. Sonja showed up momentarily and prepped her arm for the draw. The needle prick was painless in contrast to the discomfort she suffered daily.

After receiving her Procrit shot, Jolene waited in the outer office for thirty minutes before leaving, noting that Mr. Caruthers had already left. Jolene prayed Angela would respond to the treatment and survive the cancer. Like he said, God is good.

♣21

JOLENE ORDERED LUNCH at a Subway then phoned Nancy on her cell while she ate. "You done yet?" she asked between bites.

Keep eating like this and she'd be wearing tent sizes by the time she saw David again. Then maybe it didn't matter to him.

"Almost," Nancy spurted. "Kent is putting on the final touches to my new hair-do. Where are you?"

"Subway, can I bring you something?"

"Gosh, no, the gourmet sandwiches arrived about thirty minutes ago and I've had my fair share," Nancy said. "When you finish eating, come on over and take a gander."

"Do you like what you see?" Jolene asked.

"Well, I certainly look different." Nancy sighed. "I hope Buck recognizes me." She giggled like a schoolgirl.

"That drastic, huh . . .? I can't wait to see you."

"Well, good or bad, it's done."

"See you soon."

Jolene finished her sandwich and made a quick stop in the restroom before going outdoors. The noonday sun had heated up the atmosphere to an invigorating sixty-five degrees.

Luckily, she found a parking space a block from the salon, parked the Cadillac then walked. The combination of chemical fumes from perfumed products used for hair and nails assaulted Jolene's nostrils as she opened the front door and entered.

Spying a plate of leftover cookies on the welcome counter, she sampled a frosted one with pecans while perusing the shop for Nancy. "Is Nancy Blake done?" she asked the receptionist.

"I'll check. Have another cookie."

The plump brunette abandoned her computer and hurried to the back of the shop, trotting past three women seated at makeup counters. Moments later, a tall slender woman approached Jolene.

Flawless makeup enhanced the woman's youthful face, the blush on her cheeks so natural that she appeared embarrassed. A flame of wavy long hair, the dynamic bloody color of a dying sunset, set off the beauty's huge sparkling green eyes.

"Nancy?" Jolene blinked with amazement.

"Yes, Jolene, it's me." She produced a radiant smile.

"Wow! I owe Kent a bonus," Jolene exclaimed. "You look marvelous. Next stop is a boutique. We're going to buy you an outfit to match your stunning appearance; something worthy of wearing to the July singing contest when you win it."

"No, stop, Jolene!" Nancy balked. "You've done enough."

"Please let me put the final touches to a beautiful package."

Kent came up front to speak to Jolene and Nancy before they left. "Well, would you recommend my salon?" he asked.

"I might even let you do a makeover on me when I finish chemotherapy," Jolene piped as she pulled a fifty-dollar bill from her purse to tip Kent. "Enjoy a moment on me."

"That's mighty nice of you, Jolene, but it's my policy to charge fairly for my services and not accept tips. In fact, I'm giving you a ten-percent coupon to use when you come in next."

He motioned to the receptionist to fetch one.

"Okay then," Jolene stuffed the fifty in her purse, "I guess our next stop is a country-western shop to get a spiffy outfit for Nancy to wear at the singing contest."

"Oh . . .?" Kent's left eyebrow hiked. "Do we have a rising star in our midst?" His wicked gaze settled on Nancy.

"I think so," Jolene replied. "Nancy not only writes songs, she sings beautifully. Ask me, she's going to win a recording contract on July fourth if I have anything to do with it."

"Tell me, Jolene, are you originally from Nashville?" Kent inquired, his almond eyes widening with interest.

"I grew up in Charlotte. I'm just visiting for awhile."

Is that true? Jolene wondered. The longer she stayed, the less she wanted to return to her old life. But would David ever agree to give up his insurance business in Baton Rouge to join her?

"Get me a CD copy of Nancy's voice, and I'll show it to a couple of producer's wives who come as regulars," Kent offered.

"Really . . .?" Nancy blinked. "You'd do that for me?"

"Bragging rights," he said. "Never hurts to advertise." He offered a few more helpful tidbits regarding clothing.

Nancy nodded. "Thank you, Kent."

"Well, you girls have a good day. Duty calls."

They walked the block and got in the Cadillac. Nancy drove east on Interstate 40 and exited on North Briley Parkway.

The specialty shop Kent recommended was located inside the Opryland Hotel. Some years back the area had flooded, but the massive hotel was up and running gangbusters now. "A little on the expensive side," Kent had said. "Tell the owner I sent you."

"What time is it?" Nancy worried the school bus would arrive before she got home. Buck was out of town and Claire was not an option. "Kids will be frantic if I'm not there to greet them."

"Call your sitter. Ask her to stay until you get home," Jolene suggested. "We need to finish what we've started."

"I wish I had some of your backbone." Nancy paled. "You just man up and do things, trusting it'll all work out."

"Not always." Jolene thought of her rift with David.

"I don't always have the gumption to stand up to Buck's bullying," Nancy said. "Instead of talking out our disagreement like rational people, we usually end up fighting. I always hate myself an hour later, but I keep repeating my same ol' ways."

"You don't have a corner on mistakes," Jolene offered. "I had a terrible fight with David the Friday night before I caught a plane to Nashville on Saturday. I regret some of the horrible things I said to him. Now, my marriage is in jeopardy."

"Not all your fault, was it?" Nancy peered at her friend.

"No, we'd been having problems for awhile," she admitted. "We fussed a lot, but neither of us made a move to leave."

"Is that why you came here, to get away from David?"

"No, I came for myself. Looking back, our separation was inevitable. A break will help us decide what's important."

"You said it was about your parents."

"That, too," Jolene said.

"So, even if you didn't have cancer, you would've moved out." Nancy's emerald gaze rolled with speculation.

"Yes, I guess so. We both needed space."

"I'm so sorry, Jolene. David seems like such a nice man."

"He is a good person." Jolene sniffled. "I don't want our marriage to end. I've told David that, but he isn't making a move my way. I don't know what will happen next."

"Is he having an affair?" Nancy uttered.

"Possibly," Jolene said. "David's standoffishness could be work related. He promised to tell me about his Bahamas trip, but I'm still clueless." Jolene dabbed her leaky eyes with a tissue.

"I wish I could help you," Nancy said.

"Thinking about ending our marriage is depressing." Jolene stiffened. "Could we talk about something more uplifting?"

"Sure." Nancy pulled into the Opryland's parking lot and they exited the car. Inside the vaulted foyer of the gigantic hotel complex they were handed a schematic map of the complex.

After traipsing through the hotel's beautiful gardens, they located the clothing boutique Kent recommended. *High-stepping County Fashions* was the logo on the plate-glass window.

With excitement mounting, Nancy ventured inside the shop to peruse her choices. Jolene trailed a step behind. What Nancy was looking for was a flashy western outfit. A salesclerk pointed them to the rear of the store where a rack of sales items was featured. Nancy thumbed through the hanging outfits and finally selected a pair of rhinestone-studded black jeans with a matching jacket. "What about this?" She held it against her slender body.

"Looks great, Nancy!" Jolene plucked a snazzy green silky blouse from another rack. "See if this matches."

Nancy found an empty dressing room and tried on the clothes. The pair of black leather boots Buck gave her two Christmases before would work perfect with the outfit.

One glance at the price on the jeans and jacket produced a frown on Nancy's face. "I love the outfit, but even half price, this goes above and beyond. I can't possibly let you buy this for me."

"Of course you can, birthday girl. I'd be hurt if you didn't."

"You're sure?"

Satisfied with Nancy's selections, Jolene took the clothes to the register and handed the sales clerk a Visa card. However much the bill was, she was paying. To her, this act of kindness was more than just purchasing an outfit for a friend. Nancy was on target to achieve her dream of becoming a Nashville star.

During the slow drive home in traffic, Jolene recognized the happiness flooding Nancy's expression. Predictable as ocean tides rolling in twice a day on the sandy shoreline, Nancy's hope would evolve into optimism. And that was a priceless commodity.

♣22

TWO DAYS AFTER Jolene's fifth chemo treatment she developed a low-grade fever. After speaking to Dr. Blazer's nurse, she was advised to wait twenty-four hours and see how she felt. Likely her ailment was not related to her cancer treatment but rather the onset of a virus. Forty-eight hours later, Jolene felt worse and couldn't keep anything on her stomach. She phoned the doctor's office again and received a similar recommendation.

Wait another day and see if the fever lifts.

Four days after the onset of her symptoms, Jolene was running a 104 degrees temperature. Nancy thought it was time to head for the emergency room. Jolene agreed that her symptoms were serious and she needed immediate medical treatment.

At the Dickson ER, Jolene was admitted and shown into a private room to be examined. Unable to keep fluids on her stomach, she was dehydrated. The physician hooked her up to an IV drip and ordered blood samples taken. Something really bad was going on. A urine test revealed she had a nasty kidney infection, so the ER doctor injected her with powerful antibiotics.

All the while, Nancy waited out front, praying that Jolene would be all right. When a hospital attendant came out to the waiting room, she jumped up and approached him.

"Are you treating Jolene Salisbury?" she queried.

"Yes, I'm Dr. Hastings. Are you her ride home?"

"Yes. My car's right outside."

"Jolene has a urinary tract infection. She's being treated now, but we'll release her in a couple of hours. Make sure she drinks plenty of fluids during the night—water, juices, cola are good. Meanwhile, a blood culture will show if another nasty bug is involved," Hastings explained. "Any questions . . .?"

"No. Thank you, Doctor."

Nancy sat down to wait. When it was decided that Jolene would go to the emergency room, Claire had agreed to come over to the house on short notice, so the home front was covered. It seemed when she needed Buck he was always trucking.

Antsy, Nancy watched people coming and going, sounds and odors fading into the background as thoughts reached back five months. Jolene's presence in their home had changed the atmosphere. Mama and Papa were getting along much better.

If only Jolene and David could find a way to bridge their gap of distrust. Meet halfway, like one ol' country song suggested.

When Jolene emerged through the double doors two hours later, Nancy approached the nurse guiding her wheelchair.

"She's with me. I'm parked close to the door."

"Hi," Jolene mumbled to Nancy. "I don't feel so well." It was a gross understatement; she'd been run over by a Mac virus.

"Let's go home," Nancy said.

"Home, it is."

The nurse helped Jolene into the passenger seat of the Cadillac as Nancy slid behind the wheel. The night air felt refreshing after being shut up in the ER waiting room.

"We set to go?" Nancy looked at Jolene.

The patient weakly nodded.

"Do me a favor, Jolene. Don't run any marathons in the next few days. The doctor prescribes fluids and rest."

"Don't think that will be a problem," Jolene uttered, letting down the passenger side window. Above them, between the scattered clouds, stars twinkled like fireflies in the night sky.

Should she let David know she was sick?

"Thanks for your help," Nancy called out to the attending nurse before she switched on the motor.

"No problem, drive safely." The nurse waved goodbye.

"Put on your seatbelt," Nancy ordered Jolene.

"Yes ma'am." She buckled up.

It was late in the evening when Nancy pulled out of the hospital parking lot. "I guess I should call David and tell him what's going on," Jolene muttered, staring out the window.

"Your call," Nancy said.

"He might get upset if I don't tell him."

On the other hand, Jolene considered, she didn't want to use her illness to coax David to Tennessee. If he wanted to be with her, he knew the way. She grimaced at her own stubbornness.

"David hasn't called in a week, you think he cares?"

"Nancy, it's not for you to judge my marital status." Jolene's brain was stunned with meds. "He wants me to get well."

"Sorry." Nancy sassily smacked her lips. "I was out of line."

"No, it's okay. You're right, David has been ignoring me."

"Speaking of the devil . . ." Nancy shot a glance at Jolene, "I meant to tell you before we left for the hospital that a document with your name on it was delivered by UPS this morning."

Jolene was baffled at Nancy's disclosure.

"It had a Baton Rouge return address. I signed for it."

"An official document . . .?" Jolene wondered if it was from her real estate office. Divorce papers came to mind and she felt even queasier in her stomach. "I'll deal with that later."

"Okay," Nancy agreed. I just thought you should know."

"Now I know." Jolene watched as the sky darkened around them and raindrops slithered down the windshield.

Nancy exited the hospital parking lot on Highway 46.

"So, if you think you should call David, do it."

"Maybe later . . ." Jolene didn't want to worry him.

The onset of Jolene's symptoms occurred on Wednesday, two days after receiving her fifth intravenous dose of chemo. By Friday, her nagging fever had hiked despite taking Ibuprofen every four hours. Dr. Blazer's office advised her to wait until Monday to see if the symptoms diminished. Could just be a passing virus.

Then earlier today she'd raced off to the hospital for emergency treatment. Nervous over her waning confidence in the medical profession, Jolene recalled an old saying that belonged to her grandmother: WHEN IT RAINS IT POURS.

Jolene spent Tuesday in bed. As Wednesday rolled around, she began to think the worst of the infection was behind her. She had one final cancer treatment to go then she could resume her normal routine. It was a matter of hanging on another month.

"Thank God, the antibiotics are healing my urinary tract infection," Jolene told Nancy as she limped into the kitchen for a steamy cup of herbal tea. "I feel much better today."

"Before you sign up for a marathon, let's wait and see what your blood tests show." Nancy filled two stout mugs with the hot lemony liquid then added scoops of syrupy honey.

"I'm sure it's nothing bad." Jolene hoped she was right.

What else could it be?

A call from Dr. Blazer's office came around noon. Nancy answered the phone and received the message. "Okay." She nodded, writing down the instructions. "Fine, we will."

"We will what?" Jolene felt a tug of confusion.

"No, you're, uh, not fine," Nancy stuttered. "Dr. Blazer's nurse said for you to pack a bag and come straight to Baptist Hospital in Nashville. You have a dangerous blood infection."

"What kind of infection?"

"I don't know. We just need to get you there ASAP."

Jolene blinked. "I guess I'd better pack."

"Just hurry," Nancy urged.

A dangerous infection . . .? Jolene thought of the chemo patient who took the wrong medication and died.

Is this the beginning of a scary end?

Nancy phoned Buck in Clarksville and told him about Jolene's latest crisis. He listened with concern, not commenting.

"I'm not sure what time I'll be home," Nancy told Buck, "Can you get someone to cover your trucking assignment and be home before the boys get off the school bus at 3:15?"

"Sure, I care about Nancy, too. Take care of our friend."

After ending the call, Nancy went to check of Jolene's progress in packing. "Are you about ready?"

"I heard you talking to Buck. What did he say?" Jolene tossed her nightclothes into a suitcase with some toiletries. "You don't have to drive me to the hospital, I'm no weakling."

"I don't think that's a good idea," Nancy countered.

"Who's going to pick up the girls at Day Care?"

"I guess I could call my mother."

"But you don't want to involve her."

"No, but this is an emergency. She loves my kids."

"Go, call Claire, and I'll meet you at the car."

Nancy drove like a maniac all the way to Nashville while Jolene laid her head on the seat rest and wondered how this could be happening? She'd done so well with chemo, barely experiencing any side effects other than weight gain and hair loss.

"Don't be so glum, Jolene, help is on the way."

Jolene appreciated that Nancy was so sensitive to her plight. If she had a daughter, she'd want her to be just like Nancy.

"Dr. Blazer is a good doctor, she'll help heal you."

"Only God heals." Jolene removed her phone from her purse and phoned David. "Hi, it's me. Busy?"

"Yeah, sort of," he replied. "What's up?"

"I have a dangerous blood infection." Just saying those words was scary in itself. "Nancy is driving me to Baptist Hospital right now, so I can be admitted and receive care."

"When did this happen?"

"The infection started last week, two days after my last chemo. When my fever spiked on Monday, Nancy took me to the ER in Dickson. Dr. Blazer's nurse phoned a little while ago and said my blood tests revealed I have a dangerous infection."

"How long will you be hospitalized?" David asked.

"Until I'm better, I suppose."

And what if I don't get better?

"Do you want me to fly up and be with you?"

"Can you get away from work on such short notice?"

"I'll manage, you're my wife," David uttered. "First, I need to wrap up a few things at the office—oh, did you by chance receive the document I overnighted you?"

"Nancy said UPS brought something. What is it?"

"I have a buyer for our house," he replied.

Jolene's heart jolted to attention.

"We never talked about selling *our* house!"

"I didn't think you'd care."

"I do." The news flew all over Jolene.

"You said you weren't coming back."

"I don't understand why you're doing this *now*. Why didn't you ask me if I wanted to sell? Is this punishment for leaving? "

"Think what you will, but I can't go back home night after night when you're not there. I plan to put the proceeds in a money account and rent a one-bedroom apartment."

"You can't sell if I don't sign." Jolene wanted to throw up. "Does this mean you're filing for a divorce?"

"It means I don't want a house to keep up."

"Okay, I can't argue with you now, I'm too sick." Jolene inwardly groaned. "Have it your way, I'll read the contract when I get home from the hospital." *Whenever that is . . .*

"Don't be mad," he said. "It's for the best."

"I can't talk about this now."

"Ask Nancy to bring the contract to the hospital," David insisted as if impersonally solidifying a deal. "I'll see you tomorrow." He abruptly ended the call.

Stunned, Jolene held the phone limply in one hand.

"What's going on?" Nancy asked.

Jolene fought back a barrage of tears. "David is selling our home." She hitched a breath. "He didn't even ask me."

"That cad, I hate him!" Nancy scowled.

♣23

AFTER JOLENE CHECKED into Baptist, Dr. Blazer examined her and reported her portacath had to come out, it was infected. "You warned me this might happen," Jolene said.

It was springtime, she should be better not worse. David was coming to see her tomorrow. They should be going on a picnic, laughing and enjoying the day. But, he'd likely take one look at his fat, bald wife and leave again. Maybe he had good reason.

Zoned out, Jolene realized her doctor was speaking.

"Anytime a needle goes into the body, the chance of infection is possible," she remarked. "I'm sorry this happened."

"So, I guess this means surgery again."

"Yes. Then we'll treat your staph infection."

Once Jolene was in bed and an IV inserted, she insisted that Nancy go home and tend to her family. She'd be fine.

"I feel bad about leaving you alone," Nancy said. "Claire is with the girls, so I'll stay as long as you want me to."

"It isn't necessary. The sedative I took will make me sleep. Go home and phone me later. I have good care here."

"Okay, if you're sure."

"I am."

Wednesday afternoon slowly passed as Jolene battled a rising fever. She welcomed the meds at five, then again at nine. In a dreamlike state, she periodically woke up with a prayer on her lips.

God heal me. Please don't let me die.

Thursday morning arrived with a jolt as Jolene awakened to hospital doors swishing open and closing and metal breakfast carts rolling on tile floors. Food was the last thing on Jolene's mind.

"Your body needs liquids," the nurse told Jolene, holding out a glass of juice. "Cranberry is good for urinary tract infections."

Jolene drank half of her juice and set it aside. A gurney arrived at her bedside late morning and she was hoisted aboard.

"Where am I going?" she asked.

"Surgery," the tech said, "to remove your portacath."

"Oh, that." She'd forgotten.

Gliding down the long hallway with her back flat on the gurney and eyes peeled on the acoustical tile ceiling, Jolene struggled to keep fear at bay. A quick spin and the medic rolled her onto an elevator. Down they went six stories to the basement level. Jolene just wanted all this over and done with.

"You doin' all right?" the young medic with lazy nickel-gray eyes asked Jolene. "This is a piece of cake compared to ovarian cancer surgery. You won't feel a thing, trust me."

"Until I wake up," she huffed. "I was told the same thing when they installed my portacath. It wasn't a walk in the park."

"Almost there," he said, moving with skill.

The elevator doors yawned open and antiseptic odors from the operating room assaulted Jolene's nostrils. She stared up at the gleaming florescent lights above her as she rode the gurney into the operating room. It halted and the male nurse handed the surgeon his clipboard then said, "This is Jolene Salisbury."

The same surgeon who had installed Jolene's portacath looked down at her. "You're going to get a local anesthetic. You'll feel woozy, but aware, so try to be still."

Jolene nodded and closed her eyes. After receiving intravenous Benadryl, she relaxed and began to pray.

Lord, whatever happens . . . never leave me.

After the procedure, Jolene was taken back to her hospital room. David was standing by the window, a welcome sight. Handsome with a winter tan, his blond hair was a bit longer.

"Hi. How to you feel?" Hazel eyes perused Jolene.

"Better now that you're here," she admitted as David's warm hand wrapped around her slender fingers and squeezed.

Two nurses hoisted Jolene into bed and fluffed the pillows behind her head. The younger one hooked her up to an IV and started an antibiotic drip while the other checked her pulse and temperature. When they were alone, David pulled up a chair beside the bed, took her hand again and gazed into her face.

"When did you get here?" she asked.

He glanced at his watch. "Thirty minutes ago. Dr. Blazer filled me in on your condition." His expression exuded concern.

"Did she say how long I'd be hospitalized?"

"Depends on how well your immune system handles the infections," he replied. "You're a sick puppy."

"Yeah, I suppose my white blood count has bottomed out."

"It looks like you're getting excellent care," he noted.

"Yeah, I guess. I feel awful." Jolene's head throbbed as she stared at the ceiling. She couldn't recall when she'd last used the bathroom. Constipation from chemo was a constant problem.

David said, "I didn't realize there were different strains of staphylococcus. I read where some are antibiotic resistant."

"What's the good news?" Jolene tucked the cold sheet under her chin. "Mind turning up the heat, I'm getting a chill."

He adjusted the wall thermostat and came back, sat down beside Jolene. "You're going to get better," he said as if he knew.

"That's encouraging." *Be nice, Jolene.*

"You sound mad. Do you want me to leave?"

"No, please." Fear strangled Jolene. "I don't want to be alone. I'm sorry I'm just not—decent company."

"No, I'm sorry." He abandoned the chair, walked over to the window and stared down at the pavement.

"Do they know what kind of staph I have?" she asked.

He shrugged. "I assume so. I expect the antibiotic you're taking targets all strains," he replied. "We'll see in a few days."

"Can you stay that long?" Jolene asked. "What if the antibiotic I'm taking doesn't stop the infection?"

David faced Jolene. "That's why I've requested a team of doctors specializing in infectious diseases to examine you. I want to make sure you're receiving the correct treatment."

"Thank you." A ghost of a smile curled Jolene's lips. "Ever consider changing professions and becoming a doctor?"

"Nah . . . I like selling insurance."

Jolene grew sleepy as David sat in the padded recliner a few feet away and read a magazine. His statement woke her up.

"About the sale of our house—" he came closer, wide hazel eyes piercing Jolene. "I wish you'd sign the contract."

"I feel too ratty to make a rational decision today."

"Nancy's bringing the contract over tomorrow so you can read it." He hitched a breath. "Trust me this is for the best."

Is it? Jolene glared at David, scrutinizing his motives.

"I want you to be satisfied with the equity cash-out."

She glanced past him at the cloudy day. "You did list the house with Latter & Blum?" she thought to inquire.

"No, Jolene, I sold it myself. Is that a problem?"

Jolene grimaced, blue eyes set afire. Becky would be upset that she didn't get the listing through a referral.

"I wish you hadn't done that, David, without discussing it with me first." She squeezed her eyelids, growing angry.

"You want to pay a brokerage fee?"

"No, I guess not!" she snapped.

This was not a discussion they should have *now*. Jolene turned her head away so David wouldn't see her teary gaze.

He glanced at his watch. "Supper will be arriving soon. I'm going to the motel and rest. It's been a hectic week at work." He plucked his jacket from the recliner. "Get some rest."

Oh, no, buddy, you don't get to leave like this.

"About work, David, what happened in the Bahamas over Christmas?" Her words caused him to spin around, mouth open.

"Give it up, Jolene! I'm leaving now."

"Wait! Answer one question."

He glared down, lips set firm like concrete.

"Have you already replaced me with a mistress?"

She had not expected him to haughtily laugh.

"I thought you knew me better than that, Jo."

Jo? He hadn't called her that in years.

"I'm going now. See you tomorrow."

"Go." She turned away, trembling with resentment.

After David left, Jolene slept. Later, fully awake, she phoned Nancy and learned that Makeover-Kent had called a buddy in Dickson and arranged for Nancy to create soundtracks for her original songs. Buck was still skeptical about the music industry, but told Nancy to go ahead and make the demo.

Good news. It was about time.

Jolene's secret plan was moving forward. Even if her own life shattered, at least she could help Nancy achieve a lifetime dream. Yet, Jolene trusted that God was faithful, even if David had not been. With that in mind, she prayed for strength.

Mitzi called Jolene just before the lights dimmed at bedtime. She hated hearing about Jolene's double infection and promised to bring her granddaughters for a visit as soon as it was allowed.

Jolene got a refill on her IV bag and more meds at nine o'clock. Clammy and in pain, she rolled over and slept.

♣24

THE PHYSICIANS SPECIALIZING in infectious diseases reported that Jolene wasn't getting well after a week because the antibiotic she was taking was ineffective.

When Jolene's meds were changed, she was released after three days. All total, she spent ten days in the hospital.

David had gone home at the end of the first week, so Buck came to pick her up in his truck. As they drove west on I-40, Buck asked how she felt. "The pick in my right arm smarts," she replied. "Dr. Blazer has arranged for a representative of Home Health Care to deliver the treatment supplies I'll need."

"What kind of supplies?" Buck was unaware Jolene was receiving more treatment. "Are you contagious?"

"Goodness no, I have enough antibiotics in me to heal an elephant." She grinned. "Actually, I feel as huge as one, too."

She'd gained fifteen pounds in three months, less the ten she'd lost during her hospital stay. "I have to take a month's worth of antibiotics intravenously. That's why I have a pick."

The IV pick was a tubal device inserted in Jolene's left arm. Via the device, she would receive more antibiotics twice a day for a month. Dr. Blazer warned the kind of staph Jolene had liked to hide in organs. The month's treatment was a precaution.

"You look fine, Jolene; beautiful, in fact," Buck said. "Nancy and I are just glad you're better. Kids miss you like crazy."

"It's good to know someone is missing me." She thought of David, who was starting to feel more like the enemy. Reluctantly, she'd signed the papers for the house sale. Half the equity was to be deposited in her account. How impersonal was that?

"You don't think David misses you?" Buck kicked up the pace and passed two cars on the interstate. "The guy would be crazy to let a smart woman like you go."

"He'd agree with the crazy part." Jolene chuckled.

"Don't be so hard on yourself, Jolene. I was thinking of taking off work and painting the outside of our house," Buck revealed. "Nancy's been after me to do that for awhile."

"Four years," Jolene reminded him. "She told me."

"Okay, so I'm a procrastinator." He chuckled. "But I love my family. Though I don't always show it," he admitted.

"I know you do and that's why I enjoy staying with your family. I can't think of any place I'd rather be." Jolene lowered the window and felt the cool breeze wash over her face.

When they arrived at the house, Nancy met Jolene at the door and hugged her. "Are you hungry?" She had vegetable soup and cornbread made and warming in the oven. A pitcher of tea, freshly made and sweetened, sat on the counter. *Home . . .*

Jolene inhaled the familiar odors and felt the love surrounding her. As expected, the children bombarded her with questions, curious about her hospital adventure. What was it like? Did the boo-boo in her arm hurt much?

"Can we take your temperature?" Cloy asked.

Jolene answered the children's questions the best she could, ignoring the gory details—like her constipation trauma that lasted four days because of a colon impaction. And the fact a doctor tried to insert the pick and had hit a nerve that sent her up the wall. She'd reacted with a blood-curdling scream.

No, the hospital stay was not fun.

After lunch, Catherine served everyone oatmeal cookies on a plastic tray while Nancy scooped bowls of vanilla ice cream to be passed around. Jolene's appetite was beginning to return.

Chocolate syrup dripped off Carla's plump little cheeks to prove how good the dessert was. Fully satisfied, the family ventured into the living room to continue their conversations.

Buck lit a pipe and kicked back in the wooden rocker. The children sat on the floor listening to the adults talk while they played board games. Ten-year-old Cloy, Nancy's first, was quiet-natured, well mannered, and clearly in charge of the game rules. His younger brother, Craig, tested his patience with opinions.

Seven-year-old Claire, bearing her grandmother's namesake and overflowing with girlish antics, was more like Craig than Cloy, a loaded pistol about to go off after a high dosage of sugar.

Constantly interrupted, Nancy finally asked her daughters to play quietly. As the afternoon waned on, fatigue pulled Jolene down until she excused herself and retired to the guest bedroom.

The fresh pink sheets were pulled back, a welcome sight. Jolene caved into the soft pillow-top mattress. After sleeping for hours, she dragged herself from bed for a necessary potty break.

Night fell without Jolene's knowing it. She'd skipped supper, thinking her body needed sleep more than nourishment. Dreams came in swarms during the night, but the pain pills she'd taken at ten helped her sleep. In everything, she felt David close.

Morning came and Jolene felt refreshed. The house was ominously silent, signaling she was alone. The family had gone out on an excursion. Jolene welcomed the quiet as she stepped outdoors on the front porch and inhaled the cool refreshing air.

A wave of hunger suffused Jolene as she smelled kitchen odors sifting through the open window in the living room. Still dressed for bed, she shuffled back through the house and into the kitchen in noisy flip-flops. A pan of biscuits sat on the stovetop.

In the oven, she also found a bowl of scrambled eggs. And there was still fresh-brewed chicory coffee in the percolator.

Prepare for a feast, she told her stomach.

Hungry after skipping supper last night, she polished off every morsel of food leftover from breakfast then returned to the bed to rest some more.

Today will be better, she thought.

~

On Monday, a Home Health Care truck drove up to the house and delivered the supplies Jolene needed to receive the intravenous antibiotics. The efficient medical technician showed Nancy how to administer the drug via the IV pick implanted in Jolene's arm. She would sit for thirty minutes twice a day while the cold dosage slowly drained directly into her bloodstream.

The worst part of receiving the treatment was the chill that came with it. Two weeks passed with a great deal of bed rest. To pass the monotony of each challenging day, Jolene read her Bible and prayed for hours. When the children came home after school, the house was again filled with chaotic noises and laughter.

A month passed and the hair on Jolene's body was growing back. As if her baldpate had been fertilized, the fine gray fuzz became a mass of thick curly hair, dark with streaks of gray.

As a testimony of her illness, the faint shadow of eyebrows over Jolene's blue eyes were ringed in dingy dark circles. And her ghostly white face was a reminder she hadn't been to the beach.

"Dear God, I look awful," she repeated more often than not, optimism difficult to muster on some drab days.

David had phoned twice since Jolene was released from the hospital. His voice sounded distant, like he was distracted, and Jolene decided not to complain about her maladies, immensely grateful to be in the recovery process. She'd always known that life was unpredictable, that bad things happened to good people.

But it usually happened to others.

Unfortunately, she'd been ill prepared to face a deadly disease at the age of forty-five. *Too young to die*, she'd foolishly believed.

~

The third Sunday in April was Easter. Buck and Nancy had decided to take the children to church and invited Jolene to join them. Their decision to attend was prompted by Claire, who had purchased new outfits for her five grandchildren the weekend before. After the service, they planned on taking the children to an Easter Egg Hunt sponsored by the Charlotte City Council.

"Are you feeling well enough to go?" Nancy asked Jolene.

"I think so. I'll sit at the back of the sanctuary and stay away from people, so I won't catch anybody's cold."

Jolene's gaze landed on the Easter lily plant that arrived yesterday, a gift from David with a card stating, "I'm glad you're on the mend. I have something I need to discuss with you."

Was this discussion how her marriage would end?

The idea of living the rest of her life without David was frightening. Sometimes life offered you a bowl of lemons. You could either savor the bitter taste in your mouth, or choose to make lemonade. Hardships either made you bitter or better.

Jolene prayed God would let her grow older gracefully.

It was no easy feat to get the Blake family organized and ready to leave the house in time to make the 10:00 service. At 9:45, Buck gathered the boys in his truck while Jolene rode with Nancy and the three girls in the Cadillac. The drive over to the Baptist Church took ten minutes. The family train filing into the sanctuary reminded Jolene of a pack of Indians on an excursion.

Feeling like the caboose to the train, Jolene selected a seat on a wooden pew near the back, soaking in parishioners' stares.

It will be okay, Jolene told herself. *In time, I'll look normal.*

During the church service Jolene couldn't get her mind off what David wanted to tell her in May. Was he springing a divorce contract on her, like he had their house sale? Surely, he would give her some idea of what to expect. Finally, with determination, Jolene was able to concentrate on the pastor's Easter sermon.

"Jesus is our Sustainer in times of trial," Brother Danny Crouch preached. "He's our Healer in seasons of sickness. He's our Backbone when life looks impossibly dismal. . ." Jolene could readily identify with those kinds of statements. *Dismal* . . .

"But when Jesus rose from the grave, He did something wonderful few people expected. He conquered death and defeated Satan's plan to eternally separate us from our Heavenly Father. Those who trust in Jesus will be changed in the twinkling of an eye, taking on a body like His, to live in Heaven with Him eternally. Now, because of Jesus' supreme sacrifice, nothing separates us from the love of our Heavenly Father."

Preach on, Brother Crouch. . .

Light filtered through the stained glass windows as Jolene sat quietly in the pew and listened to the sermon. She missed her church in Baton Rouge, her pastor and the friends she'd cultivated over decades. But enduring cancer made her realize that no one comforted like Jesus—not your spouse, family, or friends.

Following the pastor's sermon an altar call was given as the choir sang "Amazing Grace." Then the service was over.

People stirred like flies after watermelon.

Jolene was nearly out the door when an attractive older woman in a blue suit approached. "I'm Claire Wilkes," she sputtered. "You must be Nancy's friend, Jolene."

"You're Nancy's mother." Jolene's heart skipped a beat.

"Beverly told me you stop by my B & B pretty regularly."

"Yes, I do." Jolene peered at the woman.

Claire wore her bleach-blond hair cropped. Laser-green eyes, the same color as Nancy's, hit their target as she spoke her mind.

"What exactly are you doing, Mrs. Salisbury?"

Jolene was surprised by the question.

"What do you mean?"

"Why are you so interested in my daughter?"

Jolene felt uncomfortable with Claire's remark.

"Nancy's a sweet girl. We're friends. She invited me to stay with them while I recuperated from cancer. As soon as I'm well, I'll get a place of my own." *Is this any of your business?*

"Exactly how long do you intend to sponge off my daughter?" Claire's plump ruby lips trembled with anger.

"Mrs. Wilkes," *Okay, so now we're on a formal basis*, "I assure you I am financially contributing to the family. The last thing I would do is take advantage of Nancy, or impose on her life." She defended herself. "Is this the right place for *this* discussion?

Humph. Claire's pug nose turned up. "I guess not."

Those left in the sanctuary glared in horror at the ensuring conversation. A chilly moment of silence filled the airways.

"Claire, you have a beautiful, talented daughter and—"

"I don't want to talk to you about Nancy!"

"I'm sorry, but we really do need to clear the air. Why don't we get together for coffee," Jolene offered. "Please."

"My phone number is listed in the book."

Left in the wind, the mayor's wife scurried off to fraternize with her friends, leaving Jolene feeling unwelcome at church.

Outdoors, the atmosphere was electrified. It was evident that Nancy had overheard Jolene's conversation with her mother.

"Get in the car, kids!" Nancy helped her daughters buckle their seatbelts. "And keep your mouths shut, Mama's upset."

Jolene got in the car. "It's okay Nancy, I'm fine."

"Okay doesn't begin to describe my feelings." Nancy slid behind the steering wheel and jammed in the key. "Well, I guess that's what church is like. They can have it, I'm done."

"I got bubblegum from a nice man." Claire popped her gum.

"Spit it out, now!!! Both of you!" Nancy turned around and angrily faced Catherine. "It's bribery, pure bribery."

"Whut's bri-berry?" Claire asked. "Is it good to eat?"

"I'm sure Claire didn't intend to be rude to me." Jolene prayed Nancy wouldn't create another public display.

"She meant it!" Nancy scoffed. "I'm done with her."

"I'm sorry you feel that way, Nancy."

Jolene felt inadequate to suggest a solution to the feud between mother and daughter that had lasted a decade.

"God loves you, Mommy," Catherine mumbled while Carla hummed *Jesus Loves You.*

"Why aren't you mad?" Nancy locked eyes with Jolene as they drove out of the church parking lot. "She's terrible."

"No problem is too big for God." Jolene trusted that was so. Her problem with David was growing worse every passing day. Like Nancy and Claire, they weren't communicating well, either.

"Well, considering your situation with David, that's a brave assumption." Nancy cut a corner and rammed the engine.

The two little girls in the backseat said nary a word. Jolene held onto the doorknob, preparing for a rough ride.

Buck was waiting with the boys in the truck when they arrived at the house fifteen minutes later. Nancy got out of the Cadillac, hands parked on her hips, a snarl marring her pretty face.

"What . . .?" She queried Buck.

"Did you forget we promised the kids hotdogs and sodas at the park," he told Nancy, eyes skittering quizzically to Jolene.

"I'm not in the mood, Buck. Kids will get over it."

"No, Nancy. I'm taking them whether you go or not."

"Fine, go!" She stomped on the porch and hit the screen door with purpose, disappearing into the cavity of the house.

"I'll keep an eye on her, Buck. You and the kids go on, have some fun." Jolene followed Nancy into the house.

"Are you okay?" She caught up with Nancy.

"No, and I don't want to talk about it." The young mother ran into her bedroom and slammed the door.

Jolene imagined a "Do-not Disturb Sign" posted.

When Nancy didn't come out to the kitchen, Jolene ate a bowl of warmed-over chicken casserole and laid down to rest.

Later, she heard Nancy in the kitchen, punishing the pots and pans for Claire's outpouring unwelcome speech at church.

At least, Jolene thought, *she's working off some steam.*

Finally, Jolene joined Nancy in the kitchen.

"It's not your fault, honey." She empathized with Nancy. "Claire's a work of bad art, no doubt about it, but she is only trying to protect you from a predator like me."

Nancy spun around, pointing her spatula, "You see why I can't sign up for the July 4th contest? Claire's a terrible person and I absolutely hate her." Tears streamed down her flushed cheeks.

"Hate is a strong word, Nancy," Jolene warned. "You have to separate the person from their deeds. Nobody is perfect. We all have sinned and fallen short of God's grace."

"I don't know if I can separate my mother from her deeds." Nancy washed the dishes like they were her enemies.

"The singing contest is not about your mother, or Buck, or the children. It's about you fulfilling *your* dream, the one God imparted in you when he blessed you with talent."

Nancy's gaze softened as her hands lifted from the sink.

"Don't ignore your future," Jolene pleaded.

Nancy dried her hands on a towel and peered at Jolene. "Why can't my mother be like you? Am I such a terrible person?"

"Relationships aren't always easy." Jolene knew for a fact. "I'm going to have a talk with Claire as soon as possible." *And figure out a way to get you registered for the contest*, she privately added.

When Buck returned with the children late that afternoon, Nancy apologized to him for her earlier outburst then told him why. Jolene felt a measure of relief, trusting she'd gotten through to Nancy about the importance of forgiveness. But would mother and daughter ever be able to reconcile their polarized differences?

♣25

DAVID FLEW TO Nashville in mid-June. Jolene picked him up at the airport and they drove over to the public park and took a walk. "I'm glad you came, David."

"It's good to see you, too. I like your hairdo, babe, it's really cute," he said with a teasing grin. "We could sell your curls for a wig." He winked. "Of course, you'd kill me first."

Jolene giggled like a school girl. "Dr. Blazer says the curls will fall out as the chemicals wash out of my blood."

"Doesn't matter, I like it."

"My food supplements will help with the cleansing process."

Jolene skipped down the stone steps onto a walkway that cut a path though the park. The paved trails were lined with a variety of perennials, ranging from red to deep purple flowers that ignited the lush greenery. Oaks, maples, and birch trees shaded Nature's walkway. The pleasant atmosphere was permeated with earthy decaying odors. In the distance, the Bell Tower, or the Batman Building, as it was fondly labeled, towered on the city's horizon.

"I'm glad you took my advice and dressed casual." Jolene felt joyful, like she was ready to run a marathon.

"It's pretty here in the spring." David kept step with Jolene in his blue cotton warm-up suit and comfortable tennis shoes.

"Louisiana has its share of beauty, too."

"Yes, but no hills like Tennessee," he said. "Besides, going for a walk is not as much fun when you're not with me."

Jolene hitched a breath and slowed her pace.

"Are you sure you're up to jogging?" David asked.

"I'm in pretty good shape, considering." She'd been taking long walks to increase her stamina. "I might even sign up to run a cancer marathon next spring, who knows?"

"The weight looks good on you." He inhaled deeply.

"You didn't see me before Kent did his magic on me."

"Who's Kent?" David frowned, a bit jealous.

Jolene waived a hand and smiled. "Are you jealous?"

"I might be. Who's the guy?"

"Kent owns a beauty salon downtown."

"So you got a beauty makeover."

"I'm pleased you noticed." Kent had dyed Jolene's curly hair a deep auburn to accentuate her blue eyes and recommended a makeup that would and bring youthfulness to her face.

"How did you meet Kent?" he asked.

"A couple months back, I arranged for Nancy to have a makeover, as a birthday gift. I used the coupon he gave me."

Through talking about Kent, David said, "The air feels great, a little on the warm side today but less humidity than back home."

Jolene paused, bent over to catch her breath. "You didn't come here to discuss the weather, David." Jolene caught his eye. "What is it, mystery man? What's on your mind?"

He pointed to a green wooden bench up ahead. "Let's sit a spell, if that's okay with you."

"I'm all for that."

"Race you?" He sprinted toward a clearing in the woods.

"Okay, you're on."

Jolene skipped toward the long green park bench positioned a few feet in front of a natural-flowing spring fountain. David raced past her, laughing as he called out, "What took you so long?"

"You won this time, big boy!" she breathlessly called out. "Stay in shape, buddy, because I'm working out regularly now. Plan to run a cancer marathon next year and show you!"

"I believe you." He laughed.

"Thanks." She felt his gaze hot on her body. "I sense a serious conversation coming on. Shall we?"

They sat down. David slouched on the green bench, head resting on the top rung, long slender legs stretched out in front of him, the toes of his white tennis shoes pointed at the blue sky above while Jolene perched at a decent distance from him, unsure what profound statement was coming. *I want a divorce?*

"The run was refreshing, lady. Good idea, fun."

"You should taste the spring water."

"Is it sanitary?" He sat up.

"Of course, it is. Artesian, it's reported."

Jolene hopped up, circled the bench, and walked ten paces to the spewing well. Bending forward, she sipped from the flowing mineral water—cold, arctic in nature, and most refreshing.

"Scoot over." David booted Jolene out of the way with a taut hip and drank from the fountain like a thirsty camel.

A few minutes later, they were seated on the bench again, eyes locked on each other. Jolene rolled her shoulders.

"Is this trip about getting a divorce?" she asked.

"No, Jolene." Eyes lit up with surprise. "Do you want one?"

"Don't make this trip about what I want, please!"

"Well, at least the cancer didn't steal your spunk." He pulled a letter from his shirt pocket. "Take a gander, love."

"What's this, David?" She rolled the letter over in her hand. "It's postmarked from Japan. I don't understand." Her forehead furrowed as she locked inquisitive eyes on him.

"Do you remember the important client I signed last winter?"

"Yes." It was the day she told him about her cancer. "As I recall, your two business associates took you to the Bahamas to celebrate the victory," Jolene said, "over Christmas holidays."

"There's more. My client, Hoyt Claymore, had lived in Tokyo most of his life. His parents were Christian missionaries."

"Okay." Jolene grew more interested.

"He told me about his work in Japan when I treated him to a golf game at the country club in February," David revealed. "We've become pretty good friends over the last few months."

"That's nice." Jolene raised an eyebrow for more info.

"Anyhow, to shorten my story, it turns out that Hoyt's wife comes from a prosperous Japanese family. Sosha's father earned his business degree at California Tech and returned to Japan to launch an insurance company. He's expanded into ten countries."

"Good for him." Jolene failed to see David's connection.

"Well," David wickedly grinned, "Hoyt asked me if I'd be interested in running my own branch of the company."

Surprise suffused Jolene's expression.

"Needless to say, I said yes, but lacked the required funds to launch a business." David's hazel eyes brightened.

"Maybe you should just read the letter."

Jolene unfolded the pages: *Mr. Salisbury: Hoyt speaks highly of you and tells me you are a fine insurance salesperson. Currently, I have a branch offices operating in Seattle, Washington and Chicago, Illinois. I would like to open up a branch in the heart of the South. Are you interested?*

"David!" Jolene slapped the letter. "This is an amazing opportunity! Managing your own insurance company has been your dream ever since I've known you."

"Yes, it has." His gaze dropped to the grassy earth.

"What?"

"I'm sorry to say, there are extenuating circumstances that has prompted me to accept this offer." His gaze targeted Jolene.

"Did you do something to lose your job?"

"No. . ." David drew back like he'd been slapped. "I'm doing great at the office. Work couldn't be any better."

"Okay . . ." she'd assumed from his former remarks that nothing short of death could drag him from Baton Rouge. "So what has changed that prompts you to leave a lucrative job?"

"Uh, there are things going on at the office I didn't want to tell you about while you were ill." He frowned. "I learned something astounding while I was away at Christmas."

"In the Bahamas, you mean." Jolene braced for bad news.

David's hazel eyes fell softly on Jolene, his mouth open with no words forthcoming, as if concrete had been poured.

"Don't stop there!" She pounded his arm with a fist.

"My cohorts, Ben and Lyle—they're lovers."

"They're gay?" Jolene scowled. "But they were both married."

"I know. But homosexuality is a choice, and they've crossed over." David stared up at the blue sky. "I've been making preparations to leave the firm ever since I found out. I didn't want to tell you then because I knew it would upset you."

"Yes, it has." She absorbed the shocking news. "I knew they weren't living right, morally, but I thought their marriages broke up because they were cheating on their wives. With other women—who would've thought?" She shrugged.

"I just can't work there anymore."

"I understand," she said, realizing she had David pegged wrong. He'd kept this secret to protect her. "What comes next?"

"I plan to accept Sojimona's offer and open up a branch office. I can do that anywhere in the south." David smiled. "Where would you like to live?" He fondly clutched her hand.

Jolene's sparkling eyes widened with speculation. "Charlotte?"

"I said anywhere. We have to find a house first."

Jolene thought Jesus might rapture her right there as David draped his right arm around her shoulders and pulled her close.

"Money's in the bank from the sale of our house and our furniture is in storage. All we need to do is make arrangements."

"To move here, you mean."

"All we need is a solid plan."

"I don't know what to say, David." Emotions trickled over Jolene like a warm spring rain. "I thought our marriage was over, that you didn't love me anymore." Tears clouded her vision.

"I had a long talk with Burt James," he explained. "Our pastor helped me see that our marriage is worth saving. From the way I feel right now, it won't take much to rekindle that fire."

"Oh, David!" Jolene planted a lingering kiss on his lips. "There is no other man for me! I've been so unhappy apart from you. I was afraid coming to Tennessee had ruined everything."

"We both erred."

They had a tender moment of intimacy.

"I hope the police don't arrest us for indecent behavior." Jolene tenderly bit her husband's ear as lovers sometimes do.

"As long as they put us in the same cell, I'm fine by it."

She pulled away. "So we need a plan. How can I help?"

"Have you considered getting licensed to sell real estate in Tennessee? I don't want you putting your career on hold."

"Actually, I've done very little thinking about my own future." Jolene told David about Nancy's ongoing drama with her mother.

"Claire won't forgive Nancy for getting pregnant in high school, dropping out before graduation, and marrying Buck."

"That would upset any mother," he said.

"It gets worse. To spite Claire, Nancy has birthed five children in her twenties and would have more if she could afford it."

David chuckled. "That's quite a family feud."

"Nancy is musically talented," Jolene said. "She has a marvelous contra-alto voice and writes beautiful songs." She paused to reflect. "She should have been on stage long ago."

"Except . . ." David rolled his hand for her to continue.

"Nancy realizes her anger has only hurt everyone around her. She wants to change, be a more forgiving person, but Claire is making it difficult." Jolene told him about her uncomfortable conversation with Nancy's mother on Easter Sunday.

"What?"

"On a good note, I sense Claire is as tired of the feud as Nancy is. But they're both too stubborn to apologize."

"So what is your plan, babe?"

Jolene caught David's eye. "Claire is spending more time than previously with her grandchildren. It's obvious she loves them dearly. In fact, she bought all five new outfits for Easter and would've taken them to church herself if Buck and Nancy hadn't."

"Even that sounds like a contest." David chuckled.

"Laugh if you will but it's all foreplay. I think Nancy and Claire are close to making up." Jolene blushed.

"Foreplay . . .?" His gaze widened with interest.

"I have to find a way to get Nancy entered into the singing contest in July," Jolene continued. "Claire has blocked her application for five years, and it isn't fair."

David shook his head. "I guess it's hard for some people to forgive. Could we back up to the part about foreplay?"

"Obviously, I've done everything I could to bring them together." Jolene stretched her arms skyward. "Nancy's children need their grandmother, and Claire needs her daughter."

"This is about you, too, Jolene." David realized. "You've been mad at your father since Kate died and Kirk remarried. You've carried guilt for years, running away from your feelings."

"How did you get so smart: David Salisbury?"

"What goes around comes around," he said.

"Yes, so true." Jolene spied two red birds in the tree.

"Don't be so hard on yourself." David patted her knee.

"For me, this trip to Tennessee has been like a sabbatical. I've done a lot of soul-searching, and realized it was selfish of me to exclude my parents from my life. I ignored Mama when she was sick with cancer and dying. I refused to attend Daddy's wedding when he did married Olivia. But I can't undo the past."

"I'm sorry, Jolene. I suppose we've both forgotten what love requires," he said. "It's long-suffering and forgiving. It seeks no harm." He peered into Jolene's eyes. "Can we start over?"

"Does fire burn?"

Jolene leaped toward David, arms tightly wrapped around his neck as she kissed him firmly on his wet lips.

"How's that for an answer?"

They laughed and kissed, finished their walk, then checked into a hotel. A little honey-making goes a long way. Later, Jolene phoned Nancy to tell her she was spending the weekend with David. They were making plans to move to Tennessee.

♣26

WHEN JOLENE ARRIVED at Nancy's late Monday morning, she was anxious to share the nitty-gritty details of her visit with David. "We made up." Jolene's face was radiant. "He really loves me, Nancy." She danced around the kitchen like a diva.

"Did he say why he'd been so distant?"

"I'm still peeved at him for that," Jolene mouthed. "He thought keeping his secret would ease my mind. Wrong."

"What kind of secret?" Nancy inquired while stirring up a pound cake for supper.

"The Bahamas, over Christmas, what happened," Jolene replied. "I can't believe I read David so wrong."

"Are you going to tell me or not?" Nancy huffed, pouring the batter into a greased tube pan. "Best friends don't keep secrets."

"It's about David's two business associates . . ." Jolene eyed Nancy. "They're involved." No need to elaborate.

Nancy's hands flew to her mouth. "No wonder David kept quiet. If you'd known, what would you have done?"

"Flown straight to Baton Rouge and confronted him about quitting his job and moving to Tennessee," Jolene admitted. "I guess he needed more time to plan his exit."

"So he is moving here." Nancy smiled. "David did right by not telling you. Two wars on his hands would've been too much."

"I thought he was in love with someone else."

"But he wasn't, and the wait has been worth it."

"Yes." Jolene was grateful for a virtuous husband.

"So, has David quit his job yet?" Nancy set the oven timer and began making a pot of coffee.

"No, but the equity from our house sale will simplify things."

"Selling was smart." Nancy sat down to rest.

"After his Bahamas's trip, David talked to our pastor, Dr. Burt James—who I might add is an inspiration to everyone. Burt helped David see that praying about his decision before acting on it was the wise thing to do. That's why he didn't tell me."

"Isn't that what you've been doing, Jolene?" Nancy concluded. "Allowing God to lead you through a valley of suffering while searching for a rainbow sign?"

"What beautiful imagery! You should write that song."

"Both you and David have been on a journey, though your paths were separated for a time. Maybe God intended the rainbow's end to work out this way," Nancy said.

"God is so good!" Jolene rejoiced. "He's on time all the time. He always had a good plan. That's what trust is all about."

"Well, I'm certainly glad God led you to my doorstep. If your car hadn't stalled that day we might never have met."

"And if you hadn't left your husband for the umpteenth time, you might not have picked up a total stranger." Jolene smiled.

"I supposed you believe God is always at work in our lives."

"That's what the Bible says."

A mist clouded Nancy's emerald eyes.

Jolene sat down at the breakfast table.

"When my mother treated me so badly after she learned I was pregnant, I quit going to church." Nancy heaved a breath. "I blamed God for letting me get pregnant, when you *know* having sex was my choice." She took in a huge breath. "I want God's forgiveness. I want to feel the freedom to worship Him again."

"I understand, sweetheart. We all do things we regret."

"I was young and so stupid." Nancy burst into tears.

"And in love," Jolene noted. "People in love let their emotions rule them, not their brains."

"I wish I could talk to my mother like I talk to you." Nancy dried her cheeks with the back of her hands. "If my mother could find it in her heart to forgive me, God will, too."

"Nancy, God will anyhow. 'Come unto me you who are weak and heavy laden and I will give you rest,'" Jolene quoted the Bible. "We've both been looking for that sweet rest."

"It's about doing the right thing, isn't it?"

"Partially," Jolene said. "But no one can be good enough to earn God's gift of grace. Faith leads us down a path of conviction, so that we're ready to ask for God's forgiveness."

"Jesus made a way for us by His death on the cross."

"Yes, He did, Nancy."

The young mother felt the Holy Spirit flooding her soul.

"After dying on a cross and rising from the grave," Nancy said, "Jesus entered Heaven and offered His own pure blood."

"All we need to do is accept His gift of grace."

"See, I was listening in Sunday school."

Both Jolene and Nancy needed a moment to meditate on their futures, eyes locked on one another with admiration.

"So what's next for you, Jolene?"

"David and I need somewhere to live."

"For a real estate agent, that should be a breeze."

Jolene reassured Nancy that what they'd discussed would be their secret. "I can see that your act of confession was difficult."

Nancy winked a smile and a tear. "I do feel better after sharing my troubled heart. It's good food for the soul."

"As far as finding a house, I'll pop in on a realty company and talk to a broker," Jolene said. "I'm thinking of getting licensed to sell Tennessee properties. Helping people is a joy."

"You've certainly helped our family," Nancy said. "How soon do you think you'll need a house?"

"David told me to start looking now."

"I'm glad you and David have a plan, I don't."

"Well, I do," Jolene revealed. "I'm meeting Claire for lunch tomorrow at the B & B." Silence ruled for thirty seconds.

"What will you say to her?" Nancy nervously asked.

"I'm not sure, sweetheart. Hopefully, the Holy Spirit will guide me in saying something that brings reconciliation between a very proper mom and a wonderful, unpredictable daughter."

"If prayer has wings, it's already flying." Nancy was starting to feel optimistic. "Thank you, it means the world to me."

Nancy gave Jolene a hug. "I love you like a real mom."

Overwhelmed, Jolene placed a hand over her heart.

"I wish I could be a fly on the B& B's wall." Nancy chuckled. "Claire's like talking to a stubborn mule."

Jolene's eyebrows lifted. "Not if I have my way."

♣27

AT THE RESTAURANT, Jolene spied Beverly standing behind the counter collecting money from lunch-goers. Customers milled around the freestanding shelves, perusing the resale books. A group of children, congregating in one corner, scrambled around on their knees as they thumbed through picture books.

Tuesday was always extra busy at the B & B since customers received ten percent luncheon discounts. Jolene stepped aside as people pushed through the front door and moved about.

In the dining room, Jolene spotted Sally Crouch seated at a table with three other women. "Hi, I'm Jolene Salisbury," she introduced herself to the pastor's wife. "I attended your church on Easter and was touched by Brother Crouch's sermon."

"Why, thank you, Jolene." Sally proudly introduced her three friends. "Are you moving to the area or just visiting?"

"Actually, I'm currently looking for property," she replied. "I've been staying with Buck and Nancy Blake since January."

"Claire's daughter . . . you've been staying there?"

"Yes," Jolene reported to Sally's curious friend. "Our house in Baton Rouge recently sold, so my husband and I are trying to decide where we want to live." She wasn't sharing details.

"Do you have family here?" Sally asked.

"I grew up in Charlotte, but my parents are deceased."

"I'm sorry." A sincere expression flooded Sally's expression, her pastel blue eyes dressing up her plump face. "Come visit us again on Sunday. I'll tell Danny about meeting you."

"Thanks, I'd like that." Jolene glanced around for Claire.

"Would you like to join us for lunch?" Sally inquired.

"Thanks, but I'm meeting someone." Jolene stepped aside for a senior couple to pass. "If this crowd is any indication, the food here must be delicious." Tables were filling up.

"The cook does a good job," Sally's friend June piped.

"I've had Beverly's coffee up front, and it's excellent, too." Jolene was starting to feel Claire might be a no-show.

"Tuesdays here are the busiest. The special discount, you know, draws a crowd." June prattled on. "The working crowd typically opts for hotdogs or hamburgers at the soda shop located on the other side of the square. Shakes there are marvelous."

"Every town has their restaurant favorites." Jolene was about ready to give up on Claire and leave. "I'm glad business is good."

"Oh, Dickson County is growing by leaps and bounds," Sally said. "Our quaint country culture draws people from all over. Californians are sick and tired of taxes and come in droves."

"Except for being sick . . ." Jolene regretted mentioning her malady, "I've enjoyed my brief few months here."

"Cancer, wasn't it?" June's lips pursed. "You're okay, now?"

Nothing is secret in a small town.

"As far as I know . . ."

Sally looked relieved. "Surviving cancer, that must make you feel like a million dollars. I had a first cousin who didn't."

"That's too bad." Money won't buy good health.

"If the person you're meeting doesn't show up," Sally said, "we'll pull up another chair and you can join us."

"Actually, I'm meeting Claire Wilkes," Jolene revealed.

"Maybe you should give her a holler," Gwen, Sally's quiet friend, suggested. "She might be busy in the kitchen."

Busy? As in rude, Jolene contemplated.

"Did I hear my name called?" The mayor's wife hustled over to the table, smiling like a June bride. "Hello, Sally. Girls." Intense green eyes skittered to Jolene. "Ready, dear?"

Dear? Every head in the dining room turned on Claire at hearing her lyrical voice. *Mrs. Popularity.* Jolene thought.

"Good to see you again, girls. Enjoy your meals."

"I've reserved us a private table in the back room," Claire told Jolene and began walking like Miss Astor boarding the Titanic. Jolene waved bye to Sally and trailed Claire.

She suspected Claire's stormy personality made as many waves on life's ship as the Titanic. They passed through a door under the curved staircase and entered a private dining room.

Against the outer wall was a red-brick fireplace with a decorative metal insert. An antique, gold-rimmed mirror hung over the fireplace, glimmering with dancing reflections from the twelve-tiered candelabra burning brightly on the cherry mantel.

The bead-board ceilings, no doubt original, met with dainty floral wallpaper covering the four tall walls. To further the room's ambiance a ruby teardrop light fixture, draping from a gold chain attached to the ceiling, suffused the atmosphere with a rosy glow.

From what Beverly said, Jolene knew most of B &B's antique sales items, like handmade quilts and glassware, were displayed on the second floor. The two upstairs bedrooms were reserved for overnight paid guests when not closed during the winter season.

Jolene appreciated the trouble Claire had gone to in making the exquisite dining room a pleasant place to dine. The four square tables in the room were furbished with centerpieces of petite roses in green vases. Floral china, sparkling silverware, and cream colored linen napkins, completed the settings.

The private dining area oozed with 18th-century charm.

"Have a seat, dear," Claire said to Jolene. "Beverly will bring in our lunch shortly." She proceeded to fill a rattan-backed chair.

Dear? Jolene sat down across from Claire.

A perfect hostess, Nancy's mother plucked her napkin from a wine glass and spread it across her lap. Her frilly blouse, a brilliant pink, peeked from the opening of her beige linen pantsuit. In an unconscious gesture, she primped her recently coffered bottle-blond hairdo, as if Kent had arranged every curl and sprayed it.

Nancy had inherited her mother's lovely emerald eyes, the only physical resemblance. Personality wise, they were at opposite poles. Then Claire's stony gaze fell on Jolene. "Now that we're here and seated, what did you want to talk to me about?"

Who was Claire fooling? This was game time.

Jolene usually wasn't nervous with people, but Claire's façade of superiority made her seem unapproachable. Had Nancy grown up under such scrutiny? What about her father? Children afraid to express their true feelings often rebel against parents. Maybe Nancy's love affair with Buck was more about defying her mother than sex. Well, it was time to find out, or butt out of the family squabble. Jolene cleared her throat and jumped in.

"I'd like to talk about you, *dear*," she uttered.

"*Me*. How dull . . ." Claire's laugh was musical.

"That's not what your daughter tells me."

"Is that so?" Claire's gaze bore into Jolene. "Must we be so serious? Since this is your first meal at my B & B, I took the liberty to order the chicken salad for our lunches. The chef's yummy yeast rolls are to die for . . ." she cupped her pampered hands. "Oh, and you'll be delighted with our blackberry tea."

So Claire is not going to make this easy. Jolene coddled a smile, admiring the owner's tactics in avoidance. A full-fledged control freak, she'd even selected their menu and beverages in advance.

"What brought you to Charlotte?" Claire asked.

"My parents grew up here. Kate Gilmore was my mother's maiden name. Did you know her?" Jolene unfolded her napkin.

"Granny Mercer probably knew her." Claire rang a dinner bell to summon Beverly. "Where is that girl? I don't know why we're meeting on a busy Tuesday." She fanned herself with the menu. "I despise eating late, it gives me indigestion."

"I'm fine with a late lunch," Jolene said.

The diva winced. "I'm complaining too much, aren't I?"

"Actually, I came here more for the conversation than to fill my stomach," Jolene revealed. "I want to know you better."

"Well, my goodness!" Claire scoffed with laughter. "I'm an open book, just ask anyone in town who knows me."

How can I get through to someone like Claire?

"I commend you for your success with B & B." Jolene worked at being diplomatic. She wasn't going to get on Claire's good side by competing with her testiness.

"That's nice of you to say." Claire took a sip of ice water.

"I've met your mother," Jolene submitted another topic. "Nancy took me to see Granny Mercer. She's quaint."

Claire laughed again. "Mother is a riot."

"Did you grow up in Charlotte?" Jolene asked.

"White Bluff," Claire replied. "My family moved there when I was fifteen." Answers were short and specific.

"What about Nancy's father?"

Am I prying too much?

"Deceased," Claire said. "I assume Nancy already told you."

"Yes, she did. I was hoping to learn more about him."

"Why do you care?" Claire mouthed. "It's all water under the bridge now. Benjamin Wilkes is my second husband, a godsend."

"I can't imagine how hard it would be to lose a husband." Nancy's attorney father had died in an automobile accident five years before. Elaborating on the subject wouldn't be productive.

"Were you raised in Charlotte?" Claire asked Jolene as the door opened and Beverly entered carrying a large silver tray.

After placing it on a bi-fold serving stand, Claire's niece carefully filled their china cups with steamy, blackberry tea.

"How are you doing, Jolene?" Beverly asked.

"Great! Claire and I are getting to know one another." Jolene inhaled the bold flavor of the tea.

"I always pray before a meal." Claire bowed her head. "Lord, bless our food and keep us in Your Almighty hand."

All the right moves, Jolene thought, *yet so very cold.*

"About growing up here, the answer is yes," Jolene said.

"Aunt Claire?" Beverly said. "There's still a bunch of people coming in for lunch. I'm pretty busy holdin' down the fort, taking orders. It may be a bit before I can bring your salads."

"Now, don't panic, Beverly. Call Ann and ask if she can help out for a couple of hours." Claire dabbed her lips with her napkin. "We can't afford to send folks away, now can we?"

"No, ma'am," Beverly said, glancing at Jolene.

"Shoo, get going. Time's wasting."

Beverly hustled from the room like a frightened rabbit.

"She's really a nice girl," Jolene offered, sipping on her tea.

"My sister's child, too dumb I'm afraid to go to college."

Jolene was not surprised at Claire's statement since it fit the profile Nancy had painted. Jolene took her time sipping on tea while Claire rambled on about social issues of no interest to her.

But wasn't this lunch about bonding? Jolene asked a few more questions, but received no answers that mattered. Twenty minutes into drinking tea, Beverly brought in their crisp salads.

"Thank you, Beverly. Did Ann arrive yet?"

"We got it covered, Aunt Claire."

Jolene was not disappointed with lunch. The pecan chicken salad was delicious. After the last bite of raisin pudding, she set down her fork and made firm eye contact with Claire.

"May I be frank?"

Claire's lips pursed. "I thought you were."

"I came here today to talk to you about Nancy."

"I know that." Claire asked Beverly to bring them each a coffee with extra cream. "My daughter can be quite charming."

A mask of defiance invaded Claire's expression. What Nancy's mother didn't say made Jolene inwardly shiver.

"As you already know," Claire continued, "my daughter is quite talented. She can do practically anything musical."

"I've heard her sing," Jolene offered. "She's good."

"What you don't know . . ." Claire's cold green eyes targeted Jolene, "is that I paid dearly for her music lessons. No telling how much I've spent on that ungrateful child! Nancy was being groomed for the Nashville stage and threw it all away for Buck!"

Wow, Jolene had trouble comprehending Claire's bitterness.

"So, are you saying that your five grandchildren weren't worth the sacrifice?" *Let's get to the heart of what's important!*

Claire's lips knotted, a frown set in her expression.

"Who are you to judge? She embarrassed me. But since you have no children, I wouldn't expect you to understand."

Jolene felt a jolt in her spirit.

"Claire, this is not about you!" Jolene tried to penetrate that hard façade. "Nancy has a dream of her own."

"She'd better concentrate on feeding and clothing those children," Claire countered. "I can't help her now."

"Maybe you can," Jolene said. "Nancy wants to sign up for the singing contest held in your backyard every July."

Claire glared at Jolene. "My answer is still no."

"Please reconsider," Jolene pleaded.

"It's too late for Nancy to have a career. Who would take care of the children while she's travels all over the country? *Buck?* Ha! He's gone half the time in that rundown truck of his. I don't want Nancy starting something again that she'll never finish."

"I'm sorry you feel that way." Jolene realized Claire wasn't going to change her mind today. The bonding was officially over.

Maybe, another time . . .

"I hope you're satisfied, Jolene. You've upset me."

"I apologize if that's what I've done."

Jolene needed a God-idea that would bridge the huge gap that existed between mother and daughter. Only Jesus could make a way for their reconciliation. Claire was through talking.

"Okay, thanks for taking time for me." Jolene tossed her napkin and stood up. "What do I owe you for lunch?"

"For the excellent conversation, nothing," Claire replied.

Out the door in two seconds, Jolene walked briskly through the B & B dining room and exited through the front door.

The fresh spring air had never felt so invigorating.

♣28

DAVID PHONED TWO days after Jolene's lunch with Claire Wilkes. He was flying to Tokyo to sign a contract with Mr. Sojimona and receive training. Could she go with him?

Jolene declined on the premise her immune system had not fully recovered from chemo. Exposure to new viruses in another country didn't seem wise. In a hurry, he ended the conversation.

The odor of percolating coffee sifting from the kitchen beckoned Jolene. She found Nancy at the counter icing a chocolate mousse cake. "What's the occasion?" she asked.

"None special, I just thought the family would enjoy a delicious dessert. Who called?" Nancy topped off the iced cake with rainbow candy sprinkles then turned her gaze on Jolene.

"David. He's flying to Tokyo to sign a contract with Mr. Sojimona and receive management training," she shared. "He's opening up an insurance branch in Dickson County."

Nancy licked white icing from the spatula. "That's terrific."

"Yes, it is."

Nancy's lazy gaze drifted out the back kitchen window where her five children were playing in the mowed yard. On Buck's last trucking run, he'd brought home two half-grown collies as gifts. A bunch of whooping and hollering and barking was going on.

"Cloy told me your hound died from old age last summer," Jolene made conversation. "I guess the kids were upset."

"We all cried. Old Soldier lasted seventeen years. He was Buck's dog when we married. Not just a dog, he was family."

Nancy washed the breakfast bowls in a sudsy sink, rinsed and upturned them to dry on the drain board. While drying her hands on a terry-cloth towel, she said, "Care for some coffee?"

"Always, I'll get the cream." Jolene removed a carton from the fridge. "It's been the best spring I can remember in awhile. Thank you so much for inviting me to stay with your family."

"Let's not forget all the favors you've done for me and Buck. I don't think we'd still be married if I hadn't met you."

"It was God's plan." Jolene smiled.

"And you are His angel of mercy."

Jolene added cream and sugar to her mug and trotted over to the breakfast table to sit down. "God has a way of working things out. We helped each other. That's how friendship works."

"Yeah, it is." Nancy craned her head in thought. "You know, it's too pretty a day to stay indoors. I have an idea!" She tossed her apron. "What'd ya say we go on a picnic?"

"I have no plans, count me in." Jolene smiled.

"Finish your cup of Joe and I'll tell the kids."

Nancy dashed out the back door in her plaid shorts and a yellow tee, red hair streaming behind her like threads of fire.

Since school had let out for the summer, excitement stirred among the young. The screen door flapped as Nancy returned.

"Cloy is putting the dogs in the barn and they're coming inside to get ready," she told Jolene. "Picnics rib them up."

"Where's the best place to take them?"

"I heard Dickson has updated their play equipment at Buckner Park. If the pool is warm enough, they can swim."

"Count me out." Jolene wasn't going to flaunt her white body and loose arm flesh. She needed serious gym time.

"Okay, we'll mark off swimming. You can supervise the girls on the gym set while I watch the boys knock around a few baseballs in the outfield. Then we'll pig out on some food."

"Sounds like a plan." Jolene smiled. Sunning her body in the open air was appealing. She wanted to look healthy when David returned from Japan and came for another visit.

"Are those the only shoes you have?" Nancy leaned over and tied the strings on her dirty sneakers. "What size?"

"Eights," Jolene replied.

"I just happen to have an extra pair you can wear."

Nancy erected her slender body and dashed to the fridge to explore its contents as the children raced indoors, pushing and shoving each other out of the way as they competed for a drink of water at the sink faucet. The sight was almost comical.

"Kids . . .! One at a time, where's your manners?"

"Nancy, why don't I make the sandwiches while you help the little ones get ready," Jolene suggested. "I know there's plenty of peanut butter in the pantry. And didn't I see sliced ham?"

"Thanks, Jolene. I need to help Catherine and Carla wash up and change clothes. They've been playing in the mud, and I'm ashamed to take them out in public lookin' like hobos."

"What about the boys?" Jolene asked.

"They're fine. Qualify for admittance to the ballpark. By the time they wallow in dirt, you won't see their clothes anyhow."

Jolene washed her hands and dried them on a towel, too late to stop Nancy's youngest boy from swiping a finger over the cake icing and licking it off. Embarrassed, he ran out of the kitchen.

Laughter and giggles followed Nancy and the girls down the hall to their bedroom. Jolene was beginning to feel part of their family, more human as chemicals slowly leached out of her body. On a vegetable and fruit regiment, she hoped to lose ten pounds.

Twenty minutes later, the picnic basket was packed with fruit, a variety of sandwiches, and plenty of salty and sweet snacks. An ice chest loaded with a jug of water and cartons of juices sat on the floor by the backdoor. Nancy came into the kitchen with the girls and asked where her sons were? They were already outside.

All Jolene needed to do before leaving was fetch her purse.

"Oh, I forgot to tell you that Mitzi phoned while you were taking a walk this morning." Nancy looked at Jolene. "She said to call her, it was important." The idea lingered a moment.

"I'd better do that now before we leave." Jolene used the kitchen phone to ring her cousin. The line rang only twice.

"Hi, Mitzi, what's up?"

"It's Jack, Jolene. He's in trouble."

"What's happened?"

In the next few minutes, Jolene learned that Mitzi's husband had suffered a gall bladder attack and was taken to Vanderbilt Hospital earlier that morning. Jack's condition was critical.

"I'm so sorry, Mitzi. Is there something I can do?"

"I know it's an imposition, but could you come over to the house and spend the night? Dorothy's two girls are staying with us while she and Harold are vacationing two weeks in Spain."

"Of course, I will." Jolene made eye contact with Nancy. Plans change in an emergency. "You should be with Jack while the doctors determine how best to treat him."

Nancy rolled her eyes, hands splayed.

"As soon as I pack, I'll drive over," Jolene told Mitzi.

"Hurry," she said. "I can't leave the girls alone."

Jolene glanced at the kitchen wall clock. *9:30.*

"I'm on my way now." She ended the call.

"I guess you have other plans."

"I'm afraid so. Jack was admitted to the hospital with a gall bladder attack this morning and Mitzi needs for me to stay with her two granddaughters. I don't know how long I'll be gone."

"No problem, I can handle things around here."

"You're sure?" Home alone with five children would be a challenge. "When will Buck be back?"

"Not until Friday. Go. I survived before you moved in." Nancy buffered her emotions well. "Mitzi needs you worse."

"I'm sorry I can't help out with the picnic."

Nancy threw a hand. "If the battle gets too thick around here, I'll call timeout and send the kids to their rooms."

"What about the picnic?"

"It'll have to wait another day."

"The children will be so disappointed."

"Nothing new around our house," Nancy muttered.

"You could ask Claire to go with you."

"I don't think so. You know how she was on Easter."

"Give your mother another chance."

"Yeah," Nancy huffed, "one more chance to stab me in the back. Go to Mitzi's! The kids and I will be just fine."

"I feel bad abandoning you like this," Jolene said.

"Such is life." Nancy stared at her packed basket. "We'll have our picnic in the backyard. It will still be fun."

"We're not going to the park?" Nine-year-old Craig stood in the open doorway frowning. "Mom . . .! You promised!"

"Promises are meant to be broken," Nancy stoically uttered. "We'll go to the park another day when your dad is home."

"Aw shucks! It ain't fair."

Clearly Craig was disappointed. Jolene knelt beside the lad, eye level, and said, "This is my fault, Craig. Don't blame your mother. There's been an emergency and I have to go away for a few days." Carla bawled as she stood in the open doorway.

"Me got bee bit." She tugged at Nancy's shirttail.

"Com 'ere, Carla!" Mom scooped up Carla and carried her to the kitchen sink where she applied a wad of wet soda powder to the affected skin. "I told you not to go on the front porch!"

Carla cried even harder.

"Daddy has to knock down the wasp nest when he gits back. Please don't go out there again. Promise mama?"

Carla screamed louder as a fight between the boys brewed at the back of the house, an argument over the TV remote.

The noise level dramatically increased.

"Remind me again why I became a mother?" Nancy blew a loose curl off her forehead and headed to the playroom to negotiate a peace settlement. Jolene coddled Carla and promised her that the red knot on her arm would soon feel better.

Jolene couldn't leave Nancy alone with the chaos.

Fifteen minutes later, calm pervaded the household. Nancy had her five children seated at the kitchen table, happily licking cherry Popsicles. Ragged out, Nancy looked liked she'd lost a major battle. Jolene felt so sorry for the young mother.

"Don't be so stubborn, Nancy. Call Claire and ask her to go with you to the park. It's summertime. The children need to frolic and have fun. I'm betting Claire will be appreciative."

"Don't count on it." Nancy grimaced, fizzling out.

"Please, Mom. We promise to be real good," Craig said.

"No fighting," Cloy sputtered, "promise."

"Think about it, Nancy. You need her permission to enter the July 4th contest. Use this day to close the nasty gap."

"I'm not a hypocrite like my mother."

"No one said you were," Jolene defended the cause.

No response.

"Call it practical diplomacy," Jolene said. "I'm not talking about what you do today. Don't let forgiveness slip away."

Nancy didn't respond.

"Someone has to take the first step, Nancy. It appears Claire won't. You're a better person than she is. You are beautiful, strong-willed, and talented. There's not a better mother to her children anywhere in the universe. Do the right thing."

"I'm not so sure." Nancy mulled over the idea.

"Think of it this way: it's something God wants you to do."

Tears roiled in Nancy's glazed eyes. "Well, I guess it won't hurt to see if Claire's busy. But don't expect me to apologize."

Jolene smiled, lips trembling, a small battle won.

"It ain't gonna happen!" Nancy punctuated her position.

♣29

JOLENE WAS ON the interstate by 10:30 a.m. and made it to Murfreesboro in an hour and a half. She found Mitzi pacing the floor, fit to be tied; worried to death that Jack might die. His temperature had hiked despite the medication he'd received.

"I'm afraid something else is wrong with him. What if it's not his gall bladder? What if his appendix has ruptured?"

Fear capsized Mitzi as she eyed Jolene.

"Don't think the worst, honey." Jolene embraced her cousin. "The doctors will find out what's wrong with Jack and take care of the problem. That's what they do every day of their lives, save others. God is our ever-present help. Trust me, I'm right."

Mitzi let out a tortured sigh.

"Okay, I'll try to keep it together, for Jack's sake."

"Good. Now go see your husband. The children and I will be fine. I've had a lot of experience entertaining the young. "

"A chicken casserole is in the fridge for lunch and I've rented five movies for them to watch when you run out of things to do."

"We'll be fine," Jolene reassured Mitzi.

"Oh, did I tell you my son Chris is meeting me at the hospital to talk to Jack's doctor about his condition?" Mitzi hurriedly tugged on her jacket and grabbed her heavy purse. "Am I forgetting anything?" She nervously glanced around the den.

"No, go! Don't worry about a thing," Jolene said. "The girls know me, and I've learned how to manage children pretty well after living with Buck and Nancy for five months."

"You're a godsend." Mitzi hugged Jolene. "It's so great to have family close by to help out in troubled times like these."

"Yes, it is. I have some news, too. Good news."

"I could use a little of that."

"I'll share with you later."

"Okay, I'll leave my cell phone on in case you need me."

Mitzi headed for the kitchen door that led to the garage, taking a moment to hug Amy and Priscilla before leaving.

"Mind Jolene, okay?"

"We'll be good, Granny."

"I know you will."

Jolene stood at the front window, watching as Mitzi backed her SUV out of the driveway and sped down the street.

"Are you hungry? Granny has a good lunch made for us." Jolene motioned for the girls to go into the kitchen. "Afterwards, we'll all play a game of Junior Scrabble."

"Yeah . . .!" They leaped on the sofa and bounced around like kangaroos on a trampoline. "Off the sofa, girls, I know Granny doesn't allow you to do that!" Jolene sternly cautioned them.

In response, Amy jumped to the floor, feet synchronized for the landing. Priscilla, not as coordinated, fell hard on her knees and yelped. Jolene helped her up. "Are you hurt, Priscilla?"

She shook her head no but was rubbing her knees.

"How 'bout I give rewards for doing good deeds?"

"Yea!" they screamed. "Ice cream, cookies . . .?"

"Let me surprise you, okay?"

Jolene led the way into the kitchen, a hand on each little head to guide them. "Need some help cleaning the table, Priscilla?"

"I can do it by myself." The little girl scrubbed the table with a wet sponge then dried it with a wad of paper towels. "All done, just like Granny!" She brushed her little hands together.

The chicken casserole was served in bowls. Jolene had a glass of ice tea while they drank glasses of cold milk. After placing the dirty dishes in the dishwasher, she reminded them about the game.

"Can we have dessert?" Amy asked.

Jolene had been warned that the girls had a sweet tooth like their father. Allowable desserts were stowed in Mitzi's organized pantry. "Sure." Jolene served them each a glazed sugar cookie.

"I'll get Scrabble out of the cabinet," Amy volunteered.

"And I'll sponge off the messy kitchen table," Priscilla offered, the cookie crumbling from hand to floor.

Jolene laughed. "I hope you have a dictionary handy."

"We spell real good for our age," Amy offered.

"Good to hear, I may need some help."

The board game lasted only an hour before the girls tired.

After putting away the Scrabble game, Amy wanted to watch the video about a bear that got lost in the woods. The girls loved the colorful animation. So Jolene put on a children's movie that would last an hour, but she had four others in the wing.

Mitzi had planned a simple supper, microwave hotdogs with Ketchup on buns and salty chips. To finish the day on a positive note, Jolene read the girls books until their eyelids drooped.

After tucking them in bed around nine, Jolene collapsed on the den sofa to relax and read a *Home & Garden* magazine.

Caring for children was no piece of cake, she realized. One needed a degree in proficient meal-planning, clinical house cleaning, and sensible recreational planning. It almost took a psychological profiler to master the fine art of discipline.

But Jolene had to admit that being around children was immensely fulfilling. Parenting was an opportunity to mold a little person into a responsible citizen, teach morals by example, and pass on ethnic customs. Without babies, humanity would cease.

Maybe she and David should adopt a baby, an infant whose mother was either physically or financially incapable of caring for it. Jolene smiled. A baby is a *he* or a *she*, not an *it*.

In fact, orphanages around the world were crying out for stable families to adopt abandoned children. Or, they could take another route. *Invitro fertilization* had become a popular solution.

Jolene had read about the procedure in a magazine. There were young women willing to be surrogates, for a fee, of course.

The idea of rearing a child to carry on David's genetic line appealed to Jolene. It was certainly an option they should discuss.

The land line phone suddenly rang in the kitchen, snapping Jolene to attention. "It must be Mitzi." She rushed to answer it.

"Who is this? Where's my mother?" Mitzi's daughter Dorothy asked, failing to recognize Jolene's voice.

"It's me, Dorothy. Jolene. Your mother is at the hospital with your father. I'm spending the night with the girls."

"Why? What's wrong with Dad?"

"A gall bladder attack," Jolene replied. "But there might be some other health issues involved. Mitzi is very concerned but she's trying to be brave for Jack's sake. That's all I know."

"I see. Are the girls awake so I can speak to them?"

"I'll check."

Jolene carried the remote phone with her upstairs to peek in on the girls. "Out like lights," she reported. "Shall I wake them?"

"No, I'll talk to them in the morning. Meanwhile, I'll give Mother a buzz on her cell." Dorothy fell silent. "If Dad hasn't improved by tomorrow, Harold and I are coming home."

"I understand," Jolene said.

"Tell the girls we love them."

"Okay. Goodnight." Jolene ended the call.

Before falling asleep in the guest bedroom, Jolene read several psalms from the Bible. King David's outcry for God's mercy was particularly comforting at this time in her life.

Jolene prayed for Jack's quick recovery, and for Mitzi to be comforted during his crisis. She asked Jesus to send His angels to watch over Amy and Priscilla through the night.

"And bless David, dear Lord. Take care of him and don't let anything bad happen to him in Japan," she voiced a stirring in her heart. "Thank You for life. Don't let my cancer come back. Give me the chance to be a better person and love others more."

Amen fell from her lips and she drifted off to sleep.

♣30

MORNING CAME ON with a crack of loud thunder. Jolene bolted to a sitting position in the bed and looked at the clock. *7:30* and storming like the sky was falling. Then she heard the TV going.

Grabbing her robe, she hurried down the hall and peeked into the girls' bedroom. They were snuggled under the covers, munching on Pop Tarts while gazing at Loony-Tunes episodes.

No harm done there, they seem happy. And quiet.

Jolene limped into the hall bathroom, more tired than she thought possible. The knob on the shower was turned to hot as Jolene shed her pajamas and stepped into the spraying flow.

God is good. Bless us, O Lord, this day.

After bathing, Jolene donned comfortable cotton clothing doused in Downy, and hurried downstairs to prepare a healthy breakfast for the girls. Hunger tugging at her empty stomach, she removed bacon, a carton of eggs, and a can of biscuits from the fridge. As sumptuous food odors sifted through the house and up the stairs, Jolene heard footfalls on the stairs.

Amy and Priscilla boldly stomped into the kitchen.

"What smells so good?" Amy asked.

"We're hungry," Priscilla announced.

"Crisp bacon with scrambled eggs," Jolene told the girls. "Would you both like a hot biscuit with butter and jam?"

Priscilla's blue eyes widened with interest. "I do."

"Make me one, too," said Amy.

"Okay, wash your hands then take a seat at the table," Jolene ordered. "I'll make our plates and we'll pig out together."

The girls cleaned their plates in record time. Jolene was on her third cup of Starbucks, anticipating that the jug of OJ wouldn't last through another breakfast, and that she'd need to make a trip to the grocery store. But, that was okay. Doable.

Then the phone rang.

"It's probably your mother," Jolene informed the girls. "She called last night after you'd gone to bed."

"Me first, me first . . ." Priscilla raced to the counter to answer the phone, Amy anxiously at her sister's heels.

"Wait, it might not be Dorothy," Jolene cautioned.

Priscilla grabbed the phone. "It's Mommee!" she cried. "Are you comin' home today?" She listened for the answer. "Amy and me, we had biscuits with butter and jam. We saved you one."

"Let me talk, le' me talk." Amy tugged at her sister's arm.

It was a one-sided conversation but Jolene got the gist of it. Granddad was in the hospital, bad sick. It was raining, so they couldn't go out and play. Granny went away so Jolene could come. "Let Amy talk, too," Jolene petitioned Priscilla.

"Okay." The seven-year-old handed over the phone.

The conversation lasted another ten minutes.

"Mama wants to talk to you." Amy gave Jolene the phone.

"Hi. What did Mitzi say about Jack's condition?"

"Dad is being taken into surgery as we speak," Dorothy replied. "It's exploratory, since the doctor isn't sure what's causing his high temperature. I'm plenty concerned."

"I guess this means you're coming home," Jolene concluded.

"Yes," Dorothy replied. "As soon as we can get our tickets changed and arrange an international flight."

By the time the call ended, the girls were boohooing. "It's okay," she comforted them with hugs. "I know you miss your parents. Get dressed and we'll do something fun today."

Priscilla dried her eyes. "What kind of fun? It's raining."

"Well, we'll have to decide on an indoor game."

Amy smiled. "I like you, Aunt Jolene."

"I like you, too." Jolene was Mitzi's cousin, but she didn't correct Amy. Why did it matter if they called her Aunt Jolene?

Jack had exploratory surgery. Not only did he have a diseased gall bladder, the doctor found a cancerous growth attached to his liver. The tedious surgery lasted six hours.

Mitzi was fit to be tied while waiting for the doctor's report. Specifically, she requested that Jolene pray for Jack's recovery.

Jolene empathized with what Jack's family was going through while waiting to hear his prognosis. Fear of the unknown is the greatest threat to faith. "Let's pray about it together," she suggested. Jolene's prayer was brief but profound.

After ending the call with Mitzi, she fell on her knees and wept, pouring out her heart to God on Jack's behalf. That God would heal him in a way physicians could not—that the Holy Spirit would encourage him and remove all fear of death.

Then she called David on her cell phone.

"What is it, Jolene?" He sounded preoccupied.

"I know you're probably busy, David, but I thought you should know that Mitzi's husband Jack had surgery. The doctor removed his diseased gallbladder and found a cancerous growth attached to his liver. He's being monitored in ICU."

"I'm sorry to hear that." David's concern registered in his voice. "Can I help any way, short of coming to the states?"

"No, Jack is in the best of medical hands. We'll know if the cancer has spread to other organs when the blood tests and biopsy report comes back," Jolene explained. "I know what Jack's going through because I've been in his shoes." She started crying.

"It's okay, honey, from what little you've told me about Jack, he's a strong Christian. He'll get through this somehow. You know that cancer's not necessarily a death sentence."

"Keep a positive attitude, I know that's important."

If Jolene's cancer returned, it would be in the lining of the abdomen. Loose cancer cells in the blood would ultimately spread to vital organs. That's why she was having six-month checkups.

"Jolene, are you all right?" David inquired.

"I'll be fine." She sniffled. "Just overcome with emotion, and a little weary, and missing you. It's been a trying year."

"But you are feeling some better?"

"Physically, I am. Emotionally, I'm still struggling," she honestly replied. "What's keeping you busy in Japan?"

"Actually, I'm in a staff meeting. It's okay, I've stepped outside the conference room," he said. "Be brief."

"I didn't mean to disturb you," Jolene apologized.

"Is your hair getting longer?"

"Yeah, but I won't win any beauty contest. At least, I've been able to chunk the do-rags and wigs." Jolene actually chuckled. "I miss you so much. When are you coming to see me again?"

"Soon, babe, I've reviewed Mr. Sojimona's management contract and anticipate signing it soon." David explained. "The startup money appears to be sufficient, and the company's projection for my income is better than I anticipated."

"That's wonderful, David! I'm so proud of you."

"I can't give you a date when I'll be on a plane bound for America since Mr. Sojimona insists on putting new managers through his training program before turning them loose."

"I understand," said Jolene. "I'm still tying up some loose ends in Charlotte, working on getting Nancy signed up for the July 4th contest. Finally, I have an idea I believe will work."

"Are you going to share details with me?"

"Not yet." Some plans were best kept secret.

"How's your money holding out?"

"Fine, my listings have all sold and closed, and my referral fees forwarded to my P.O. Box in Charlotte. God has blessed me in so many ways." Jolene realized she was momentarily joyful.

"Well, I should get back to my meeting. Keep me posted on Jack's progress. If I don't answer my cell, leave a message."

"I will. David?" Jolene didn't want the conversation to end.

"Yes, Sweet Pea?"

"I love you so much."

♣31

JOLENE FOLDED HER cell phone in one hand. Concentrating on Jack's condition so diligently, she barely felt a tug at her shirttail. Glancing down, she spied Priscilla with a half-eaten frozen fruit pop that was dripping onto the kitchen floor.

"Need a cleanup, Priscilla?" She jolted to the present, grabbed a bundle of paper towels from the counter, swiped the girl's mouth, then the floor. "You're a mess, how 'bout a bath?"

"With lot'sa pink bubbles . . .?" Priscilla's eyes lit up.

"Absolutely—where's your sister?" Jolene suddenly missed Amy. The TV was blaring in the playroom but Priscilla's older sister was missing. "Where's Amy, Priscilla?"

The little girl licked her sticky fingers, baby-blues innocently peering up at Jolene. "Me all gooey, get bath."

"Did you see Amy go up to her room?" Jolene knelt in front of Priscilla, eyelevel, practically nose to nose. "Pay attention, it's important, sweetheart. Do you know where your sister is?"

Priscilla shook her head no and pointed to the back door.

"What . . .?" Panic seized Jolene. "Amy went outside without telling me?" She rushed over to the window and glanced around the backyard. Not one soul in sight as the sky rumbled.

"Are you mad at me?" Priscilla's eyes were global.

"No, sweetheart." Jolene swept the seven-year-old into her arms. "Did you see anyone at the back door?" She trembled. "Did a friend of Amy's come over and invite her outside?"

Priscilla was clearly becoming upset. "I don't know."

Jolene's questions were getting her nowhere.

"Okay, it's not your fault if Amy went outdoors, Priscilla." She grasped the child by the hand and led her to the front door.

Priscilla looked up and asked, "Are we going out to play?"

"Right now, we're both going to go outside and look for Amy. Maybe she rode her bike to the end of the cul-de-sac."

Jolene opened the front door and glanced down the street both ways. Ten-year-old Amy was nowhere in sight.

"Amy!" Jolene called out. "Amy, if you can hear me come home right now!" No answer was forthcoming.

Jolene knelt beside Priscilla. "Can you think of some place Amy may have gone? Does she have friends who live nearby?"

Priscilla's eyes filled with tears. "I don't know, Aunt Jolene."

"Okay. Don't cry, sweetheart, we'll find Amy."

Jolene hated the idea of alarming Mitzi by telling her Amy was missing. Surely, the girl could not have gone very far in fifteen, twenty minutes. *Could she?* What if she was abducted?

Mitzi should know what was going on.

Jolene went back into the house, dragging Priscilla by the hand, and retrieved the cell phone from her purse. Mitzi's number rang four times then her voicemail clicked on.

Not wanting to leave a message, Jolene hung up.

"Is Granny gone, too?" Priscilla asked.

"No, she's just busy." Jolene fought panic. "Get your coat, Priscilla. We're going to take a walk around the neighborhood. I'm sure we'll find your sister soon." *So don't worry . . .*

The idea of taking a walk appealed to the little girl as she skipped to her room and snagged her dolly from the closet.

Fifteen minutes later, they had knocked on three neighbors' doors and not found Amy. One concerned mother told Jolene to contact Beth Joyner, the owner of the adjoining property behind Jack and Mitzi's. Sometimes Amy played with Beth's daughter.

Jolene spied a new batch of cumulous clouds sparing on the horizon and hurried down the street. Holding tightly to Amy's hand, they traipsed across Mitzi's backyard and approached the tall fence dividing the two lots. Jolene saw no gate in the fence.

Priscilla suddenly jerked loose and sprinted around the right side of the fence, calling back to Jolene. "Birdie lives here. Go see Birdie now." She ran harder toward her destination.

"You've been here before?" Jolene caught up with Priscilla.

"Uh huh . . ." Beyond the tall fence Jolene spied a big oak tree shading the backyard. "See Birdie there!" A little finger pointed to a wooden gate. "Go through and see Birdie."

"Who's Birdie?" Jolene wondered.

Priscilla flipped a metal latch. When the gate swung open, she raced into the yard before Jolene could stop her.

"Wait up, Priscilla. Stop running."

"Birdie, Birdie, Birdie! See!"

Jolene hurried after the little girl—quick, excited and agile.

Priscilla stood at the foot of the oak looking up. Dangling from a huge limb was a huge wire birdcage. Inside it, a tropical species of some kind sputtered and squawked, perched on a wooden pole like a king. "Birdie! Birdie!" Priscilla pointed up.

As Jolene's eyes circled the backyard, she spied Amy seated in a swing, pushing off with her feet as she sailed higher and higher into the air. A little girl with red hair was in the other swing.

"Amy!" Jolene called out. "Why did you run off?"

The little girl frowned and placed both feet solidly in the sand, halting the swing. "Am I in trouble, Aunt Jolene?"

Relieved that Amy hadn't been abducted, Jolene rushed over and ferociously hugged the naughty runaway. "Don't ever go off like that without telling me where you're going!" She looked Amy square in the face. "You scared me half to death!"

"Sorr-ree." Amy bit her lower lip. "Granny lets me come."

"It's okay this time, but I'm not your grandmother, and I didn't know you came here to play." Jolene recognized the uncertainty in Amy's glassy brown eyes. "You're not in trouble, Amy, I am. Since I failed to keep a closer watch on you."

Amy burst out crying from the scolding.

"Can I swing now?" Priscilla crookedly stared up at Jolene.

"Sure." Jolene hugged Amy to reassure her she wasn't mad then launched Priscilla into the swing seat and gave her a shove.

From the house came the sound of a slamming door. Jolene looked up to see who it was. "Is there a problem?" asked a young woman from the porch. "I heard someone crying."

"No, we're fine now," Jolene called back. "I'm Mitzi's cousin, Jolene. I'm watching the girls for her." She gave Priscilla another push. "Amy came over to swing without my permission," Jolene explained. "I hope we're not intruding too much."

"Where's Mitzi?" Beth Joyner ventured out into the yard and approached Jolene. "Did something happen?"

Beth Joyner's lilac eyes registered concern.

"I'm afraid so, Jack had emergency surgery. Harold and Dorothy are vacationing in Spain, so Mitzi called and asked me to come over and stay with the girls for a few days."

"Are they on their way home?" Beth inquired.

"Yes, they are. This whole episode with Jack has been pretty traumatic for all of us." Jolene glanced down at Amy, who stood like a statue. "When Amy went missing, I practically lost it. I'm just grateful that I found her in your yard, safe and unharmed."

Beth shook a finger at the little girl. "Shame on you, Amy! Never come over here to play without telling someone."

"I'm sorry." Amy stared at her shoes.

Beth made eye contact with her daughter. "Carol, why didn't you tell me Amy came over to play with you?"

"You were talking on the phone, Mama."

"I'm so sorry this happened," Beth apologized to Jolene. "I didn't realize Amy was here or I would've phoned Mitzi. "Amy, tell Jolene you're sorry for running off without telling her."

Amy chewed on a fingernail, eyes glazed and about to bawl.

"When you make a mistake, Amy, always say you're sorry."

"Are you mad at me, Miss Beth?"

"No, dear, adults get upset, too." Beth grasped Amy's hand. "Why don't we all go inside the house and have some lemonade and cookies," she suggested. "Do you have the time, Jolene?"

"Sure." Jolene let her breath go as the terror passed.

"Yeah . . .!" Like rubber balls, the three little girls held hands and bounced around the yard in circles. Oh, the joy of youth!

The entourage soon took their frolicking inside the Joyner's house. "This is awfully nice of you, Beth," Jolene said after visiting with her for an hour. It's getting late, though. I should get the girls home and cleaned up for lunch."

"Now that you know we're here, feel free to visit." Beth handed Jolene her phone number on a sticky Post-it. "Carol loves playing with Amy. Can't say I don't enjoy the company, too."

"Me, too! Me, too!" Priscilla would not be left out.

"Let's go home, girls." The sky was churning with dark clouds in preparation for rain. "How does chicken noodle soup sound for lunch? With peanut butter and jelly sandwiches."

"Yeah!" They clapped.

Happy little girls are so easy to please.

Later, after feeding the hungry girls, Jolene addressed the problem with Amy about leaving home without telling an adult.

"Do you understand why you must ask permission before leaving the house?" Jolene queried. "It's not safe for a little girl."

Amy nodded. "You were busy and I didn't want to bother you," she explained. "Mama says not to bother Granny when she's talking on the phone." It was a believable reason.

"It's okay now, we're all safe now." Jolene said a prayer to God for His goodness. "It was just a huge misunderstanding. I'm fine if you're fine." *Am I?* Jolene couldn't tamp down anxiety.

"Will Granny be mad at me?" Amy's pink lips pouted.

"I don't think we should worry her about that, do you?"

Amy smiled as her eyes brightened. "It's our secret."

"Yes." Jolene hugged the little girl.

"Can I have a bath now?" Priscilla asked.

"I think both of you could stand a soapy dip." Jolene smiled. "After that, what do you say we pop some corn and watch a Disney movie?" *Thank God for Disney*, Jolene thought.

"Hooray!" The girls scrambled up the stairs, always in competition, always laughing and enjoying childhood.

Motherhood is treacherous, Jolene realized, releasing a pent-up breath; but far more interesting than she'd believed possible. What had she been missing by not raising her own family?

♣32

JOLENE STAYED WITH Mitzi's granddaughters two more days, until their parents returned from Spain and came to get them.

"We had a good time," Jolene told Dorothy.

"Did the girls obey you?" the concerned mother asked.

"They were perfect." Jolene winked at Amy.

"Can Aunt Jolene come home with us?" Priscilla asked. "Pleeze . . . she cooks real good peanut butter sandwiches."

Jolene and Dorothy both laughed.

"Sure. Can you spare the time, Jolene?" Harold asked. "We owe you, Jolene. How about we treat you to lunch? Downtown: at one of Nashville's swanky dives . . .? Say yes."

"Can I have a rain check?" Jolene returned. "I need to get back to Charlotte and see what's going on." It was time to convince Claire to forgive her daughter and end the feud. "I need to get my friend Nancy ready for the July contest."

"What kind of contest?" Dorothy inquired.

"It's a singing contest," Jolene answered. "The prize is a recording contract with a Nashville company."

"Is this contest held in Charlotte?" Harold asked.

"Yes, it's sponsored by the city council, but since it's held in the mayor's backyard, the audience is invitation only," Jolene explained. "I know the mayor's wife, would you like to come?"

"We might." Dorothy eyed Harold for an opinion.

"Okay, I'll see if I can reserve four tickets for you."

"Maybe Dad will feel like coming, too," Nancy told Harold. "We could make it a family affair." She smiled at the idea.

"I'm game." Harold tapped Priscilla on the head. "What about you, Sweet Pea? Want to go to a singing shindig?"

"What about your brother and his wife?" Jolene asked.

"They'll be in Australia, trudging around the countryside," Harold replied. "My brother-in-law's a real renegade when it comes to vacation time. The moon's the limit."

"Sounds like a beautiful trip," Jolene commented.

"Ready to go, Pun' kin?" Harold knelt down and scooped up his least daughter, Priscilla. "Com' on, Amy, we'll pick up Rufus at Sue's house on our way home. I bet he misses you."

"What kind of dog do you have?" Jolene inquired.

"An Irish Setter. He's still a pup and into everything imaginable," Dorothy declared. "We didn't think Mama needed an extra mouth around to feed, so we boarded Rufus."

"Good thing, too," Harold said. "That pup's a handful."

"Rufus is a good dog." Amy defended her pet. "He just gets bored. I would too if somebody put me in a cage."

Everyone laughed as Amy frowned. "Well, he does!"

"Okay, Amy." Harold patted his daughter's head. "We weren't laughing at Rufus, he's the best." His eye caught Dorothy's, who was still snickering at Amy's honesty.

"Where's that husband of yours?" Harold asked Jolene.

"In Japan, receiving training from an insurance company that plans to open a business in Dickson County," she replied. "David will soon be managing a branch. I'm so proud of him."

"That's wonderful!" The dark pupils in Dorothy's eyes danced. "So David is pulling up his tent in Louisiana and moving to Tennessee, after all. That must please you immensely."

"That's the plan." Jolene beamed.

"What changed David's mind?" Harold asked.

"Several things happened at his office that pointed him here," Jolene replied, afraid she's opened the door for more inquiry.

Dorothy gave her husband a look.

"It's very personal." Jolene's cheeks flushed.

"Some things are best left unsaid," Dorothy sputtered.

Jolene glanced down at the children. "Not here."

"Okay. But you definitely have my ears perked for more."

"God has been working on both of us while we've been stewing over where our lives are headed."

"Marriage has its quirks," Dorothy noted.

"David and I have been evaluating what's important. I suppose, in a way, God has been checking out our faith."

Harold chuckled. "God is like that, isn't He?"

"You can usually count on tomorrows to present us with the unexpected, both good and bad." Dorothy profoundly stated.

"Stuff happens." Jolene identified.

"Just look at what's happened to Dad. When we left for Spain he felt just fine. Six days later . . ." Dorothy shook her head.

"Who knows how long I had been walking around with cancer inside me?" Jolene spurted. "Now that the tumors are out, and I'm finished with chemotherapy, I feel like God has given me a new lease on life. The experience has definitely changed me."

"Maybe you should write a book, tell others what you went through," Harold suggested. "Lotta people think cancer is a death sentence. You're living proof it's not."

"I'm not out of the woods yet," Jolene voiced. "I'll be getting checkups for the next five years. Dr. Blazer says the cancer can come back even a decade later." *One day at a time.*

"We'll pray that doesn't happen," Dorothy promised. "I've never heard you complain about your pain even once. You are one brave woman, Jolene Salisbury. A walking miracle."

"You weren't my nurse in the hospital." Jolene chuckled. "I gave them some grief, believe me."

"Well, we'd better take off, my dear ones." Harold called a halt to their visit. "Girls, go get your bags from upstairs and haul them down. We'll get your jackets from the hall closet."

"I'll take a walk around the house to see if we've missed anything," Dorothy said. "Mama's always finding a sock here and there. Heaven's, I keep Wal-Mart in business."

"Oh, I did wash clothes late last night," Jolene informed the attentive parents. "Check the dryer, too."

The two little cherubs raced upstairs, grabbed their packed suitcases from the bedroom, and hauled them down the stairs, chattering at one another like excited squirrels.

Harold took their bags at the bottom of the stairs.

"Hey, girls, these suitcases feel a whole lot heavier than when we packed them. Did Jolene buy you gifts?"

"Aunt Jolene gave us dolls. They're riding inside," Amy said.

"We made a quick trip to the mall," Jolene admitted.

"You shouldn't have spent money on them," Dorothy scolded Jolene as she returned to the living room with a pair of Priscilla's white socks in hand. "Watching them for Mama was above and beyond the call of duty. Let us pay you for them."

"No, it was my pleasure. But thank you for offering."

Everyone laughed, hugged, let go of a few tears, and said their goodbyes. When the family had driven away, and the house was once more silent, Jolene walked into the kitchen and checked to see if she'd left anything undone. The coffee maker was clinically clean, as was the counter. All perishable items in the fridge had been frozen in care packages to be served later as mini-meals. Plus, she'd made a huge pot of vegetable soup and frozen it in serve-size containers. She could check off kitchen duties.

Jolene glanced inside the two bathrooms upstairs.

Clean and ready for occupancy.

Earlier that day, she'd stripped the sheets off on the girls' twin beds and put on fresh ones. All the dirty sheets had been washed, folded, and placed in the linen closet. Jack and Mitzi's house was in order. It was time to leave for Nancy's.

♣33

WHAT A GLORIOUS day for a drive in the countryside! Jolene recalled last December, five days before Christmas when she'd made the trip to Tennessee. Much had seemed askew in her life back then. Her marriage to David was failing. Her health hung in the balance as cancer invaded both ovaries.

Life had never looked so dismal.

Not at all like today. While the sun spread its warmth over the rolling green hills and deep valleys of Middle Tennessee to bring forth new life, hope was blossoming inside of Jolene.

With God's blessing, anything is possible.

Everywhere Jolene looked, budding trees unfolded their emerald leaves while flowering plants paraded in an array of colors, flaming against nature's greenery like decorations on a Christmas tree. Wildflowers everywhere dotted the grassy fields.

All of nature is praising God.

As Jolene steadily drove toward Charlotte, it appeared that other folks shared her excitement. At this time of year, parents ventured outdoors with their children to share in a variety of activities. Americans had much for which to be thankful. Freedom still reigned, while the individual rights of some nations were utterly crushed under the weight of dictatorships.

In the past months, Jolene had undergone cancer surgery, endured the side effects of chemotherapy, battled a nasty staph infection, and won. Plus, she and David had finally bridged their differences. It seemed today that love conquered all.

Jolene had forgiven David for keeping secrets, for not telling her about his conflict with his two business partners over morality issues. With enlightenment, to her it made good sense that he took it upon himself to sell the house and set aside the assets. All this time, David was preparing for their future together.

Now, like the ending of a fine romance movie, husband and wife would soon be reunited. David would be relocating to Dickson County to open up an insurance office. They would find a suitable home and move in. Happiness lay before them.

Also, Jack was on the mend following surgery. Mitzi would soon be bringing him home from the hospital. Jolene's prayer was that Jack's cancer had not spread and his prognosis was a healthy future. Hardship sharpened a person's appreciation for life.

Having bonded with Harold and Dorothy's daughters, Amy and Priscilla, Jolene felt like she was a real aunt, though in reality she was Mitzi's first cousin. Life was settling out to an even keel.

What else could possibly go wrong?

That was not a question Jolene should have asked herself. A halo of gloom hung over the Blake's house when she arrived.

"What's wrong, Nancy?"

A harried expression flooded the girl's face.

"Everything!" she cried. "Buck and I had a huge fuss and he stormed out of the house! I don't think he's coming back."

"You're exaggerating. Buck's done this before, right?"

"This is different."

Nancy was a mess, eyes red from bawling, flaming curls tangled and tumbling in her pretty face. A hug wouldn't solve the problem but Jolene grabbed Nancy in a tight embrace anyhow.

"He'll be back," Jolene assured her. "Buck loves those children as much as you do. He's just blowing off steam." She held Nancy at arm's length. "Wanna talk about it?"

Nancy sniffed and dried her tears on the coattail of her stained floral apron. "I guess."

"Where are the children?" Jolene heard no frolicking.

"Claire picked them up. She's taking them to the park."

"Does she know—I mean, about you and Buck?"

"Yes, I told her." Sadness clawed at Nancy's face.

"How did she respond to the news?"

"Ha! How to you think? My mother said it was about time I kicked out the loser," Nancy exclaimed. "She's keeping her fingers crossed we'll divorce. Our pain is pure joy to her."

Jolene blinked at the harsh statement. "Well, I can't say I agree with Claire. Your spouse is a great guy, Nancy. If David and I can get past our grievances, so can you and Buck."

"Do you really think there is hope for us?"

"Get dressed and let's go over to the B & B, I want to have a talk with Beverly." Jolene nudged Nancy out of her hopelessness. "Hurry up, get ready and let's go before the restaurant closes."

"Why do you need to talk to Beverly?" Nancy puzzled over Jolene's invitation. "Claire treats her like a slave."

"I have an idea I want to run by both you and Beverly, one I believe will get you accepted into the singing contest in July."

"You're nuts if you think Mom will change her mind."

"Did you hear yourself, Nancy? You called Claire Mom."

"I did, didn't I?" Nancy shrugged.

"Let's go, time's running out."

"But the deadline for signing up for the contest has already passed," Nancy pointed out. "Even if Claire agrees, how can you possibly get the rules changed at this late date?"

"Trust me: rules won't matter when you hear my plan."

~

Friday's B & B menu included blackberry cobbler.

Jolene and Nancy arrived around 1:15 and invited Beverly to join them for lunch as soon as the crowd cleared out. The lunch special was mixed greens with fresh crabmeat, served with a cup of tomato basil soup and a blueberry muffin. Beverly instructed Jolene and Nancy to park their things in the back dining room, that she would join them shortly. They took off walking.

"Are you going to tell me what you have in mind?" Nancy asked as they sat down at a table. At Jolene's insistence, she'd donned a summer dress with a pair of sandals. A string of antique pearls draped her neck as she toyed with a matching earring.

"You look elegant," Jolene complimented Nancy. "You wear your new poky-dot black-and-white sundress like a real country star. And you have a radiant tan. You'll look great on stage."

"If I ever get on stage . . ." Nancy shrugged, feeling a little chilly as the air-conditioning unit raced on full blast. Summer's brutal Tennessee heat had arrived and wasn't going away soon.

"Tell me what happened between you and Buck."

"It was a silly argument," Nancy shrugged, glaring out the window. "He got mad because I cancelled the lawn service at the end of May." She looked at Jolene. "I thought he would mow."

"Oh." Jolene knew that lawn care was major with Nancy.

"He's just being a heel."

"I'll be glad to pay for it to be reinstated," Jolene offered. "Breaking up with Buck over grass seems senseless."

Nancy frowned. "There's more." Fear clouded her gaze. "I found marijuana in the back of his truck."

"Was it Buck's? Is he using?" Jolene was alarmed at the idea.

"He said it wasn't his," Nancy replied with a stone-cold expression, emerald eyes reflecting bewilderment.

"But you didn't believe him," Jolene concluded.

"Why should I? He used before we married."

"That was ten years ago, Nancy."

"When I lit into him about smoking pot, he packed his bag and stormed out of the house," Nancy explained. "What was I to think, the evidence was right there in his truck?"

Jolene hitched a breath and said, "Buck has been going to church with you and the kids. Could you be mistaken?"

"I wish . . ."

"He seems like a responsible adult."

"Most of the time he is."

Jolene peered at Nancy. "Did you give Buck a chance to explain before you accused him of a crime?"

"Whose side are you on?" Nancy moved to attack mode.

"Everybody's," Jolene replied. "Yours, Buck's, and the children's," she clarified. "I love all of you."

Nancy slumped down in her seat. "Somehow I knew you'd feel that way." Emerald eyes misted as she nervously shivered.

"I'm right, admit it." Jolene scrutinized the troubled wife. "You didn't bother to hear Buck's side of the story. You just assumed the worst. Did you consider that was how your mother would handle the problem? Do you want to turn out like her?"

"Yes, you're right! But all that doesn't matter now."

"Here." Jolene handed Nancy her cell phone. "Call Buck and apologize. Ask him to come home."

Obviously contemplating Jolene's suggestion, they were interrupted by Beverly as she popped into the room carrying a tray with three glasses of fruity tea. "Is there a problem?"

No answer came forth.

Beverly's curious gaze flitted between Jolene and Nancy. "Did I interrupt something?" She placed the tray on the table.

"No, we're finished talking," Nancy replied. "Join us."

Beverly filled the third chair at the table.

"Are you sure something's not wrong?" she asked.

"Positive." Nancy's lips were clamped.

Beverly's gaze targeted Jolene. "It's good to see you again. How are you feeling these days?"

"I'm getting back to normal," Jolene replied.

"Are the children enjoying their summer vacation?" Beverly asked Nancy, who looked like the Grinch had visited her.

"We've been having a serious discussion," Jolene offered.

"Kids are fine," Nancy piped. "My mother's with them now, spoiling them rotten." She could not deny tears.

"Because Buck's left you," Beverly said, hands covering her mouth. "Sorry, but I already heard. News travels fast in a small town." She glanced at Jolene. "Gossip: shame on us all!"

"Especially bad news," Jolene grimaced.

Nancy's mood flipped to furious. "So my mother has already blabbed to everyone in the family that I kicked Buck out of the house?" Nancy shook with anger. "It wasn't her place!"

Beverly's lips twisted. "Maybe he'll come back."

"Girls . . .!" Jolene intervened.

She had their attention.

"I didn't invite you to lunch to talk about Buck or Claire. I have another important agenda in mind, and I need your help."

"What?" they simultaneously inquired.

"Can we call a truce first? Anger won't solve problems."

Beverly's lilac eyes drifted to Nancy. "I'm sorry Aunt Claire has been such a butthead. I'm sure Buck will come home when he has time to think about what he'll lose if he doesn't. For what it's worth, Nancy, I think you're a wonderful person."

"Really . . .?" Nancy lit up like a light bulb. "You don't still see me as the black sheep of our family?"

"Why would I? Because you made a mistake? Who hasn't?"

Jolene cleared her throat. "Back to why we are here . . ."

"What's your plan?" Beverly folded her hands on the table.

"The kind that will get Nancy registered for the singing contest in July," Jolene replied. "But let's eat first."

After blackberry dessert, Jolene offered a solution to the rift between Nancy and her mother. "What if Claire's grandchildren want to perform in the singing contest? Would she refuse them?"

"You want my children to enter the July 4th contest?" Nancy blinked, clearly shocked.

"It's not like they can't sing." Jolene patted Nancy's hand. "I've heard the boys in the yard harmonizing. Craig has a voice as pure as Bing Crosby's, and Cloy is a natural performer. I'd say they both inherited their mother's singing talent."

"Your girls aren't so bad, either," Beverly recalled, already sold on the idea. "I've heard them before, singing nursery rhymes with Claire. Jolene, I think you're on to something."

"What about me?" Nancy asked.

"Of course, you'll be part of the family act, just not the main part," Jolene answered. "The judges aren't stupid. When they hear you sing they'll want to hear more."

"You think?" Nancy made eye contact with Beverly.

"I know," Jolene said. "We just need to decide what the children will sing and how you will fit into their act."

"But the cutoff date was last Friday," Beverly pointed out.

"Do you have an application on hand?" Jolene asked.

"Yeah, I think I stuffed a handful under the cash register—oh, we could fill one out today and postdate it. No one would know the difference." Beverly wickedly smiled.

"Isn't that cheating?" Nancy asked.

"Let's just say we're bending the rules for a good cause. Your mother has cheated you out of a chance to succeed long enough."

"It's a great idea, Nancy." Beverly sided with Jolene.

"I know for a fact that Claire hasn't had time to go through the latest applicants," Beverly said. "What will you call the act?"

"Five Little Angels on a Mission . . .?"

"I like it," Nancy excitedly exclaimed. "In fact, I think I can write a song around that theme."

"Okay, get the application, Beverly, so Nancy can fill it out."

After doing business, the three of them sat outside the porch, laughing and joking over shared family stories of days gone by.

Jolene learned from Beverly that one of her classmates, Joy Hogan, was in town for her niece's wedding. "Beverly, do you have the phone number for Joy's niece?" she asked.

"No, but I can look it up in the phone book."

"Good. I'd like to see Joy."

♣34

JOLENE AND NANCY were back at the house an hour before Claire returned with her grandchildren. She seemed surprised when Nancy invited her inside for a glass of lemonade.

"How was your day, Mom?" Nancy lightheartedly inquired.

"*Mom?* What's up, Nancy?" Claire scrutinized her normally sassy daughter. "You haven't called me that since you were in the tenth grade." Her surly gaze slid to Jolene. "I suppose *you* had something to do with Nancy's mood swing."

Jolene shrugged her shoulders, offering no opinion.

"What's so different today?" Claire locked eyes on Nancy.

"Excuse me?" Jolene raised a hand in a defensive gesture. "Think about it, Claire. Isn't it time to mend family fences?"

"She listens to you, not me!" Claire shot back at Jolene.

"If I didn't know better I'd think you were jealous."

"That's idiotic." Claire wrung her hands, clearly flustered.

Honey, if the shoe fits, wear it. Jolene knew she'd struck a nerve.

Claire mirthlessly laughed with a satisfied expression. "You know, Jolene, you're right! Now that Buck is out of the picture, I don't see why Nancy and I can't talk about reconciliation."

Nancy clearly didn't know how to respond, looking to Jolene for help. "Don't count on Buck and Nancy's marriage breaking up!" Jolene jumped in. "I'm positive they *will* work out their differences, given a little time. Leave him out of the equation."

"Ha! After the way Buck has treated Nancy all these years, don't tell me divorce isn't in the picture!" Claire barreled down.

"There you go, Mother! Judging us like you're our jury!" The glass pitcher of lemonade slipped from Nancy's trembling hand, hit the floor, and shattered into a thousand pieces.

Jolene ran to get the broom, hoping the two of them would get all that anger out of their systems and makeup.

"That boy's always been wrong for you from the start!" Claire held her chin high. "You just never wanted to face the truth. How can you be so dumb when it comes to men?"

"What has Buck done to you, Claire? Besides love me?"

Nancy emotionally wilted, close to the breaking edge. But there was nothing Jolene could do but watch the drama play out.

"Why don't you like Buck?" Nancy asked. "He's a great guy, underneath all that male ego. Down deep, I know he loves me."

"Ego . . .?" Claire's mouth was open in shock. "Is that what you're calling emotional abuse now?" She spewed venom.

"Could we call a truce?" Jolene stepped into the middle of the squabble. Clearly, this reunion wasn't going well. Mother and daughter were at opposite ends of the pole when it came to Buckley Dodge Blake. "Surely, you two can agree on something."

Nancy inhaled deeply. "This conversation is over."

"I believe I've expressed myself pretty well." Claire's foot crunched on a sliver of broken glass. "Somebody's got to clean up this mess." She spied Jolene holding the broom.

"I can do it!" Nancy marched over to Jolene and grabbed the broom. "Some messes get cleaned up faster than others."

"No, I'll do it." Claire snatched the broom from Nancy.

Jolene nearly laughed at their ridiculous power-play.

"Just make sure the children stay outdoors so they won't get their little feet cut on glass," Claire ordered Nancy.

Jolene shot Nancy a warning glance to let it go.

"Whatever . . ." Nancy recalled the need to be in her mother's good graces when she reviewed the last of the talent applications.

"Claire, let me clean up the mess," Jolene offered. "Please."

Claire's face scrunched with indecision.

"I can handle this, Claire. Really. Why don't you and Nancy go out on the front porch and watch the children play?"

And talk some more like two reasonable human beings.

Claire handed Jolene the broom. "I know my daughter thinks I'm terrible, but I do have one nice thing to say." Emerald eyes hit their target. "I need to thank you for paying for the yard service and swing set. That was going above and beyond."

"My pleasure," Jolene said, surprised at the compliment.

Like a persistent blade of grass pushing up through a crack in the concrete until finally it broke through and touched sunlight, Jolene was slowly making progress in mentoring Claire and Nancy's marred relationship. In time, they would realize how much they belonged together. At least that was her prayer.

Two days later, Nancy received word that the children's application to sing in the July contest had been accepted. "I can't believe it worked," she told Jolene as she swept the porch.

"Believe it, because it's true."

It was a rewarding moment.

"You are a genius, you know that?" Nancy leaned on her broom handle. "I'm so pleased to have you as a good friend."

"God's way of working out our problems is always best." Jolene smiled. "Have you written your theme song for the show?"

"Not yet." Nancy's mouth screwed into a knot.

"Better hurry, you still have to teach the children the words and melody," Jolene advised. "Just let your creative juices flow."

"What if nothing comes to mind?" Nancy plopped down in the swing. "I've never been mentally blocked before."

"You've never had such a serious reason to write a song."

"You're right, I just need to relax and let the ideas flow."

"A prayer won't hurt. Talents are a gift from God."

"Right again. I've been centered on myself far too long when it comes to Claire. Correction: *Mom*. She's gone more than half way to meet me." Nancy had many moments to regret.

"Then you should go the rest of the way." Jolene inhaled the odor of freshly mowed grass, thanks to a lawn service. "Has Buck returned your call yet?" It had been three days since he left.

"Has David?" Nancy asked back.

"I guess we both need to pray harder."

Jolene took the broom from Nancy's hand. "Why don't you get your guitar and work on a song? I'll sweep the porch."

"Five Little Angels on a Mission," Nancy uttered.

"Yep, and this song better be dynamite."

~

Jolene met Joy Hogan for coffee at the B & B later that day. "It's been how long?" Joy laughed. "Twenty-eight years since we walked the aisle and received our high school diplomas. My, my, how time flies!" The dental assistant sipped on a vanilla latte.

"After I graduated from the University of Memphis I worked for a collection firm in Jackson, Mississippi," Jolene explained. "That's where I met my husband, David."

"I'm divorced," Joy said. "We just grew apart and decided it was best to part as friends." Sadness flooded her expression.

"How long ago was that?"

"Three years and counting . . ." Joy frowned. "I still love him. Sometimes I think we didn't try hard enough to stay together. Divorce is the easy way out of problems."

"I understand," Jolene uttered. "David and I have our differences, too, but we're working at compromising."

"I'm glad. It's for the best."

Jolene asked, "Is reconciliation possible?"

"No, Greg has remarried." Joy sighed and avoided tears. "He tried to make me see his point of view, but I didn't listen."

"Was it an affair?"

"Yes, his, and I was unforgiving." Joy paused a long moment to reflect. "He slept with my best friend, Pam."

"Are they happy together?" Jolene pried.

"Goodness, no!" Joy exclaimed. "My twin boys tell me they fuss like cats and dogs. They hide their problems well."

"Do you have custody of them?"

"Yes, but they're with Greg vacationing in Florida. That's why I was able to attend my niece's wedding. The ceremony is this Friday," Joy revealed. "Would you like to go with me?"

"Which church?" Jolene asked.

"No church. Their vows and the reception are being held at the Dickson Country Club. Tina and James are atheists."

Jolene's heart sank. "How can they not believe in God?"

"I thought the same thing, but America's family values are changing. People today seem to think they know better than God how to live their lives. They make their own rules as they go."

Jolene sensed she'd hit on a raw nerve that would ruin their visit. "Tell me about your boys, Joy."

"Phillip and Clayton are fourteen, good kids who love playing sports." Joy shrugged. "They have to fight off the girls."

"I'm sure you're a wonderful mother, Joy."

"Do you have children, Jolene?"

"I wish." Jolene debated whether to tell Joy about her cancer experience. She already seemed troubled enough.

"What?" Joy sensed her friend's hesitation.

"I had double-ovarian cancer surgery in January."

"Are you okay now?" Alarm flooded her expression.

"I'm finished with chemotherapy and mending well," Jolene reported. "Part of why I came to Tennessee was because of my illness, but there's another reason."

"It must be something important."

"I don't know if you knew my parents well," Jolene said, "that both of them died at fairly young ages from diseases."

"No, I hadn't heard." Joy peered at Jolene. "I'm so sorry."

"The reason I'm in Charlotte is to make amends. I left town after graduation because I didn't want to live here anymore. I was determined to get a college education and do something more important with my life than till the land or work in a store."

"America is made of hardworking folks, Jolene."

"I understand that now. I was a selfish young adult, after a golden ring that would lead me to higher social status. I was ashamed of how my parents lived. I treated them badly."

"Wow. I can't imagine judging myself so harshly."

"Even when my mother came down with cancer, I avoided coming back for visits. After Kate died, my daddy remarried a woman he worked with at the post office. That ticked me off."

"You think he was seeing her before your mother died?"

"Pretty sure," Jolene shared. "I hated him for his betrayal."

"Yet, you also betrayed Kate, from your own admission."

"Yes, I did." Jolene grimaced at past choices. "After learning I had cancer, I needed to find a way to forgive my parents and my own shortcomings. I need to move forward, guilt-free."

"We all do. What kind of amends are you making?

"I'm still trying to learn all I can about my parents—what they did with their spare time and who their friends were."

"That's a pretty tall feat," Joy pointed out.

"I just need to know what happened during the years I was absent from their lives. One thing I know for sure, I failed them as an only daughter. I need their forgiveness, and God's."

"Oh, now that makes sense." Joy's nose squinted.

"Actually," Jolene continued, "I was hoping you might know something about Kirk and Kate Lancaster's lives. Gossip gets around, so your parents may have heard something. . ."

"Dad's dead, but I can ask my mother," Joy offered. "She's in a nursing home in Dickson. I'm going to visit her today."

"It must be hard on both of you, living so far apart."

"Alzheimer's is a terrible disease that attacks people, even middle-age folks." Joy sighed. "Shoot, I'm halfway there myself."

"I guess life goes pretty fast, doesn't it?"

"Yeah, but if we can learn from our mistakes, maybe we can help future generations understand what they're facing," Joy uttered. "Maybe, my boys will make better choices than I have."

"When you see your mom, ask her about Kirk and Kate."

"I will, Jolene. And it's been a pleasure talking to you."

The classmates finished their coffees and parted ways, possibly never to cross paths again, unless someone planned a fiftieth class reunion. In that vein of thought, Jolene saddened.

♣35

DAVID PHONED JOLENE Wednesday afternoon. "How are you?" he asked. "I'm fine, where are you?" she returned.

"Back in Baton Rouge," he replied. "I have to pack up my office and put my things in a storage unit with the rest of our belongings before I can come to Tennessee."

"That's really good news, David."

"Have you looked for us a house yet?"

"Actually, no, I've been pretty busy for a homeless woman."

They laughed over her comment.

"When I come, I'd like to see some properties," he said.

"I'll call a realtor and ask what's available."

"Get something beautiful and extravagant, we can afford it."

"I'm more interested in comfort and scenery."

The conversation paused for a reflective moment.

"This purchase will likely be our last," Jolene said. "I want to own a property that will serve us well till death do us part."

"What's this morbid obsession with old age?"

"Sorry, I didn't mean to put a damper on your day," she said. "I had coffee with a classmate and her life hasn't gone so well."

David chuckled. "Bumpy roads come along."

"Joy's mom is in a nursing home," Jolene revealed.

"I don't want to talk about Joy or her mother."

A moment engulfed them.

"How soon can you open a business in Dickson County?"

"Soon," David reported. "I'll get a good yearly base fee plus commission on all the business I bring to the company."

"I'm so proud of you." Jolene swelled with pride.

"We netted two-hundred-fifty thousand from the sale of our house in Baton Rouge so, as I indicated, we can afford to buy a really nice place to live. Don't let the list price scare you off."

"Okay." The idea settled in her brain. "Is country property doable?" She loved Middle Tennessee's rolling hills.

"Sure. I can rent commercial space in Dickson and work from home part of the time. You're a great realtor, so I trust your judgment. Find something and we'll negotiate the contract. If you like it, I'll love it," he said. "Hey, phone's ringing, gotta go."

"David—" he was gone. "I wanted to tell you about the contest." Jolene's words fell on deaf ears. "And that I love you."

"Was that who I think it was?"

Nancy stood in the doorway.

"It was David. He wants me to look for a house."

"Great!" Nancy smiled. "I have some news, too."

Jolene hoped it was an answer to her prayers.

"Buck called. I apologized to him and he's coming home."

"Oh, Nancy, that's wonderful!" Jolene embraced the girl. "I also spoke to Mitzi and Jack is doing great. God is so good."

"Yes, He is."

"Did you tell Buck the children are singing on the fourth?"

"I forgot." Her hands flew to her mouth. "Imagine that."

"What else? You look like the cat that ate the mouse."

"I wrote our theme song, and the kids love it."

Jolene felt her spirit lift to heaven. There was one last person she needed to see before David came: Olivia Kemp.

Lancaster, now, Jolene recalled.

Joy had phoned late yesterday and told Jolene that her father's second wife lived alone in one of the early 20th-century houses on Main Street. Though Kirk had been dead for fifteen years, Olivia had never remarried.

Why not, if she was the kind who stole other women's husbands?

~

It was mid-morning on Friday when Jolene tapped on Olivia's front door. A woman looking to be in her late sixties cracked the door and peeked outside. Lean as a carrot stick, slightly taller than Jolene, surprise exploded in her chestnut eyes.

"Do you know who I am?" Jolene inquired.

"Lord, yes! Jolene! Come inside, girl!" Olivia pulled her indoors like she was a long lost, rich relative. "Your daddy kept your picture on the mantel—it's still there." She pointed a finger at the gold-framed photograph. "You must've been sixteen."

Sure enough, there it was: Jolene's photograph. It had been taken at a church picnic social. Her hair was longer then.

"Why did you keep it, um—am I intruding?"

"Not in the least." A huge smile materialized. "You're always welcome here." The retired postal employee waved to the well-used sofa. "Sit. Take a load off your feet, honey."

Jolene felt a bit foolish. She had not expected so warm a greeting. "Thank you for seeing me, Olivia. I should have phoned first." It was rude to barge in here unannounced.

"Call me Livvie; all my friends do."

Kirk's second wife possessed a winsome personality, though years of hard living registered age in her sun-baked face.

"I'm not exactly your friend." Jolene glanced around the room and spied a few pieces of her mother's antique glassware. "But I'm not here to fight with you either."

"That's a relief." Olivia chuckled. "Kirk said you were a handful. Guess you're just living up to your reputation. As you can see, I don't have anything worth fighting over. If you've come for your mother's glass collection, you're welcome to it."

Jolene was unsure how to take Livvie's overt friendliness.

"I was about to have my afternoon tea. Will you join me?"

"Sure." Jolene was not anxious to leave. Olivia was her last hope for gleaning information regarding her deceased father.

"Make yourself comfortable, I'll just be a jiffy."

Choosing the plush, velvet-pink vintage sofa, Jolene sat down to wait. The spry woman wearing fluffy blue house shoes and an old-fashioned brunch coat shuffled back into the living room.

She placed the silver tray loaded with a floral tea pitcher, two matching china cups, a cream pitcher, and bowls filled with lemon wedges and brown sugar crystals, on the coffee table. Two silver serving spoons and a stack of napkins completed the offering.

"It's nice to have company." Livvie smiled.

"You've done a wonderful job preserving history."

"Your gratitude belongs to Kirk."

Jolene was puzzled.

"Your father picked out all the furniture and paint colors in the house," Olivia recalled as she handed Jolene a cup of tea.

"I had no idea he enjoyed decorating."

"Cream or sugar . . .?" she inquired.

"Both please!" Jolene replied.

A few uncomfortable moments slipped by.

"I never realized Dad was interested in antiques," Jolene said.

"Children don't often know who their parents are until they've lived a while themselves." Livvie shrugged.

"I'm learning that," Jolene said. "You are quite the hostess, Olivia." Jolene accepted a napkin. "Do you have children?"

"Livvie, please," the hostess insisted. "No, Kirk was my first and last husband. I married late in life."

"Oh." Jolene hadn't known that.

"Tell me, dear, why you've come to see me." Olivia added a sprig of lemon to her cup then made firm eye contact with Jolene.

"I almost didn't come here," she admitted. "The past scares me, but I need to talk to someone about my father."

The truth was out and Jolene felt better.

"To be honest, I'm surprised you came."

Jolene inhaled the steamy odor of the hot liquid then added ample cream. "Almond flavored tea is my favorite."

"It was Kirk's, too." Olivia took a sip from her cup.

Jolene stirred two lumps of brown sugar into the murky liquid, unsure how to begin her inquiry. She lifted sad blue eyes and inquired, "How was Daddy doing before he died?"

"Oh, he was a trooper." Olivia's gaze brightened. "The day before his heart attack we took a two-mile hike in the woods."

Jolene blinked. He never took leisure walks while working.

"The whole time, all he talked about was you—did you know he kept a scrapbook with newspaper clippings spotlighting the honors you won while attending the University of Memphis?"

Jolene shook her head, ashamed.

"Kirk was so proud of you for graduating from college."

"I never knew." Astonished, Jolene choked back tears. All those precious years wasted on anger. *God, forgive me.*

"The scrapbook he put together is on the bottom shelf of the bookcase, if you care to see it, Jolene."

"I'm surprised you've kept it." Jolene had never expected their conversation to center on her achievements.

"I think you'll be pleased," Olivia added.

"When I finish my tea, I'll thumb through it."

"Kirk added wedding pictures from the Jackson, Mississippi paper when you married David. He kept up with you."

But I didn't keep up with him.

"I just took a butter cake out of the oven, care for a slice?"

"Is that what smells so enticing?"

"Cooking is about all I can manage these days."

"Can I help with anything?" Jolene asked.

"Sit tight, sweetheart." Olivia pattered back into the kitchen, fetched two slices of cake then reappeared in the open doorway.

"The recipe calls for real butter and umpteen eggs, but the taste is worth the calories. It was your father's favorite dessert." She handed Jolene her portion on a plate with a silver fork.

How can I stay mad at this gracious woman?

♣36

JOLENE ACCEPTED A piece of Olivia's cake. Light and flaky, the recipe would win a baking contest at any county fair. Vanilla mingled with almond made her mouth water. "This is the best cake I've ever eaten." Jolene cast a gaze at her hostess.

"I love to bake," Olivia imparted. "It's part of Tennessee's cultural heritage—good home cooking with vintage recipes passed down through generations of hardworking pioneers."

"I've always been too busy. First, it was finishing college. Then working at a job that required most of my time," Jolene explained. "I guess that's why I never took an interest in baking."

"Well, I'm sure you're good at anything you try."

"I know for a fact David loves home-cooked meals."

Olivia's expression turned serious. "When you didn't come home to get married, Kirk made a cake and decorated it himself."

"I had no idea." Jolene had not known her father at all.

Olivia revealed, "Kirk was always celebrating your life in small ways, Jolene. Never doubt he loved you very much."

Tears stung Jolene's eyes as she gazed out the window. She felt like a first-class heel, judging her daddy like she'd done.

"I'm sorry if I've upset you." Olivia touched Jolene's hand.

Jolene swiped away a tear. "This may have been a bad idea, my coming." She got up. "I'm not ready for this conversation."

"No, stay, please." Olivia restrained Jolene with a touch on her arm. "You need to hear what I have to say, child. Then I know you have questions." Jolene nodded and sat back down.

"When your daddy got sick, and you didn't come to see him, he was distraught. But he never wanted to pressure you."

"What do you mean?"

"He knew you were upset when Kate died. Kirk didn't know how to show you he loved you. So he let you go."

Jolene nodded. She was a lot like him.

"When Kirk was laid to rest, and you didn't show, I realized the problem was nearly insurmountable." Bronzy eyes gazed softly at Jolene. "If you want to talk about *that* now, I'm here."

In her wildest imagination, Jolene never thought the woman who took her mother's place would be the one who showed her the pathway to forgiveness. Bewildered, Jolene gazed at Olivia.

"They say you broke up my parents' marriage." Not knowing for sure had prayed on Jolene's mind for what felt like forever.

"I didn't, Jolene. Kirk and I had known each other forever."

"What do you mean?"

"Our friendship went way back to high school days. Your grandparents and mine were the best of friends, did you know that?" Olivia blossomed in the presence of pleasant memories.

"I had no idea. What about my mother?"

"After Kate fell ill, Kirk was devastated. He started going over to my parents' house to vent his feelings. Being single, I was often there when he visited. We'd worked together at the post office for decades, so talking about Kate's illness came easy."

As Jolene listened to Olivia's explanation of her relationship with Kirk, she longed to go back in time and change the way she'd reacted when she received an invitation to their wedding. Father and daughter could have shared that sacred moment. She'd miss out on so much because she never knew the truth or asked.

"Kirk and I had meals together many times at my parents' home before he ever asked me out on a date," Olivia continued. "When he did ask me to marry him, I was surprised."

"But you were married so soon after Mom died," Jolene uttered. "I thought—" words fell away from her lips.

"Six months to the date, dear, but that's because we knew one another so well. In a small town like ours, it's hard to find happiness. Fact is, your mother and I were good friends, too."

"I never knew that." Jolene was astounded at her ignorance.

"I wished you had talked to me before you decided not to attend Kirk's funeral. It might have saved you a lot of grief."

"I'm so sorry."

Olivia threw a hand. "I know town folks gossiped about us, said we were having an affair before your mother died, but it wasn't true. I respected Kate." By this time Jolene was weeping.

"I had it all wrong, Olivia. I am so sorry. Can you possibly forgive my stupidity?" She hugged the woman she once despised.

"You've given me joy, child. I've always prayed you would come around one day so we could have this talk. My folks are dead now, and I don't have any close relatives."

"I'm pretty much a loner, too. Except for David," Jolene admitted then shared her encounter with ovarian cancer. "I ran away from home and nearly destroyed my marriage."

Olivia was a good listener and empathized over Jolene's plight. She was delighted Jolene was resolving her differences with David. "Where have you been staying?" she inquired.

"With Buck and Nancy Blake," she replied. "They graciously took me into their home while I was recuperating from surgery."

"Had you known them before?"

"No, Nancy and I met by chance. It didn't take long to form an unbreakable bond. I love her like she is my own daughter."

"I have a guest bedroom, Jolene. If you like, you're welcome to stay with me while you and David are house hunting," Olivia offered. "Will you let me be a part of your family?"

How can I refuse? Jolene rejoiced in her spirit.

"We'll certainly make it a priority," she promised.

"That's all I can expect."

Jolene had learned a valuable lesson: *the truth will set you free.*

In one afternoon, her mind had undergone a revolutionary transformation. Hatred for a woman she hadn't known had been miraculously dispelled as she forged a river of forgiveness.

Acts of love were liberating, cleansing.

All this time Jolene had diligently worked to liberate Nancy and Claire, to bridge the wide gap of distrust in their relationship. But God, in an act of great wisdom and kindness, had worked a double miracle for her, not only with David, but with Olivia, too.

Today, Jolene viewed her future through enlightened eyes. Tomorrow's promise was one of hope perpetuated by faith, the substance of the unseen power of God at work in human lives.

♣37

JULY 4th CAME IN like a lion as a summer storm roared through Middle Tennessee spawning tornados and leveling trees. Mayor Wilkes was distraught, thinking he might have to cancel the yearly contest due to debris the storm had dumped in his backyard.

Proclaiming that the show must go on regardless, Claire hired a yard cręw to clean up the fallen limbs and set erect the folding chairs and tables. By two o'clock that afternoon, their half-acre backyard had been renovated into a Garden-of-the-Month with f lush greenery and flowering bushes standing in decorative pots.

"There!" Claire proudly announced: "The show will go on!"

As if hearing Claire's summoning, a brilliant sun magically appeared overhead and the atmosphere cooled to a comfortable seventy-five degrees. Mother Nature dare not interfere with the Charlotte Society for the Promotion of the Arts. The civic organization sponsored all kinds of affairs. Artists, sculptors, musicians, and persons of craft, depended on the committee.

Today, fifteen applicants would perform their original tunes in the singing contest. It was inconceivable that the event would be cancelled under any circumstance, short of total destruction of the town. Contestants would be devastated if they missed an opportunity to compete for a Nashville recording contract.

Claire Wilkes made sure everything was in proper order for the shindig. A popular radio host was scheduled to emcee the talent show, broadcasting the acts live. It was the biggest July event in Dickson County. Three hundred tickets had been raffled off in January to finance the show, some resold for great prices.

This event was a national treasure to Charlotte citizens.

Three Nashville producers would be present to judge the contest, awarding the winner with a recording contract and promotional package that guaranteed radio airplay. The winner's career would be launched; the rest left up to the artist to succeed.

~

"I'm a little scared," Nancy confided in Jolene as she brushed on her lipstick and added the finishing touches to her makeup. She'd revisited Kent's salon the day before and looked fantastic.

The jeweled-studded black pantsuit that Nancy wore fit like a glove over her perfect five-foot-eight-inch figure. Fire-engine-red hair tumbled across her squared shoulders. Laser-green eyes rimmed in black eyeliner were electric with excitement.

"What if we don't win?" the contestant uttered.

"Don't think about winning, Nancy." Jolene was bent on bolstering the potential star's confidence. "Just sing your heart out, like you do on your own front porch. Folks will love it."

"I don't know why the kids aren't nervous."

"They're too young to know fear," Jolene said. "Your children are well rehearsed, even look like little angels."

"You really believe in me, don't you?" Nancy stared at Jolene. "I don't know how I'll ever thank you."

"Thank me by singing." Jolene assessed Nancy's appearance through the mirror. "Just go out there and be you."

Claire had made the children's outfits. No doubt she wanted them to put on a good show. Nancy brushed additional mascara on her long eyelashes. "Too much . . .?" she queried Jolene.

"Camera lights are bright, so I don't think so. You might add a little more blush to your cheeks." Jolene snagged the tool from Nancy's hand and applied the blush as she'd seen Kent do.

"Where are the kids?" The noise level had diminished to zero. "Don't tell me they're gone outside to play!"

"Stay calm, Nancy," Jolene advised. "Buck's already taken them with him to the mayor's house. He promised me they wouldn't budge from their seats until after they performed."

"Does he have our soundtrack?" Nancy asked.

"I packed up everything and sent it with him." Jolene reassured Nancy. "You're ready, sweetheart, and the children are very excited. I think they were born to entertain."

Excitement swept down Nancy's spine. "What if we had never met? Where would I be today? You've changed me."

"You've changed me, too." Jolene felt a kindred spirit. "It's a God-thing, two people on a journey to find their rainbow."

"You're right. Miracles do happen."

"Well, you still have a ways to go. Claire can be stubborn."

"I can, too. But I'm really trying to be reasonable."

"God will help you, Nancy. I'm so pleased you and Buck joined the church last week," Jolene said. "Your children will hear God's message of grace and soon follow in your footsteps. It was the right thing to do." She and Buck were both baptized.

"I hope we have the good judgment to set the right example for our kids." Nancy squeezed Jolene's hand. "I've always heard that families who pray together stay together."

"It's God's way of blessing humanity."

"What time is it?" Nancy nervously asked, turning around to glance at the wall clock. The moment was about to arrive.

"Time to go, the contest starts in exactly thirty minutes."

"Okay, I guess I'm ready." The wannabe star studied her image in the mirror. Her hair was as red as a fiery sunset, her eyes bright as Colorado jade. No freckles shown on her nose with the new, expensive makeup Jolene had purchased from Kent.

"I'll drive the car," Jolene said. "Say a prayer."

♣38

WHEN JOLENE AND Nancy arrived at Mayor Wilkes' impressive home, they discovered his backyard jamming with social activity. Country music flowed from loudspeakers strategically positioned and nearly every folding chair was filled.

Heads turned in every direction to observe who was there and what they were wearing. Nancy spotted Buck seated on the front row with their five children—probably hoping she had the nerve to appear. "I see Buck," Nancy whispered in Jolene's ear.

"Where are the other contestants?" Nancy glanced around.

"Trust me, they're here somewhere." Jolene led the way down the grassy aisle toward the white picked-fence line.

"I guess this is it." Nancy let go of Jolene's hand and walked toward the stage, smiling as she joined her husband and kids.

"I'll see you in a bit." Jolene headed in the opposite direction.

"Where's Jolene?" Buck craned his neck looking.

Nancy shrugged. "My guess, she's going to find Mom and offer to help with food preparations."

"It's good that Jolene and Claire get along so well," Buck remarked, inwardly nervous at the upcoming performance.

"My mother thinks Jolene hung the moon."

"No, her eyes are only for you, Nancy," Buck countered. "Isn't it obvious? She's totally into you."

Nancy drew in a quick breath. "How much longer is it before show time?" She looked at Buck's wristwatch.

"Not long, hang in there, sweetheart." Buck kissed his wife on the cheek, gave her a hug. Their children were stone-faced.

"What did you do to the kids?"

"You don't want to know," Buck replied.

Jolene negotiated her way through the crowd and entered Claire's elaborately furnished kitchen. The hostess was missing, but two male chefs were preparing meat-and cheese platters.

A variety of fresh fruits sat on the counter in two glass bowls. There were also jugs of lemonade and tea. It appeared all was in order. Not needed, Jolene ventured outdoors again.

It was time to find a seat and watch the show.

Deep in concentration, gazing at the ground as she walked, Jolene sensed a presence near her before recognizing a pair of polished brown loafers on two large feet. Heart skittering, Jolene's gaze slowly climbed up the man's pants, past his belt and crisp blue shirt, until she spied a face that made her smile.

"David. You're here!" She grabbed him.

"I told Nancy not to tell you I was coming." He embraced his wife and fondly kissed her. "Are you surprised?"

"Totally, I can't believe it."

David clung tightly to Jolene, like she'd evaporate if he let go. Jolene nearly melted with love until a loud applause broke out.

Laughing joyfully, she pulled away. "We have got to stop meeting like this, husband! It's show-time, let's go watch."

"Where, the place is packed?"

"Not to worry, we have reserved seats."

"Did you find us a house?" David whispered as they took their seats, his voice breathy with minty Listerine.

"I have a property in mind," she whispered. "Maybe we can do a drive-by after the contest ends."

The radio announcer approached the microphone erected on the stage platform and raised a hand. "Well, this is it, folks!"

In response, the audience clapped.

Jolene crossed her fingers, all prayed up.

"Welcome to the eighth talent contest sponsored by the Charlotte Society for the Promotion of the Arts!" The emcee flashed a Dentine smile. "I'm Randy Taylor, your host for today."

A round of applause broke out.

Randy put up a hand. "The talent acts are listed on your brochure. Please refrain from clapping until everyone has performed. You may express your opinion to the judges with your comments on the back of your program, although this isn't a popularity contest. The winner will have to earn the prize."

Smalltalk erupted in the audience.

"We'll take a break half way through the show and enjoy the mayor's refreshments," Randy said. "Be prompt in returning to your seats so we can maintain a timely schedule. Participants are anxious to perform. Are we ready to begin? Are we ready?"

The audience responded with clapping.

The panel judges were introduced, all three reputable producers representing Nashville recording companies.

The first act commenced.

Nancy sat with her family, on pins and needles as she anticipated her time to come. Her "Five Little Angels on a Mission" were the first scheduled act after the half-hour break.

The first hour passed quickly. When Randy announced the break, people scrambled from their seats. Port-A-Potties were available through a gate outside the fenced yard. The temperature had risen to eighty-five degrees and folks were thirsty.

Nancy asked Buck to watch the kids while she searched for Jolene. Ten minutes later, she returned with two bottled waters.

"Did you find her?" Buck inquired.

"No, but I saw David."

"Did Jolene know he was coming?"

"I don't think so," Nancy replied.

A grin spread over Buck's lips. "The guy probably doesn't realize anybody's here but Jolene. They act like newlyweds."

"Have you seen my mother?" Nancy asked.

"Last time I saw Claire, she came and fetched the kids, herded them off toward the refreshments. By now, she's fussing over them, making sure they don't spill anything on their outfits."

"That's my mom, thinks of everything."

"We have company," Buck said, rising to his feet.

"I'm Jolene's husband," David introduced himself to Buck with a firm handshake. "Hi, Nancy, you look amazing." He pecked her on the cheek. "Jolene's told me all about your family."

Nancy's gaze fell on her children as Claire returned with them and stood stoically at a distance, offering no comment.

"Uh oh, should I be worried?" Buck laughed at David's remark regarding his brood. "We're a riot sometimes, I admit."

"No, no," David uttered, thinking he'd misspoken. "It was all good. Jolene loves you and Nancy like you're her own family."

Offering no input into the conversation, Claire slipped off.

"And we love Jolene, too," Nancy beamed with pride. "I just wish the next ten minutes would hurry up and go by, I'm getting the jitters real bad." Perspiration dotted her forehead.

Jolene arrived and looked at Nancy. "How are the kids?"

"Not as nervous as I am," Nancy admitted. "Claire took them to the refreshment table so they wouldn't be thirsty when it came time for them to sing." The mom smacked her lips.

"Do you need a snack?" Jolene asked.

"No, I couldn't possibly eat until after I sing."

"Well, at least drink some more water," Jolene said. "I don't want you fainting on stage when you get up to sing."

Nancy unscrewed the cap and took a swig.

Buck glanced at all the people milling around the mayor's yard. "Sure are a lot of people here, Babe," he told Nancy.

"Don't let that rattle you, just sing," Jolene cautioned.

"I'm already rattled," the would-be star admitted. "I haven't performed on stage before a crowd since I turned seventeen."

"You'll be fine," Jolene said. "I know you're a winner."

"I sure hope so." Nancy took in a huge breath.

"I guess it's time to shine, Nancy." Buck spied Randy hop on the stage then tap the microphone to test if it was working.

"Attention everyone, please take you seats."

"See you later." Jolene waved as she and David moved to the second row. "I sure hope Nancy gets over her nervousness."

"From what you've told me, the woman is practically a pro."

"You're right, she'll do great."

"We ready to go another round?" Randy announced through the speaker system. "Let's put our hands together to show the first eight acts our appreciation." He started clapping. "Didn't they do a great job?" The audience responded with catcalls.

"Our next act is truly special," Randy announced. "Claire Wilkes' grandchildren will be performing for us shortly."

Another big round of applause resounded.

"Mrs. Blake, are you and the children ready?" Randy gazed at Nancy. "Bring those little angels on stage and let us see them."

Gulping air, Nancy patted each of her children's backs as they stepped on the stage and lined up in a row.

"I'm Nancy Blake, and these are my five little angels," she announced over the sound system. "We're going to perform an original song I wrote for the contest." She strummed her guitar as the soundtrack commenced playing. After the brief musical intro, the children's bell-clear voices peeled forth in perfect harmony:

The music has gone out of the song,
When folks can't find a way to get along . . .
When wars are fought for faith; and love's replaced by hate,
If forgiveness waits too long, the music goes out of the song.

♣39

WHEN THE FIVE Little Angels on a Mission finished their performance, the audience scrambled to their feet with loud applause, though it was clearly against the rules.

Emcee Randy, impressed to the max, raised a hand to shush the crowd. "Don't think I've ever heard a more beautiful presentation," he said over whistles and catcalls ringing out from the yard. "Thank you, Angels. You, too, Nancy!"

More applause as Nancy and her children returned to their seats. Buck's face beamed with pride as he grasped Nancy's hand. Jolene, holding tightly to David's arm, lifted a prayer of thanks to Almighty Father for bringing this day together. The performance was even better than she'd anticipated. Nancy was radiant.

When the final act was performed, Claire hustled over to give her grandchildren hugs, reminding each of them how wonderful they were. Nancy and Buck stared at one another, holding hands like teenagers, proud of their clan. Behind them, David clung to Jolene like she might vanish. Love was in the air.

The judges gathered at a table, notes spread out, to determine the winner. Finally, the announcement came as Randy was handed the results. "And the winner of Charlotte Community July 4th singing contest is . . . Five Little Angels on a Mission."

After the applauses diminished, the judges surrounded Nancy and her children and asked a lot of questions. Afterwards, a line formed to congratulate the winners on their accomplishment.

Jolene clung to David's hand, vowing she'd never let him go. *Ever!* "I think it's time we slip away," he said. "Show me the property you found for us." They slipped out the side gate.

"There was plenty of food, we could've eaten."

"Food is the last thing on my mind," David opened the door of the Ford Explorer, his hazel eyes gleaming with passion.

The newness of their romance engulfed Jolene.

"We could go back to your motel room."

"I like the idea of taking it real slow, the anticipation . . ."

Jolene road shotgun as David drove his rented SUV away from the mayor's house. Like a cowboy maneuvering the reins to guide a perky filly, he controlled the powerful vehicle with finesse.

Jolene couldn't help but think how handsome he looked. His tan was golden and flawless. Wearing tan chinos and a navy blue short-sleeve shirt, wisps of his blond hair teased his long forehead.

"Don't look at me like that or plans will change."

Jolene felt giddy from the day, like it wasn't real. "Being together feels right," she said. "It's like we never were apart."

"But we were, and a lot of life's road went by," he said. "I feel like I've been liberated from prison." He grasped her hand.

"Were these past few months so bad?" She'd only begun to sense the pressure he'd been under. She'd wrongly assessed his motives for distancing himself from her. "I'm sorry," she said.

"What happened at work isn't your fault."

"I know, but I never should have doubted you."

"And I should have told you what was going on." David shook his head. "Hindsight, it was a huge mistake."

"Life for me has been pretty intense. I've learned some life lessons during our separation." Jolene thought of Olivia.

"I couldn't make my move until I had another job," David said. "When you walked away in December, I still had bills to pay. After my trip to the Bahamas, I knew I had to sell the house."

Jolene peered out the window. Guilty as charged. "I was too absorbed into my own problems to think about anything else."

Reaching over, David grasped her hand.

"That's behind us now, Babe. All is forgiven, right?" He wanted to hear it from her lips.

Jolene slowly turned her face toward David. "I'd like to believe this is the first day of the rest of our married lives."

"Make that a ditto." A mellow expression flooded his handsome face. "So, where is this great property located?"

"I'll key in the house address on the GPS."

The two-year-old house was constructed of timber and stone. It stood on a grassy hill on a twenty-acre slice of land with a half-acre road frontage. David turned into the long driveway; wheels kicking gravel as the vehicle slowly climbed the sloping terrain.

As they approached the house, David spied a freestanding workshop twenty feet into the backyard. Behind the shop, the countryside rolled with mature hardwoods.

"Hunting will be good here," he noted.

"I've always wanted to try my hand at pottery," she said.

It was a fairytale property. The exterior logs cast a yellow glow in the presence of the receding sun, sharpening the green color of the tin roof. "I hope you like listening to the pecking of rain on that roof," he told Jolene as he shut down the motor.

"Isn't the view of the countryside spectacular?"

Jolene exited the Ford, raced to the front of the house, and mounted the steps leading up to a wraparound porch. From this vantage point, she viewed miles of rolling countryside covered with timber. Flashes of color sparked by sunlight looked like specs of confetti. Gusty winds threaded seeds in the air.

David caught up with Jolene. "Wow."

"Well, what do you think of this view?"

He took in a huge breath. "Picture perfect, I'd say."

The air was cooling quickly as the sun prepared to set.

"I love it," she said.

Jolene relished the serene moment. This house was nothing like the one they'd shared in Baton Rouge. It represented a new beginning, the promise of a better life for them both.

"Are we going to stand here or go inside?" he asked.

Jolene plundered through her purse for the house key.

"Is the realtor coming out?" David asked.

"No, I have a key."

"Here, let me help." He opened the door and they stepped into the foyer. "Wow! This is fine."

"Yes, it is." Jolene shared his excitement.

She flipped on the lights. The foyer merged into the spacious den with walls climbing sixteen feet to meet the rafters. Plucking a flyer from the side table, she handed it to David.

The floor plan featured three good-sized bedrooms, each with its own bathroom. The master was down, two up.

Stairs led up to the loft, presently used for office space.

The designer kitchen located at the back of the house had everything a gourmet cook would want—not that Jolene qualified as one. But with Olivia's help, she was determined to improve.

"Coming?" She led the way down a short hallway.

"Hey, wait up!" David lightheartedly caught Jolene by the waist. "Have I told you today how much I love you?"

"Not nearly enough times," she said, laughing.

David was interested in viewing the loft. Jolene jaunted up the stairs after him. On the back wall, three windows brought in the outdoor light and a view of the countryside. The floor was commercially carpeted and a side wall featured custom built-in cabinets. A rectangular TV screen nearly filled the opposite wall.

"The sellers left all this behind?"

"Yes, as a perk for a quick sale," she replied.

"Wow! Who's the builder?"

"An architect out of Nashville," Jolene replied. "He moved to California after the couple's divorce, so I was told."

"Should've rethought that decision," David said, cuddling Jolene. "What about the wife? Did she get the house?"

Jolene shrugged. "Not privy to those details."

David faced Jolene and grasped her shoulders "Promise me you'll never run off again without taking me with you."

"Do you want my signature in blood?" She arched her back and kissed him on the lips. "I love you too terribly much."

They took a moment just to be.

Jolene led David by the hand downstairs and into the master bedroom. It was a spacious fourteen by sixteen feet with a vaulted ceiling. A picture window opened a panoramic view into the front yard and the rolling hills beyond the road.

"I like this setup," he said.

They entered the deluxe master bath featuring an oversized Jacuzzi. The sink countertops were white marble, and the cabinets were constructed of Old Pine. The stain-glassed window facing the backyard provided plenty of natural light. After looking in every nook and cranny, David wanted to see the workshop.

The freestanding shop was wired for electricity and plenty big enough to accommodate a lawnmower, tractor, and bass boat.

"I hope you like work," Jolene said. "This is the country."

"As long as I still have time to feed the baby deer, I'm all for sweating." David chuckled. "I hope you don't get bored."

"What do you think? Should we buy the property?"

"Remind me of the list price," he said.

"Three ninety-nine, nine," Jolene said, eying David. "The listing agent has an appraisal on it for four-fifty, but obviously the owners are anxious to sell and settle their financial affairs."

"With a loan, we can manage that, I expect."

David pulled out his pocket calculator and figured the monthly payment based on the current interest rate.

"Call the realtor and see if she can meet us at her office," David said. "I think we should solidify this bid today."

♣40

KATIE THE LISTING agent of the property was delighted to hear from Jolene and said she'd meet them in Charlotte at her office. After cutting off the lights, and locking up the house, Jolene walked back to the car with David.

He opened the passenger door and she climbed in. The engine was soon rumbling. "You did a great job finding this property, Jolene. Are you going to sell Tennessee properties?"

"Maybe after we settle in, I'll take my test."

"You're a natural at helping people."

"I want to practice being a wife first. I was never really good at it. And this house is big enough for a family, don't you think?"

"What do you mean?" His forehead furrowed.

"Don't you think it's time we have our own family?"

"A baby . . ." surprise cornered David. "Gosh, I never thought I'd hear those words from your lips."

He ignited the engine and turned the truck around.

"What brought on this change of heart?"

"Being around Nancy's five children and Mitzi's two granddaughters," she replied. "I can't see us not having a family."

"I can't either. As long as you are in the family picture, I'm game for a dozen little ones." David slowly drove down the steep curved driveway and turned on the main road toward Charlotte.

On their way, Jolene made eye contact with David and said, "I've done some reading. We should consider all our options."

"Adoption, right . . .?"

"I don't have an egg to contribute, but you still have a viable sperm. There are women who will bear our child for a price."

"Hire a surrogate mother . . .?" He blinked and turned a curve hard. "Wow, Jolene, that's thinking out of the box."

"Or, we could adopt an older child who needs good parents."

David grinned. "Funny you should mention that. I visited an orphanage while I was in Japan. After the 2011 quake, a lot of children lost parents. From what I've learned, the need is great."

"We don't have to decide at this very moment." Jolene's mind was whirring with ideas. "But, if anything, I've learned it's not wise to put off a good plan." She smiled at him.

As David drove down the highway he thought about their options. What did God want for them? "We need to pray about our decision, Jolene. This is a giant step and we're in our forties."

"I know," she said. "But together, we are stronger."

~

After signing the residential purchase contract at Katie's office, and setting up a loan application appointment, they decided to drive over to Murfreesboro and tell Jack and Mitzi their good news. Jolene phoned Mitzi to tell her they were coming.

"Will we be interfering if we pop in for a visit?"

"Actually, we're in the middle of a family picnic," Mitzi replied. "Was there a big turnout at the contest?"

"Yes, and we really missed your family."

"Who won?"

Background noises were chaotic. "Say that again?"

"Who won the contest?" Mitzi raised her voice a decibel.

Jolene exclaimed, "Nancy and her children, of course!"

"Sorry we couldn't make it," Mitzi apologized. "Jack just wasn't feeling up to the hour and half trip."

"How is he handling the chemo?" Jolene inquired.

"A day at a time, I'm sure you can readily identify."

"Oh, boy, can I." She shot a glance at David as he maneuvered the Ford in the hectic Nashville traffic.

"It's after six, but if it won't be a big imposition, we're thirty minutes away and rolling. David wants to meet your family."

"If you're hungry, there's still plenty of food left."

"I think we're too excited to be hungry."

"What's going on?" Mitzi asked.

"I'd rather tell you in person. I want to see the look on your face." Jolene was bursting to tell her about the house purchase.

"I hate cliffhangers." Mitzi laughed.

"I promise you, this news is worth the wait."

"Okay. We have grilled ribs warming, and if you hurry, you can join us for homemade peach ice cream before it's all gone."

"We're coming as fast as we can."

"I know Amy and Priscilla will be happy to see you. We've heard tales about the good times they had with you while Jack was in the hospital," Mitzi revealed. "They love their Aunt Jolene."

Jolene laughed and ended the call. "What?"

"It's been a big day, are you sure you're not too tired?" David asked Jolene, aware she was still recovering from chemo.

"I'm too excited to recognize fatigue if it hit me in the face."

"Are we spending the night with Mitzi?" he asked.

"No, we'll visit the family for awhile, tell them about our purchase in Dickson County, and find somewhere private to spend the night." A sheepish grin materialized.

"I hope you're not planning to take advantage of me tonight." He envisioned a private moment with his wife.

Jolene laughed. "I do have some pillow talk in mind."

"Sounds like a plan." He drove with purpose.

♣Epilog

IF ONE BELIEVES in happy-ever-after endings, this story qualifies. Jolene's adventure to Charlotte changed her perspective of truth. Finding a way to resolve her guilt by revisiting the past was a success. She learned that assumptions never led to the facts. After Jolene and David moved into their new home, Olivia Lancaster became one of their best friends.

In time, Olivia taught Jolene how to bake and cook meals like a real Tennessean. Jolene became licensed to sell real estate but made it a point to spend quality time at home.

David never regretted leaving Baton Rouge. After opening a branch of Mr. Sojimona's insurance business, he worked between his downtown Dickson office and home, always making time for long walks in the woods with Jolene. A year later, they adopted two young boys, siblings from the Nashville Children's Home.

` Meanwhile, Buck and Nancy stayed together to raise their five children in a Christian home. Nancy and her children got their promised recording contract and were received by the radio-listening audience so well Nancy was scheduled to make a second CD as the soloist. Buck was on board one hundred percent and gave up trucking to be a stay-at-home dad and support her career.

Though a challenge, Claire Wilkes learned to tolerate Buck, a gesture to please her popular daughter who was gaining stardom. Since Mayor Wilkes had no grandchildren of his own, he took Nancy's two sons under his wing and taught them gardening.

Jack fully recovered from his cancer surgery, and Mitzi stayed in contact with Jolene and David on a weekly basis. The families shared holidays, rejoicing over God's goodness.

Everyone learned valuable lessons after enduring hardships. Life is truly like a bowl of lemons. You can either eat them sour or make sweet lemonade. God blesses those who keep their eyes on Him. What is your hope? Do you dare to dream?

Explore your faith and see where it takes you.

About the Author

Author-publisher M. Sue Alexander has been involved in writing most of her life whether in penning a children's story, an article, novel, or gospel song. Reared on the grounds of Western State Hospital where her father was the resident dentist for the mentally ill, she acquired a vivacious imagination that threads her work.

A 1958 graduate of Central High School in Bolivar, Tennessee, Sue earned higher educational degrees from Union University and the University of Memphis, taught school before establishing Suzander Publishing, and later embarked on a real estate career.

After moving to north Dickson County Sue was diagnosed with double-ovarian cancer in 2001, underwent surgery followed by chemo, and later developed a staph infection in her portacath.

In *Tomorrow's Promise* Jolene Salisbury mimics Sue's experience with ovarian cancer. Sue currently resides on a farm with her husband and writes daily, believing God gives ordinary people extraordinary assignments to accomplish His purposes on earth.

Sue is also the author of the *Resurrection Dawn 2014* Christian fiction series. View her other books at www.resdawn.net